TAKE
NO
PRISONERS

Also by Cindy Gerard

Show No Mercy
Into the Dark
To the Edge
To the Limit
To the Brink
Over the Line
Under the Wire

TAKE
NO
PRISONERS

Cindy Gerard

POCKET **STAR** BOOKS

New York   London   Toronto   Sydney

Pocket Star Books
A Division of Simon & Schuster, Inc.
1230 Avenue of the Americas
New York, NY 10020

First Pocket Star Books paperback edition November 2008

POCKET STAR and colophon are registered trademarks of Simon & Schuster, Inc.

Cover design by Lisa Litwack.

Manufactured in the United States of America

ISBN-13: 978-1-60751-078-9

This book is dedicated to the men and women of the United States military—both active and retired. There are no words to adequately express my gratitude and respect for the sacrifices you and your families have made and for the losses many of you have endured to protect and defend our nation and our way of life.

ACKNOWLEDGMENTS

Special thanks to Kylie Brant and Roxanne Rustand, problem solvers extraordinaire—and a darn good time to boot :o)

Again, thanks to Gail Barrett for her excellent assistance with the Spanish translations.

Susan, Leanne, Glenna, Ben, Joe—you know I luv ya!

People sleep peaceably in their beds at night only because rough men stand ready to do violence on their behalf.

—GEORGE ORWELL (attributed)

1

Las Rosas, Honduras

A gecko, low slung, forked feet flying, skittered across the sill of an open window, hauling ass as if it actually had somewhere to go.

Lucky little bastard.

Sam Lang watched him through world-weary eyes—jealous of a damn lizard because at the moment, Sam had exactly *nowhere* to go. And nothing to do.

Nothing but sit here, slouched at a crude wooden table in a shadowed corner of a crumbling adobe cantina, like he'd sat here for the past three days. Nothing but amuse himself watching insect-eating egg-laying reptiles and wishing he were anywhere but Las Rosas, Honduras, on yet one more wild-goose chase.

No, he was not having fun yet.

While the action in the cantina was stagnant and slow, years of caution and force of habit had Sam sitting with his back to the wall. Thirst and boredom had his fingers wrapped around a lukewarm can of Polar.

He wiped his cuff over the lip of the can, then tilted it to his mouth as the gecko shot away again.

Fast little sucker. Speed-of-sound fast compared to the rest of the populace in this dusty and rodent-infested hamlet where time crawled, stalled, and stopped dead in the noon heat of the Central American sun. The gecko obviously knew something Sam and the handful of patrons of this squalid, sweltering cantina didn't because, hell, even the flies didn't bother to buzz over pools of stale, spilled beer. Nope. Not a lot of action—with the notable exception of the gecko and the X-rated show taking place in the middle of what could loosely be called a dance floor, where a man and a woman performed what could loosely be called a dance.

Sam had known better. He should have dragged his partner, Johnny Duane Reed, out of this dive three hours ago when they'd officially decided their guy wasn't going to show. So far, the "tip" that they might get the goods on Fredrick Nader hadn't panned out. With each tick of a very slow-moving clock, it became more apparent that they'd run up against one more dead end.

Big surprise. Sam had been tracking the elusive German for months. He'd set trap after trap, harassed the hell out of Nader, whose "legitimate" international enterprises were merely fronts for every type of terrorist activity known to man. Drugs, weapons, bioterrorism—you name it, Nader was in it ass deep. Yet his blue-blooded lineage and the bottomless cache of payola that came with it kept every international agency off his back.

That's where Sam and Black Ops, Inc. came in. Nader was an off-the-books operation. Sam had finally found the man's Achilles' heel. The pompous bastard had a penchant for sparkly things—Nader craved stolen gems—which Sam was counting on to be Nader's downfall.

Last week in El Salvador, Nader had gotten a little sloppy and Sam had come within minutes of nailing him—only to lose him one more time. Just like this last attempt had turned out to be one more lost cause.

"We've been here for three frickin' days," Reed complained earlier when Sam had decided to give up the ghost and get the hell out of Dodge. "Another hour or two isn't going to change the course of the world. Besides, we deserve some R and R."

Deserve, in this case, was Johnny Duane Reed–speak for "I've been eating dust and drinking mud-thick coffee for three days and I'm ready for a beer—or ten."

Three hours ago, Sam had been hard-pressed to argue with Reed's stand, but that had been three long hours ago. Now he realized the error in that line of thinking.

He glanced toward the dance floor again. Shook his head. Reed was a pretty boy, but Sam knew from experience that there was strength in those broad shoulders, speed in those lean legs. He'd relied on the former marine despite his smart mouth, Rambo strut, and weakness for the ladies in more than one dicey situation.

The kid had never let him down and he delivered few surprises. That's why it came as no shock that nothing good would come out of a situation when Johnny Duane Reed had time on his hands and a yen for alcohol and a woman.

A scratchy merengue played from a dusty jukebox as Sam watched Reed through dim light and a haze of sweet-smelling smoke. Both the smoke and the scent hung in the air like fog. No one mistook the scent for anything but what it was: prime Colombian weed. Just as no one mistook the woman with the swaying hips, barely haltered breasts, and sex-and-whiskey laugh for anything but what she was: a past-her-prime Honduras whore.

No one but Reed, who'd been without the company of a woman way longer than the cowboy liked. Give a fisherman a hook and he'll catch dinner. Give Reed a beer and he'll catch a hooker.

Kee-rist.

Reed was in lust. He was also *bolo*—drunk off his ass. It made for a perfect combination. Or a perfect storm.

If Sam didn't break the lip-lock the hooker had planted on the tall blond cowboy, whose hands were now kneading the hell out of her ass, dawn would find Reed rolled, robbed, and in need of a good delousing.

He heaved a weary breath, then couldn't help but grin at the cowboy's sloppy attempt at a salsa move. Sam tried to remember the exact point in time when he'd been appointed Reed's keeper. Somalia? Beirut? Sierra Leone? Hell. Could have been any one of a hundred third world hellholes. Years ago, as team members on Uncle's top secret Task Force Mercy, they'd saved each other's lives more times than Sam could count. More times than he wanted to.

Lot of years ago when they'd been lean and green and full of God and country. *Hoo-rah!*

Years ago, when they'd been soldiers.

He drew deep on his beer. At least Sam had been a soldier. He'd been Delta Force, U.S. Army. Reed was Marine, Force Recon and in or out of uniform, he'd be a marine—not a soldier, he was quick to point out— until the day he died.

Sam squinted through the smoke. They'd all paid a price through the years. Which was why, from time to time, they needed to let off a little steam. Case in point was stumbling around on the dance floor, probably not as drunk as he wanted everyone to think he was.

"You want to party, too, gringo? Maybe a private dance? *Vaya pues?* Okay?"

A pouty brunette had sidled up next to Sam and wrapped herself around him like a faded ribbon on a Maypole. Once upon a time he might have taken the *ladina* woman up on her offer. Once upon a time when she'd been young and pretty and he'd been young and stupid. A time when better judgment and discerning taste had been no match for randy youth, raging hormones, and the superior intellect that could be found in a bottle of tequila. Before control had become the name of Sam's game and the mantra that he lived by.

Sam wanted to ignore her, but his mother had taught him better manners. "Not tonight, darlin'."

While he'd thought he'd been gentle, he could see by the look in her eyes and the way she'd skittered away that he'd done it again. Scared the shit out of her with one hard look. Apparently it was the same look that Reed was always telling him was more intimidating than an M-16.

Whatever.

He headed for Reed. The cowboy may have tipped a few but that didn't negate the fact that Reed was still six lean feet of solid muscle and sinew. Thirty-plus years of stubborn warrior blood pumped through his veins. And he was horny.

This wasn't going to be fun.

And it wasn't going to be pretty.

But it *was* going to get done.

Sam tapped Reed on the shoulder. "Yo. God's gift. Time to roll."

"Fuck off."

Reed's response was typical and expected. It was also remarkably articulate given the fact that his tongue was buried halfway down his lady love's throat. "Get your own woman, Sammy. This one's mine."

"I said, let's go." Sam stood, hands on hips, waiting for it to seep into Reed's alcohol-soaked brain that he'd just been issued an order.

"Aw, come on," Reed actually whined when Sam didn't buckle.

Lolita, or Rosalita, or whatever the hell her name was, spewed a string of Spanish curses in Sam's direction when she realized her customer was slipping away.

"Yeah. Things are tough all over," he agreed and pried her arms from around Reed's neck.

"But our guy didn't show," Reed pointed out, hopeful it would buy him a little more time.

"It's not happening. Let's go."

As sure as two plus two equaled four, Reed drunk plus horny equaled belligerent. Lang had no expectations that either his math or his take on Reed were anything but dead-on right.

The cowboy didn't disappoint. "Fifteen minutes. That's all I need."

"No."

As only a drunk can, Reed squared off in front of Sam, bleary eyes narrowed. "You ain't the boss of me."

Sam couldn't help it. He grinned. "That's the best you can do?"

Reed sniffed. Cocked his chin. Shot for a glare. "I don't want to have to drop you, Sam."

This time Sam actually laughed. It was as much bluff as amusement because even drunk, Reed was one of the toughest, meanest, dirtiest fighters Sam had ever seen in action.

Sam pulled the older, meaner, wiser, bigger card out of the deck. "Yeah, that's gonna hap—"

He never finished his sentence.

A car roared to a screeching stop outside the cantina and grabbed his full attention, jarring him straight to red alert.

He was already diving for the dirt floor, dragging

Reed down with him when the swinging cantina doors burst open to a hail of AK-47 fire. Together they rolled, overturning tables as they went, scrambling to reach their go bags, where Sam had stashed an H&K MP-5K and Reed had packed a mini Uzi.

Wasn't gonna happen. The gunmen's fire steered them in the opposite direction, where they finally found cover behind a thick wooden support post and a half-baked adobe wall near the bar. They bellied down on the floor behind it as the deafening burst of automatic-weapon fire sprayed through the cantina. The women screamed and everyone ducked out of the line of fire.

Beside him, Reed was all business now as he unholstered his gun. "What the fuck!"

Nothing like an AK to snap a man out of a drunken stupor.

Sam peered around the wall for a quick look-see, then ducked back behind it when another round of fire slaughtered the bottles lined up behind the bar, shattering them into oblivion along with the cloudy mirror. Gunpowder and *guaro*—rotgut whiskey—stank up the air as Lang cut a glance to Reed. Like Sam, Reed had flipped to his back with his pistol in a two-handed grip, waiting for a break in the action.

It came as fast as the barrage of gunfire.

Silence—acute and potentially deadly.

Unexpected silence, except for the ringing in their ears and the creaking swing of the cantina doors.

Car doors slammed, an engine roared, and a vehicle sped away.

Sam glanced at Reed. Nodded.

Sam rolled left, Reed rolled right, flat on their bellies, Sam's Kimber Tactical Pro 1911 A1 and Reed's Sig Sauer 9mm aimed at the door—where they met nothing.

No one.

There was nothing in the cantina but residual smoke, broken glass, spilled booze, and quietly weeping women.

A single mason jar sat in the threshold beneath the cantina doors.

"Party's over?" Reed croaked, carefully assessing the bar for any remaining threats, his Sig still in a two-handed grip, muzzle pointed down and at the ready.

Sam stood slowly, did the same with his Kimber. "Seems so."

He glanced around the room. "Anyone hurt?"

One by one, figures emerged in the gloomy and hazy light. Except for a glass cut on the bartender's face there appeared to be no casualties. The conclusion was clear. With that much firepower, they should have all been dead, which meant the bad guys hadn't been aiming to kill.

They wanted someone's attention.

Reed nodded toward the dirty jar. "I'm gonna take a wild guess and figure that's for you."

Sam grunted, his footsteps crunching on broken glass as he walked across the room. He chanced a careful peek over the top of the chest-high doors. The walkway outside was littered with spent cartridges. Other than a boiling dust trail, the street was empty.

He stared down at the jar.

It was exactly what it looked like. An old, scarred, and well-used mason jar. He slipped his Kimber into his waistband, squatted down, got a better look.

"There's a note inside."

"There always is," Reed said, rubbing at bloodshot eyes.

Sam picked up the jar, cautiously fished out the sheet of paper and unfolded it.

All the blood drained from his face when he read it.

Jesus. Jesus.

Eyes wild, he sprinted for his go bag, unaware of the gecko scrambling for his life to get out of the way.

"What?" Reed pushed aside an overturned table, racing to catch up with him.

Sam shoved the note in the general direction of Reed's chest. "I need the SAT phone."

"Christ, Sam." Reed's eyes were watery with shock and disbelief when he finished reading.

Sam dug into his bag, shoved the H&K, ammo, and a dozen other pieces of equipment aside until he finally found the satellite phone. His fingers shook as he dialed the number, heart thudding, breath choppy.

"Dad." He forced himself to calm down when his father finally picked up. "Dad . . . it's Sam."

The moment of silence before his father spoke told the unthinkable truth.

"Sam . . ." His father's voice was weak. Shaken. Sam's chest tightened into a mass of white-hot lead.

"I . . . I've been trying to . . . to get a hold of you, son." Then he dissolved into desolate weeping.

Sam gripped the phone tighter. Waited, eyes burning, while his father composed himself and confirmed what Sam feared.

Wild with rage and grief and guilt, he disconnected, then burst through the cantina doors, staggered outside.

So he could breathe.

So he could think.

Only when Reed touched his shoulder did Sam realize the younger man had followed him.

A dust devil spun down the debris-strewn street, scattering powdery grit in his eyes, burning until tears ran down his face.

"Come on, Sam." Reed's voice, painfully gentle and rock solid sober, made Sam's chest ache.

"Come on," Reed repeated and urged Sam toward their car. "We need to get you home.

Sam knew he was dreaming, did his damnedest to wake up. But he was mired in images and sensations that sucked him deeper into the nightmare.

He felt like he was swimming through mud. Slogging through quicksand. Watching a movie in slow motion through a distorted wall of glass. Behind the glass, traffic shot by on the bustling Las Vegas Strip. A blur of color and motion.

On the other side of the glass wall, he saw his sister,

Terri. She was walking toward her car. Laughing at something his brother-in-law, B.J., had said. Love in her eyes. Fun in her heart. Completely unaware of the danger.

He had to get to them. But he couldn't get through the mud and the quicksand and stop them before it was too late.

"Terri!" Through an echo chamber he heard his sister's name.

A man's voice shouting. His voice. Begging.

Then roaring. "Stop . . . stop . . . for God's sake, stop!!!"

But she kept going. Straight for the car.

He could still stop this. Maybe he could still stop this. "Terri!!!!!"

Frantic to get to them, he pushed through air as thick as foam and finally reached the distorted glass wall. Behind it four lanes of city traffic crawled in an eerie, choreographed dance. Cars sped then slowed, transformed to jeweled and painted carousel horses that danced and spun in a kaleidoscope of dazzling prisms, brass rings, and gilded manes.

Rhythm and light, glowing and golden—perfection out of place with the horror that was about to happen.

"Terri!"

He rammed the wall. Slammed hard with his shoulder . . . again, again, again . . . until finally, glass shattered and parted, flew around him in glittering, knifelike shards.

He sprinted past it. Sank into more quicksand. More

mud, as Terri opened the passenger door and B.J. slipped behind the wheel.

Oblivious to his shouts.

Sweet and pristine and good with the sun on her face, the breeze in her hair, and the heat of the Las Vegas morning baking down.

"Terri! Terri!!!!"

Sweat trickled down his back, ran into his eyes as he dodged a minivan, then rolled over the hood of a fast and flashy red sports car.

Fast like life. His sister's life.

Red like blood. His sister's blood.

His sister, who he could see reaching for her seat belt as B.J. shoved the key into the ignition.

"Terri!!!!!!!!!!!"

He ran faster, shouting her name, praying he'd still make it in time . . .

Then time stopped. Life stopped.

The car exploded in a blast of fire and smoke and a breath-stealing concussion that blew him off his feet . . .

Sam shot awake like a bullet. Heart hammering. Drenched in sweat. Aware of someone talking.

Talking to him, he realized after several moments.

He blinked. Blinked again, focused on the FASTEN SEAT BELT sign lit in red on the bulkhead in front of him. Heard the clunk and shift of landing gears.

"I'm sorry to wake you, sir."

A sense of time and place finally assembled. He was

on a plane. On a flight from Tegucigalpa, Honduras, to Vegas.

"We'll be landing in a few minutes. Please return your seat to the upright position."

He dragged an unsteady hand over his jaw, nodded absently to the cabin attendant, did as she asked.

"Someone special?"

He glanced up at her. Barely noticed nice blue eyes, a cover-girl complexion. Her name tag identified her as Dana. She was smiling at him. Expectant. Flirtatious.

"I'm sorry?"

"Terri? You were calling her name. While you were sleeping. Is she someone special?"

He felt himself go cold beneath the clammy layer of perspiration dampening his back.

Dana must have taken his silence for affirmation. And a rebuff. "Well . . . hope she knows how lucky she is."

With a wistful, regretful smile, she headed down the aisle.

. . . how lucky she is.

Sam stared at the seat back directly in front of him. He fought the burn of tears that had been pushing since he'd talked to his father yesterday.

. . . how lucky she is.

Yeah. Terri was lucky.

Lucky enough to be dead along with her husband.

Lucky enough to be buried in two days.

Lucky enough to have been killed by a bomb delivered as a message for Sam to back off.

He reached into the breast pocket of his shirt. Unfolded the dog-eared scrap of paper delivered with the help of AK-47 fire and a fucking mason jar.

He reread the words that still made his heart lurch, his breath catch, his hatred coil like a snake in his belly.

"Better call home. Boom, boom. She's dead."

Guilt washed through him. Weighty. Desolate. Acute.

His sister was dead. Because Sam had pissed off the wrong person.

Fredrick Nader.

There was no question in Sam's mind that Nader was behind Terri's and B.J.'s deaths. Nader's signature was all over the hit.

Nader wanted Sam to back off. When he wouldn't, and because Nader couldn't get to Sam, he'd found a way to hit Sam where it hurt the most.

The bastard murdered Sam's kid sister with a fucking car bomb.

As a warning.

As a means to ensure that Sam understood: Back off or Nader's organization could get to any of his family members anytime he wanted and Sam couldn't do a damn thing about it.

Not one thing but bury his kid sister.

2

"What about yours?"

Abbie Hughes glanced up from her chocolate malt and pressed at the sharp pain in her temple where the ice cream had shot her into a temporary brain freeze. "What about my *what*?"

"What about your qualifications for the ultimate male?" Crystal Debrowski reminded Abbie of their current topic of conversation. "I told you mine, now you tell me yours."

Abbie fiddled absently with a French fry. Outside the window, neon flashed, sirens screamed, and people of every age and ethnic heritage ambled along the street, laughing and talking, limping and exhausted. It didn't matter that it was nearly 1:00 a.m. It was bright as noon twenty-four-seven, three-sixty-five, on the Vegas Strip.

Crystal glared impatiently at her friend. "You may think you've gotten good at practicing avoidance, but, my dear, it doesn't work with me."

Abbie grinned at Crystal. Well, she'd tried. With Crystal for a friend, Abbie practiced avoidance a lot. Not that practice made perfect—and not that Crystal ever let her get away with it.

Abbie dragged her gaze back to Crystal. "Why is it that every time we get together the conversation eventually drifts to men?"

"Because," Crystal said with the patience generally reserved for the mentally challenged, "conversations about men always lead to conversations about sex—and sex is my all-time favorite subject."

Abbie lifted a brow. "I have no idea why that logic escaped me."

Crystal snorted. "Yeah, well, I do. It's because you're too busy to think about sex, let alone participate in it. The way I see it, I'm your best chance to live vicariously since you obviously have your priorities all screwed up."

Priorities. Well, there were those, Abbie thought, and tried not to worry about her kid brother, Cory, who should have returned home last night. Not only was Cory a no-show, Abbie hadn't heard word one from him about where he was or why he'd been delayed.

It wasn't that Cory hadn't pulled something like this before. Before and often. Cory wasn't exactly known for his reliability and good judgment. She just kept hoping that he had finally found a little stability in his life.

So much for what she'd hoped.

Reminding herself that it was his life, not hers, and that she had to literally stop trying to be her brother's keeper, she tuned back into what Crystal was saying.

" . . . later?"

Abbie grinned sheepishly. "I'm sorry. Later what?"

Crystal slumped back in the booth, expelled an elaborate sigh. With her pixie features, spiky red hair, and fairy-green eyes, Crystal had to work hard to look stern, but somehow she managed it. "I said, do you want to go casino crawling later?"

"I don't know how to break this to you, Tinkerbell, but one, it *is* later. Two, I just came off a double shift, which means that I just *crawled* out of a casino. And three, I can't think of a single incentive strong enough to compel me to crawl back into one."

Chin in her palm, Crystal swished her straw around in her glass. "How do you ever expect to meet men if you don't go out and party with them?" She looked and sounded put out.

"I've met plenty of men. You may recall I was even foolish enough to have married one."

Not that Don was the yardstick by which Abbie now measured all others, but once had been enough, thank you very much. She'd given it two good years. The problem was, Don had only given it one. By the time Abbie found out he was sleeping around, it was all over but the shouting anyway.

Yeah, Abbie had regrets. She'd loved Don. She'd planned on making a life with him. She hadn't suspected that he'd had the fidelity of a tomcat and the integrity of a Kleenex. And she hadn't banked on being such a poor judge of character. That was probably what upset her the most out of the whole deal.

Her confidence in herself had been badly shaken. Confidence in her judgment, in her self-worth. In monogamy in general. True, she'd been only twenty-three when she'd married Don. Twenty-three was young. She recognized that now, yet two years after the divorce, she still didn't feel that she had fine-tuned or adequately honed the skills required to fight the good fight again.

"You probably haven't even noticed the hunk in the booth across the aisle from us," Crystal said in a low whisper and with a little head hitch to the right. "He's been checking you out ever since he got here."

Abbie glanced across the aisle. She'd noticed the guy all right. It was hard not to. Hair too long and too blond, eyes too blue, body too buff, jeans too tight. Oh, yeah, let's not forget the heavy five o'clock shadow and snakeskin boots. She knew the type. Don had been just like him. Pretty and petty, with an ego the size of Lake Mead.

"Do not—I repeat," she uttered under her breath with an I-mean-business glare at Crystal, "do *not* make eye contact. Do not encourage him. Do not even think about playing dating service."

She glanced involuntarily at Mr. Blond and Blue, ignored his "I like what I see and I'm interested" grin and fired Crystal another warning glare.

"You are sooo not fun," Crystal muttered with a roll of her eyes.

"You like him? *You* go after him."

"Why bother?" Crystal sighed. "He's probably gay

anyway." Another sigh. "Or a cowboy. Or a cop. One's as bad as the other."

Abbie pushed out a sympathetic laugh. With anyone but Crystal, it would have been a difficult leap of logic to follow. But, since Crystal had fallen for all three types and had gotten her heart broken each time, Abbie understood. She also understood that Crystal talked big about sex but the truth was, she was monogamous in her relationships. That's not to say she didn't take very seriously the old axiom of love the one you're with and practice it with enthusiasm.

"I suppose you have class tomorrow," Crystal muttered, looking and sounding as disgusted as if she'd just said, "I suppose you have foot rot."

"I suppose I do." Between Abbie's job at the casino and her accounting classes at UNLV, her free time was short. So was her sleep time. "Which is all the more reason for me to head home and get to bed."

Abbie slid out of the booth to Crystal's mumbled, "And we all know what that means for you."

"Yeah. Sleep. I need it."

As they walked to the register to pay for their burgers and fries, Abbie was aware of the sidelong looks they got, not only from the cute, blond, gay, cowboy cop who was still sitting in the booth watching them with his bedroom-blue eyes, but from the other patrons of the little diner. They'd been getting those looks for years. Individually, the two of them were each capable of turning a head or two. Together, they never failed.

It wasn't that either of them was a raving beauty, although one of the most common lines Abbie heard as she dealt at her blackjack table five nights a week was that she was striking. The same could be said about Crystal. As a pair, though, they presented ample cause for curious stares.

While Crystal was green-eyed and tiny—in her four-inch platforms she had to stretch to make five foot five—Abbie's eyes were so brown they were almost black. And she was tall. Put *her* in a pair of four-inch platforms—and Lord knows, Crystal had tried—and Abbie pushed six feet. In addition, while Crystal's fair skin would fry to a crisp under the Nevada sun and she wore her fiery red hair short and spiky, Abbie had been blessed with a Mediterranean complexion.

Her olive skin loved the sun. She wore a perpetual honey-colored tan that complemented the hair she'd inherited from her mother. Sable brown, thick and lush, she wore it in a simple cut, the same length all over. When she wore it down, it hit just between her shoulder blades; when she wore it up, which she had tonight, it added another couple of inches to her height.

Where Crystal bounced when she walked—all round jiggling breasts and saucily swinging hips—Abbie had been told that she glided, her figure lean and fine-tuned from the five miles she ran every morning.

"See you, toots," Abbie said as they walked out the diner door. "And be careful out there," she added in her best warning-cop voice.

"Wish I had a reason to offer you the same advice." Crystal fluttered a wave over her shoulder.

Abbie just smiled, headed for her car, and drove straight home, enjoying the new-car smell, the luxurious leather, the quiet purr of the smooth-running engine. Lord, she loved this car. Her very first *new* car.

Once home, she engaged her security system, double-checked the locks, and before she went to bed, spent too much time worrying about her brother and wondering about the boxes that arrived a couple of times a week from Honduras.

"Relax," Cory had said the last time he'd called and she'd asked what was in them. "It's nothing illegal. You think I'd stick you in the middle of something like that? Give me a little credit."

Abbie had been giving Cory credit for most of her life. Most of her life, though, he'd disappointed her. Yet she chose to believe him because she loved him and because of all they'd been through together. If she didn't believe in him, no one else would.

"Check 'em out if you want to," he'd said, sounding wounded. "All you're going to find are trinkets. Native craft items I picked up for a song in Honduras. You know. Drums. Baskets. Knockoff Mayan figurines. As soon as I find the right wholesaler, I'm going to make a small fortune off that stuff."

Cory was always going to make a small fortune off something. Of course, Abbie hadn't checked the boxes she had stored in her garage. Cory needed that from her. Needed to know she trusted him.

She hoped it had been the right choice.

She checked her e-mail before she went to bed, just

in case. Nothing from Cory. Before she finally fell
asleep, she was still thinking about him, worrying about
where he was and how he was. And yeah, she spent a little time wondering about the blond Adonis who had all
but followed them out the door. Cowboy? Gay? Cop?

Cop, she decided finally. Despite the obvious invita-
tion in his eyes, he had an edge to him. What didn't
make sense, though, was why he'd seemed so interested
in her, and that had her wondering about Cory's boxes
and fretting again about where he was as she drifted off.

San Pedro Sula, Honduras

Cory Hughes sat behind the wheel of the rented Jeep,
tapping his fingers restlessly on the steering wheel.

"Sit and wait. Sit and wait," he muttered. He spent
half of his life on the sit and wait.

It would be different if he could afford to. As it was,
he was living on borrowed time.

He felt it. Just like he sensed the clock ticking. Just
like he knew that if he didn't get out of this cloak-and-
dagger crap he was going to end up sliced and diced
into little pieces and scattered like chum bait from the
Gulf of Honduras to Cuba.

Exhaust fumes and jet fuel clogged the sweltering
air as he sat and waited for Derek Styles outside the San
Pedro Sula airport, trying to figure out how he'd come
to this. One day he'd been selling his knockoff Honduran artifacts on a Vegas street corner. The next thing
he knew he'd agreed to do a favor for a friend in exchange for a free ticket to Honduras, where he could

select his inventory firsthand instead of relying on long-distance contacts. All he'd had to do to earn the ticket was bring a package back with him to Vegas.

How could he say no? All his life he'd been scrambling to make a dime. The job market was slim to none for a high school dropout. He'd needed rent money. He'd needed to eat. And he'd promised himself he wouldn't hit up his sister for cash again. So he'd made the delivery. End of story—or so he'd thought.

God, he'd been stupid. He should have known there was something illegal going on. Turned out the package had contained drugs—something he'd fought all his life to stay clear of. It also turned out that his so-called friend had been an enforcer for an international criminal and warned Cory that if he didn't continue to play along and deliver the occasional package, bad things would happen to him.

He didn't want bad things to happen, so now he was in the stew up to his neck and barely managing to stay afloat. He knew without a doubt that if he crossed these guys, he'd end up dead.

That fact became crystal clear six months ago, when he'd been taken to meet Mr. Big in Puerto Cortez. Fredrick Nader had asked to see him. To be introduced to the "promising young protégé," as he'd put it.

Cory had never been anyone's promising young anything. Knew he wasn't now, even when a limo had picked him up and driven him to the docks, where a cigarette boat right out of *Miami Vice* had run him out to Nader's yacht.

And Nader—he acted like royalty or something. Looked like it, too. The dude was old—fifty-, sixty-something. Thin and fit. Hair as white as his pants. Cory had never seen pants so white. Shoes so shiny. Nader had been getting a manicure when Cory had been introduced to him while a crew of servants had stepped and fetched him pricey wine in a glass so fine and thin he was afraid it would break in his hand.

Then things had gotten real. Cory had been shown what happened to someone who "opted out" of Nader's employ. The man—what was left of him—had fallen out of favor with Nader and under the blade of Nader's muscleman, Rutger Smith, a guy with a real skill with a knife.

Cory had been scared straight ever since that night. Just like he'd been looking for an out ever since.

"Hey, man."

Cory jumped when Derek Styles, another one of Nader's mules, jerked open the passenger door and threw his duffel into the back. "How's it shakin'?"

He tried to look cool. "You're late."

"Bitch to the airline."

Derek was tall and scrawny, his hair a shaggy, dirty brown. He smelled like sour sweat and sweet weed as he crawled into the passenger seat and slammed the door behind him. "Home, James."

Cory grunted, checked the rearview mirror, and pulled away from the terminal and into traffic.

"Big deal going down," Derek said, tapping his fingers on his thigh.

Yeah, in this business, there was always a big deal going down. "Don't want to know about it."

Derek shook his head in disgust as they headed for open highway and the wind dragged his hair back from his ferret face.

"Nader—he's got more money than God, you know?" Derek said, ignoring Cory. "Me, I'd spend it on women and blow. But Nader has this thing for diamonds."

Didn't surprise Cory. Nothing about Nader surprised him anymore. Nader's main business involved cocaine and heroin, stolen arms, and chemical weapons. That Nader also had a thing for diamonds just stood to reason. Diamonds and stolen art and anything else that was hard to come by and illegal to own fit the MO.

"That's why I'm back in Honduras," Derek went on. "To move hot rocks for the Man."

"Must be some diamonds." Cory's curiosity got the best of him when Derek told him how much Nader paid for the diamonds. "How do you know what they cost him?" It wasn't like Derek was in Nader's inner circle.

"I overheard Smith make the final transaction on the phone."

Cory suppressed a shudder when he thought about Rutger Smith. He was one big scary dude. Carried one big scary knife.

"Package arrives tonight. Coming into port at Muchilena."

Muchilena was a small Gulf of Honduras port less

than an hour north of San Pedro Sula. Nader liked to mix up the drop spots. Last pickup had been on the Caribbean side.

"You know, we could get there first. You and me. Beat Smith to the transfer."

Cory stared at Derek like he was tripping on E when he realized what Derek had in mind. "Are you nuts?"

"Come on, dude. Get a backbone. Don't you ever get tired of being Nader's errand boy?" Derek taunted. "Don't you ever wonder what it would be like to have the lion's share of the sale instead of groveling for table scraps?"

"Hell, yes, I wonder. But I'm not crossing him. No way."

"Not even for a cool half of five mil? You really think you're going to make anything but chump change with those native craft knockoffs you keep sending back to the States?"

Those knockoffs were Cory's bid for legitimacy. He bought them for a song down here and shipped them back to his sister in Vegas. And, yeah. When he finally figured a way out from under Nader's iron fist, his little stash of merchandise was going to set him up in business. Rich Americans dug that kind of stuff. He'd get twenty times his cost once he broke into the market. He could finally leave this life behind and get back to being legit.

Not that half of five million dollars wasn't tempting as hell. But so was living. "A little hard to spend if you're dead."

Derek snorted. "With that kind of coin, you can go to ground for a year. Buy yourself a new face. New ID. Nader can't kill a dead man."

Cory checked his mirror. Switched lanes. "I don't want to talk about it."

So he didn't. Didn't say another word as he drove Derek to a cheap motel and dropped him off.

"Don't do it," he warned when Derek got out of the Jeep.

"Last chance," Derek baited him.

Hands raised, Cory shook his head, then drove away. Hoping to hell that if Derek was lame enough to attempt his idiotic plan, Nader wouldn't come looking in his direction for an accomplice.

He decided right then and there that he had to figure a way out.

                                                    2:00 a.m.

Cory shot up in bed, jolted out of a dead sleep. Someone at his door, he realized as a muffled pounding had him scrambling to his feet. He stumbled into a pair of cargo shorts and scrambled across the room.

"Who is it?"

"Le' me in."

Derek.

Cory cracked the door to the hostel room he rented by the day. Deadweight pressed against it, then Derek fell into the room. Blood soaked his shirt.

"Jesus. Jesus." Cory caught him, broke his fall. "What the hell happened?"

He stared into unfocused, feverish eyes. Derek struggled to breathe.

"Damn. You did it, didn't you? God, Jesus God." Panic slammed to the beat of his heart as Derek coughed up blood and folded into himself. "You stupid bastard."

"So s-stupid I'm carrying . . . m-millions of dollars in . . . diamonds."

"And you brought them here? Led Nader to me?"

Derek's breath rattled. "Lost 'em. Those . . . fuckers who shot me . . . lost 'em."

"Yeah," Cory wailed. "For now. Fuck. You need a doctor."

He started to rise. Derek grabbed his arm, stopped him.

"My pocket." Derek wheezed with the effort to even whisper. "It's all . . . there. The goods. The d-deal I set up. Your . . . d-deal . . . now."

Then the bastard died.

Died.

Holy God.

For a moment, all Cory could do was stare. He was frozen with panic, stunned by what had just happened. Derek wasn't a friend. But he was a human being. And now he was dead.

Heart pounding, Cory stood, stared at the body, dragged his hands through his hair. Knew the door was going to burst open any moment and Nader's thugs would blast him, too.

That's what he had to think about now. No matter which way he sliced this, Nader was going to kill him. Even if he went to Nader and told him what Derek had done, Nader would figure Cory was in on it but that he'd gotten cold feet. If he ran, Nader would just find him. He always found who he was looking for.

He stared at the blood on his hands. At the body on the floor. Then his survival instincts kicked him in the ass.

His hands shook as he fished around in Derek's pockets. Finally, he pulled out a blue velvet pouch. He turned it upside down. A necklace of the biggest diamonds he'd ever seen poured out into his hand.

His mouth dropped open.

Shit. Oh, shit. He'd seen this necklace before. On the local news on TV. Big theft from the Honduras National Museum last week. A national treasure. Once belonged to some Honduran priestess or something. He couldn't remember.

What the hell did it matter anyway? He had the diamonds now. If he turned them in to the government, it was just one more guarantee he'd signed his death warrant. Nader wouldn't take kindly to having what he, no doubt, considered his stones given back to their rightful owners.

Five million dollars worth of stones.

Five. Million. Dollars.

It didn't matter that he didn't want anything to do with them. Like it or not, they were his now. All he had to do was figure out a way to live long enough to reap the profit.

He glanced back down at Derek. He had to have had a buyer set up. Someone who was a guaranteed quick score, because Derek would have needed a quick score to get out of Honduras.

He dropped to his knees again. Frantically searched the rest of Derek's pockets. He finally came up with a piece of paper with a name and phone number.

It took him a while to puzzle out the letters but he made himself take his time. When he finally pieced the words together, he didn't want to believe what he saw.

Desmond Fox.

Oh, Christ.

This was where Derek had planned to sell the diamonds? To Desmond Fox?

Cory wanted to fall to the floor and bawl like a baby.

If Nader was a cobra, Fox was a pit viper. The two men were archrivals. There was no love lost or honor held between these two murdering thieves and Cory was now firmly caught between them.

He clawed a hand through his hair again. Finally laughed. Shit. It was either that or curl up in a ball and wait for Smith to come after him with Mr. Knife. Or Fox to come after him with an AK-47.

"Think. Think, dammit!"

He stood, paced the floor, stumbled over Derek's body. Wondered who would stumble over his when they found him.

"What choice do you have? What choice do you really have?"

He stared at the phone number on the paper, drew a breath, and picked up his cell to make the deal with Fox. His fingers shook as he dialed the number. A voice, heavy with a Spanish accent, answered on the third ring.

"Tupacka." Cory had labored over the letters, spoke them now, according to the instructions on the paper. As soon as he said it aloud he made the final connection. Tupacka—that was the name of the Honduran priestess. The diamonds had been hers—a wedding gift from some Spanish dude a couple hundred years ago, according to that same TV news report.

"Hold, please," the contact said after a short silence.

Cory waited. And paced. Bouncing with nervous energy and fear. Until finally, he was given a time and a place for the meet. The connection ended.

His gut knotted with fear. Five days. The meet was set for five long days from now. Swearing, he started throwing his few things into a backpack. He carefully packaged the diamonds, deciding what he had to do to protect them and hopefully protect himself until he made the deal.

He got all the way to the Jeep, had the engine started, hand on the gearshift, and just couldn't do it. He couldn't leave Derek there. Styles was a thief and a druggie but somewhere, someone might care. Just like somewhere, someone cared about what happened to Cory.

Swearing, he sprinted back to his room, wrapped Derek's body in a blanket, and hauled him out to the rented Jeep. He stopped at the first church that popped up—there were hundreds of them in San Pedro Sula—and pulled up out back where it was dark. Making sure no one was around, he unloaded Derek's body by the back door.

Then he raced the hell away, ditched the Jeep, and took off on foot. He never looked back. He made himself disappear in this city of close to a million people. Five days from now he'd either be rich or dead. Providing he could stay alive in the meantime.

3

Rancho Royale, Las Vegas, Nevada

"I get the picture, okay?" Without turning away from the screen on his laptop, Sam interrupted Reed's monologue about some woman he'd just met. "She brushed you off like a piece of white dog hair on a black dress."

"Yeah. She did for a fact." A big grin spread across Reed's outrageously handsome face. Somehow, he'd managed to slouch all six feet and one hundred eighty pounds of cover-boy looks into the black leather club chair facing the desk in Sam's office.

"The woman said no. To me," Reed continued, oblivious to Sam's dark scowl. His golden grin flashed a set of perfect white teeth and a pair of dimples that made the old ladies coo and the young ones lie down and smile. "God, what a set of balls."

"Having a little trouble with *that* picture," Sam said drolly as he turned his attention back to the pedigree of the quarter horse stud he was considering buying to improve the line of the breeding program at the ranch.

Reed laughed. "You are not taking me seriously, here." He stood, started prowling the office.

"Ya think? You met her on a flight. You'll probably never see her again. End of story."

God only knew what Sam had been thinking when Reed had called him from the airport and Sam had told him to come on out for this impromptu visit—the third in the three months since Sam had resigned from Black Ops, Inc.

He wanted Reed and Nate Black and the rest of the BOIs to leave him the hell alone. The chances of that happening were about the same as Reed giving up women. Just like the chance that Reed had shown up again was so he could catch Sam up on his love life.

Sam put up with Reed's semimonthly visits for one reason. He understood that his leaving Black Ops, Inc. hadn't merely broken up the team. That's because they weren't just a team. Black Ops, Inc. was a family. They were brothers, not by blood, but by ties forged in the trenches that were as tight as the coordinates on a precision bombing run.

Several years ago, Nathan Black, the CO of Task Force Mercy, had grown tired of being hamstrung by D.C. legislators who didn't know their ass from a frag grenade and knew even less about waging war, covert or otherwise. So Black had formed his own private contracting firm. When he'd parted ways with Uncle, so had most of the Task Force Mercy team. Sam had been one of the first to join, along with Gabe Jones, Raphael Mendoza, Luke Colter, Wyatt Savage, and Joe Greene—to name a few. Once they'd served out their hitches, they had separated from their various branches of the military and joined Black Ops, Inc.

For a lot of years now, they'd worked for Nate like a family.

Sam watched absently as Reed walked around the room. Most of those years had been spent down in Argentina. All of them chasing bad guys whose names law-abiding Americans would never know, pulling off ops that would never make the paper, and never be recorded in any annals of American history attached to the U.S. war machine.

Through it all, they hadn't just worked together. They'd lived together. Fought together. Grieved together.

Sam thought back to Terri's and B.J.'s funerals. Not only had the BOIs come to pay their respects, so had Ann and Robert Tompkins, who had "adopted" them all several years ago. The Tompkinses also knew what loss was. They'd paid the ultimate price. Their son, Bryan, had been a member of Task Force Mercy. He'd been killed on a mission in Sierra Leone, fighting as a warrior who knew the stakes, knew the risk, accepted the danger.

Sam stared into space. Clenched his jaw.

Terri hadn't been a warrior. Terri hadn't signed on for any risk. She and B.J. had been innocents. But to Fredrick Nader, Terri had been a means to an end. Collateral damage, a necessary tactic to get Sam off his back.

Well, Nader had gotten what he wanted.

Sam was done. Finished. He'd resigned from BOI the day he'd helped bury his sister. Nader's message had been clear. Back off or someone else Sam cared about would die.

So he'd walked away.

Yeah, it ate at him. Ate at his gut, ate at his soul, ate at his will until there was no fight left in him. He was done. Done trying. Done fighting.

Nader had won.

He would not risk anything else happening to his family.

"How do you handle this?" Reed had moved to the window. He stared out at the horse barns that snuggled up to the slow rise of the foothills and the low riding mountains beyond.

Sam spared him a glance. He'd known this was coming. It was the opening line to the "aren't you ready to come back to BOI?" spiel.

And the "this" in question was life on the ranch. Sam had grown up on Rancho Royale, breeding and selling quarter horses with his dad. "I'm handling it just fine."

"It's so friggin' quiet." Reed turned, planted himself in front of Sam's desk. Head cocked, he frowned, looking genuinely perplexed. "Don't you miss it?"

Sam looked up. He met Reed's eyes with a direct stare. Did he miss the action? The adrenaline rush? Breaking bad boys and their toys and putting them out of commission?

He couldn't afford to miss it. Just like he couldn't afford to let Reed see that he did. "Nope."

Reed hunkered down on his haunches, crossed his forearms over the edge of the desk directly in front of Sam. Those baby blues studied Sam from behind lashes as thick and blond as his hair. "Not even a little?"

Sam blinked. Turned back to his laptop.

"You know, if it's the conditioning that's stopping you," Reed continued, "it wouldn't take much to whip you back into shape. Hell, it's only been three months. And thirty-five's not *that* old—you're still close to fightin' weight. Not that anyone would ever expect you to keep up with me. Not that you ever could," he added with a baiting grin.

Sam gave him a benign look. "And the horse you rode in on."

Reed laughed. Sam didn't.

He wasn't going back. Reed knew why.

Yet here Reed was. Again.

"So," Reed said, sober suddenly, "it probably wouldn't interest you to know we've got a line on Nader. No smoke and mirrors this go-round. Something solid. We can nail his ass this time."

Sam forced himself to remain perfectly still. Reed was every bit as still. His good-ole-boy grin had dissolved into a grim expression.

"I mean it, Sam. This could finally be the break we need to take him out," he said with a soft but steely resolve. "Mendoza's been in Honduras since you left, digging around, setting up contacts, working on leads, but it's been your op from the beginning. Your hard work. You deserve to make the strike and take this bastard down."

Sam closed his eyes, made himself breathe as fists of anger clutched at his chest and pummeled at his control.

What he deserved.

This wasn't about what he deserved. His sister was dead. His brother-in-law—dead.

Because Sam had been bearing down on Nader's ass.

He wanted Nader more than he wanted to breathe. But he couldn't. He just couldn't.

He pushed back in his chair, steepled his fingers over his mouth, and glared at Reed. He wanted to shout at him to get the hell off his property and drag the bait along with him.

Forty pounds of giggling energy burst through the door of the study and forestalled anything more toxic than a glare. "Uncle Sam!"

Oblivious to the tension zipping through the room, as only a six-year old can be, Tina scrambled up onto Sam's lap.

"Hester's foalin'," his niece announced breathlessly. She smelled of little girl sweat and hay and sunshine. It was painfully sweet to see her smile after listening to her cry herself to sleep most nights. "After waitin' and waitin' it's finally time. This baby's mine, right, Uncle Sam? Mine and Hester's."

Sam smiled into Tina's dancing brown eyes. Love for this beautiful child overwhelmed him. She looked so much like her mother had at this age. Terri had been as bright and as bubbly as the ginger ale she'd loved to drink. Tina sparkled with the same effervescent energy.

Fredrick Nader may be the reason Sam was helping his parents raise his sister's little girl, but Sam was ultimately the one responsible. Just like Tina and his mom and dad were the reasons he couldn't risk going after Nader.

"Right, Uncle Sam?" Determined to get his full attention, she tugged on the dog tags he still wore.

"You betcha, baby." He pressed a kiss to her forehead. "Everything going okay in the barn?"

"Um-hum. Caesar said Hester's doin' just fine, but he wanted me to run and tell you 'case you wanted to call the vet or somethin'."

"Hey, babycakes," Reed said when he could get a word in edgewise. "How's my darlin'?"

"Johnny Duane!" Tina squealed.

In a flurry of scuffed boots and honey-brown pigtails, she scooted off Sam's lap and ran into Reed's outstretched arms. "What'd you bring me?"

Reed laughed and scooped her up for a smacking kiss. "You women are all alike. Greedy little wenches, that's all you are."

"So what'd you bring me?" Tina persisted, playing the game they'd played since Reed had charmed her on his first visit, a female secure in her element and her power.

Reed dug in his hip pocket and produced a set of handcuffs.

"Wow!" She snatched them away like a little thief. "Just what I always wanted!"

"Wish all the girls were as easy as you, shortstuff."

"Are you staying for supper?" she asked hopefully as she slid down to the floor and experimented with the latch on the cuffs.

Reed glanced at Sam, took his cue from a stone-cold glare. "I don't think so, darlin'. I think I'll head back to town and try my luck on the Strip. I just stopped by to give your Uncle Sam a piece of news." He slid an envelope out of his breast pocket, tossed it on the desk.

Sam's gaze shot from Reed's to the envelope. He knew there would be information on Nader inside. Very slowly, Sam rose, turned his back on the desk and any discussion involving Nader. "Come on, Tina. Let's go check on Hester."

"Call me," Reed said when they'd walked outside. The sun beat down like hot lead, weighty and oppressive.

Sam kept right on walking. Everything that mattered to him now was right here on this ranch. He wasn't leaving them alone and defenseless ever again.

The first thing Sam saw when he stepped into his office at 6:00 a.m. the next morning was the unopened envelope Reed had left on his desk the day before. He glared at it through bleary eyes, set a steaming cup of coffee beside it. Then he sat down in the leather chair and dragged a hand over his face, rubbing at the stubble.

He'd been up all night with the mare. Turned out she'd had complications after all and he'd had to call in the vet. All was well now. Both the mare and a foxy little filly were doing just fine.

He wasn't.

He stared at the envelope.

Swore.

Picked it up.

Tossed it down again.

He glanced outside. Through the branches of a cottonwood framing the office window, he could see all the main buildings. The stud barn sat on the north, the foaling barn dead ahead. A large enclosure full of yearlings opened wide to the east, just beyond the pasture of broodmares turned out with their foals.

His mom stood by the paddock fence, a protective hand on Tina's back as Tina stood on the third fence rung, her little cowboy boots hooked over the rail so she could get a better view of the mommas and their babies.

As loving and giving as his mom was, as nurturing and careful as she was with Tina, the picture was all wrong. It should include Terri.

A soft knock on the door broke into his thoughts.

"Am I interrupting anything, son?"

Sam forced his shoulders to relax. Just as he forced a smile. "No, Dad. Come on in. And since when do you have to knock on your own office door?"

His dad walked into the room, glanced out the window. "It's your office now." Tom Lang turned back to

Sam, offered a smile that didn't manage to conceal the strain Terri's death had carved into his face.

"Always hoped you'd come back home. Take over the ranch someday." He compressed his lips, shook his head, and Sam could see he was fighting tears. "Never thought it'd be like this."

Sam swallowed hard. He hated seeing his father like this. Haggard. Broken. Always on the edge of tears.

For as long as he had memories his dad had been like a god to him. Strong. Proud. Invincible. Young for his years. Loving life.

Terri's and B.J.'s deaths had changed all that.

Sam had never felt helpless in his life. He felt it now. Marrow deep. Like he felt the churning deep in his gut to hunt down Nader like the dog he was and make him pay for what he'd done to Terri. To little Tina. To his mom and dad.

Helpless because, to keep his family safe, Sam had had to let the murdering bastard walk away.

"You need to fix this."

The hard edge in his father's voice startled him. For the first time in weeks, Sam saw something other than profound grief in his father's eyes. They were fired with anger and conviction.

"You can't let him get away with what he did to Terri and B.J."

His father knew, of course. One night over a bottle of Jack Daniel's, Tom Lang had called his only son out. "Let's hear it," he'd said. "Let me hear it all."

Sam had never lied to his dad. Had never been able

to keep something from him when it was eating at him. Terri's death had been tearing into him with shark's teeth.

So he'd told him. Slouched back on the leather sofa in this very room, with a half-empty glass in his hand, tears in his eyes, and midnight striking on the clock, he told him that Fredrick Nader had killed Terri to get to Sam.

"Sam."

His dad's voice snapped him back to the here and now.

"You *need* to fix this."

Sam was so tired. Of living with the guilt. Of resisting the urge to do exactly what his father was asking him to do. "I can't. You know why I can't."

His dad eased down into the club chair, met Sam's tortured eyes across the desk. "I've given you time. Knew you needed to get yourself grounded again. Needed to grieve. But now it's time for revenge."

Sam looked away, heartsick. His dad was a gentle man. Like Sam, he was also a quiet man. Tough but fair. Honest to a fault. A believer—in God, in goodness, in his fellow man. Sam's hatred of Nader ascended to new heights as he sat here and listened to his father talk about revenge.

"I can't," he said again. Pleaded with his eyes for his dad to understand. To let it go. To move on.

Like Sam was trying to move on.

Tears filled his father's eyes. "You can't not."

Tears. From this proud, proud man.

Sam's fault.

"You think I don't want to take this bastard out?" Sam's voice broke. He settled himself. "Jesus, Dad. It's all I think about."

"Then take care of it."

He lifted a hand. Let it fall. "What? And take a chance he'll come after you next . . . or Mom? What if he targets Tina? I can't live with another death on my head."

His father straightened. "I may be getting older, son, but I can still take care of my own. He won't blindside me or mine again. No one else is gonna die on my watch."

Outside, the sky was a brilliant, crystalline blue, the air hot and arid and scented of the desert. Inside, shadows filled the room—shadows of his sister's ghost that cooled the air to a grave-damp chill.

Tom Lang stood, walked to Sam's side, and laid a hand on his shoulder. "You owe it to Terri. More, you owe it to yourself. I know you. This is going to eat at you until there's nothing left but a hollow shell of the man you are. Then you'll be as gone from me as Terri is."

He squeezed, dropped his hand. "I can't lose you both."

Then he walked out of the office, closing the door behind him.

Sam sat in the ringing silence for almost an hour before he picked up the envelope Reed had left. He ran his thumb along the creased edge. Finally opened it.

Read it. Read it again.

He glanced out the window to see his dad walk out of the stud barn toward the driveway. His shoulders were stooped, his gait labored.

Sam breathed deep, then he slowly reached for the phone.

Reed answered on the second ring.

"I'm in," he said and hung up, knowing he'd just done the equivalent of stepping out of a Blackhawk without a parachute or a rope.

4

"Do you think I should be worried about Cory?" Abbie asked Crystal as the two of them stood back and assessed the placement of Abbie's new sofa and chair.

"I think you should be enjoying your new furniture. My Lord, this leather feels like butter." Crystal Debrowski sank down on the luxurious sofa with a humming sigh.

"Yeah," Abbie agreed, grinning at her friend. "It *is* pretty cool, huh?"

"More than."

"Looks good," she said, glancing around the room, approving of the arrangement after she and Crystal had moved the furniture several times.

"Looks great!" Crystal agreed.

For accessories and paint, she'd gone for soft, soothing colors to complement the buff-colored leather. With her hectic and packed schedule, she'd wanted a calm and inviting place to land when she had a moment to unwind. Sage and moss green, sand and desert browns interspersed with the occasional punch of a watery blue made this room the oasis she needed.

"So what do you think about Cory?" Abbie persisted, plopping down on the sofa beside Crystal. "He was supposed to be back in Vegas two days ago. I still haven't heard from him."

"And this is out of character?"

Abbie lifted a shoulder. "Okay. So maybe it's not."

"You're not his mother, Abbie," Crystal said gently. "And you're not his keeper."

Yeah. Crystal was right. Abbie needed to quit stewing.

"Right. Thanks. And thanks for the help." She checked her watch. "Oh, man. I've got to scramble or I'll be late for work tonight."

"Say no more. I'm off like a dirty shirt." Crystal headed for the door. "See ya when I see ya."

Abbie hustled for the shower, mentally calculating the time and wondering what corners she could cut and not be late for her shift, all the while fighting desperately not to worry about her brother.

"That's her. Second table. She's just coming back from a break."

Sam had met Reed at the Casino New Orleans ten minutes ago, where the two of them had taken up residence at a bank of Lucky Seven slot machines. Since then, they'd waited for a blackjack dealer named Abbie Hughes to return to her table.

According to Reed, Abbie Hughes was their pipeline to Fredrick Nader.

Sam fed the machine and tried not to second-guess a decision that had placed everything he loved at risk. He was back in this now. He was in it to the end.

Nader was going to die. For Terri. For B.J. For his dad. Sam would use whatever means available to make certain that happened.

He cast a glance away from the slot, sized up Cory Hughes's sister.

"She's a stone-cold fox, huh?" Reed sat at a slot beside him. "Begs the question, what's a woman like her doing mixed up in Fredrick Nader's shit?"

Over the years, Sam had learned that life begged a lot of questions. In this case, Sam's questions were the same as Reed's. Out of years of practice, he sized up Abbie Hughes with a cold, critical eye.

Reed's assessment was spot-on. The woman was stunning. She was also tall—five-eight, maybe—and willow slim. Vegas was filled with beautiful women. Wannabe models, wannabe actresses, wannabe famous. Sam's initial impression was that Abbie Hughes didn't appear to want to be anything but what she was, as she chatted easily with the players at her table.

That was his first inkling that she might not be exactly what she seemed. Yeah, Abbie Hughes made a pretty package. Sam had learned long ago not to judge a package by its wrapping. Just like he'd learned that women as beautiful as this one always had bigger, better, bolder things on their agendas—wide, guileless eyes and easy smiles notwithstanding.

Her sable-brown hair swung around her shoulders,

glossy and girl-next-door natural. Though she had an athletic body, the curves were all there, too—all the more effective because of their subtlety.

She looked wholesome and centered and sexy, and if she were faking innocence, she was damn good at it, because if Reed's intel was right, Abbie Hughes was knee-deep in international crime just like her brother. That made her Sam's best lead to flush Nader out of his lair.

Still, Sam wondered as he turned back to the machine. "You sure she's in the mix?"

"Shame, huh? But yeah. Everything points straight to her door."

Yeah. It was a shame. Because if she were involved with Nader, she was fair game. As such, Sam would use her to get what he needed and walk away from the wreckage without a backward glance or an ounce of remorse.

"Fill me in." Sam hadn't wanted Reed to brief him over the phone. Old habits were hard to break. The landline at the ranch house wasn't secure and he didn't want to take a chance with his cell. While the report Reed had left for Sam addressed the key points regarding Cory Hughes and his sister, it hadn't offered specific details.

Reed smacked the side of the slot machine and swore when he just missed a jackpot. "Abbie Hughes. Twenty-seven. Divorced. Accounting student at UNLV. Deals here five nights a week. The brother, Cory Hughes, is twenty-two. Single. No visible means of support."

"That much I got. Why'd you look at him in the first place?"

"That watch list you'd been tracking on Nader? Cory Hughes's name started popping up with a bunch of known accomplices shortly after you left the team."

Sam dropped more money into the machine. Punched the button. The *ding-ding-ding* and whirl of bells joined the unending cacophony of sound resonating through the crowded casino and insulated their conversation. "Can you pin him with anything specific?"

Reed shook his head. Swore again when he just missed another jackpot. "What we do know is that Nader likes to play cat-and-mouse with U.S. customs. He's scrambled the paper trail, but Hughes looks good as a facilitator."

"So you're tagging Cory as one of Nader's mules."

"Low level. At least until recently. Like I said, Hughes has never had steady income. It looks like Nader hooked him hard with drug deliveries. Mostly out of Central America. Specifically Honduras."

Nader's favorite playground. Sam's biggest nightmare.

"Hughes was spotted in San Pedro Sula within the last week," Reed continued.

Which meant the trail was fresh. It also meant they needed to start moving on this fast before it went cold.

"Other than the fact that family is usually the first line of resistance, what points to the sister?"

"First, it would figure that an 'entrepreneur' like Cory Hughes would have an accomplice on the inside, right? Someone he could trust."

Sam glanced at Reed. "Yeah, it would figure. But you've got to have more than that."

Reed scowled at the machine, dug into his pocket for more change. "Couple of things. Little brother rents a flop in Northwest Vegas—just past Circus Circus. Nice neighborhood—if you're a rat. Lots of rent-by-the-hour or -day or -week motels. Plenty of meth labs."

"I take it you paid a visit."

"And wouldn't you know it, the door to his room just sort of swung open when I got there."

Yeah. Sam knew how handy Reed was with a pick kit. Lots of doors "just sort of swung open" for Reed.

"Anyway, like I said, the place is a dive. Nothing there but roaches, and there's no room to store anything. But I did find a slug of shipping orders tucked in a locked desk drawer."

"That drawer fall open like the door?"

Reed grinned. "Go figure. Anyway, guess whose address was on those shipping orders?"

"The sister."

"That would be a big blackjack. So, I checked out her place."

"Jesus, Reed. How many laws you going to break?"

Reed effected a wounded look. "I do not break laws. I take advantage of opportunities. But in this case, not so much. Part of town where she lives is several steps up from her brother's digs. Not high end but respectable. Small house. Modest suburban bliss. Lots of security. A suspicious amount, in fact. Gated lot. I also spotted a couple of cameras on the roof. Kind of makes you won-

der what she might be hiding. Add that to the neigh-
bors who are plentiful and nosy and I didn't get inside.

"But I did watch it for a few days," he added to the
ding of his machine making a small payoff. "She gets a
lot of deliveries. Gotta make you wonder what's in them.
If they're from the brother, they could contain anything
from drugs to laundered money to stolen gems."

"And if that's the case, we might be able to convince
her we're on to them and that she's in deep weeds if she
doesn't tell us what she knows," Sam surmised.

He cut another quick look at Abbie Hughes. Her
table was full. She flashed her gamers a killer grin as she
shuffled multiple decks, offered the cut card to the first-
base player, then expertly slipped the cards into the
shoe. Sam watched as she dealt around the table. He
found himself wishing she would turn up clean, even
though it would mean they'd hit a dead end.

"Anything else?" he asked Reed.

"Odds are she's cashing in on the brother's merchandise. The pretty lady has a brand-new shiny ride.
Bought it just last week. Top of the line. And check out
the sparkly hanging around her neck."

While she was wearing it over a pristine white shirt
that buttoned at the throat to accommodate a black tie,
the necklace was what Sam called a cleavage piece.
The rock of a diamond hung from a gold chain. It
didn't take much imagination to figure that if she
hadn't been wearing that shirt, the diamond would
hit just at the point where Abbie Hughes's breasts
squeezed together above her bra cups.

Sam dragged his attention back to the slot and away from her breasts. "Maybe they pay their dealers well here."

"Yeah, right," Reed said. "A little above minimum plus tips."

"Did you run her credit history?"

"One card. Zero balance. And there's no lien on the car."

Which begged another one of those questions that Sam couldn't discount as coincidental: How did a minimum-wage dealer who was also paying tuition come up with the coin to buy a new car and a hunk of carbon that could choke a horse?

If Reed was right, Abbie Hughes could do it because she was working with her brother, who was working for Nader, who was a badass with a penchant for—among other things—stolen gems.

Gems like the diamond hanging around Abbie Hughes's neck.

"By the way," Reed said as he worked the machine, "Mendoza sent some info today that adds a new wrinkle to the report I left with you."

Raphael Mendoza, like Reed, still played on the BOIs team with Jones and Colter and the rest of the guys. Mendoza had been nosing around Honduras for the better part of three months looking for an in with Nader.

Sam waited.

"You did *read* the initial report, right?"

"Yeah. I read it." The Tupacka diamonds—a necklace valued in the millions, had disappeared from the

National Museum of Honduras a week ago. Aside from it being worth upward of five mil, it was also a national treasure, complete with an ancient legend attached. While they had nothing concrete, Nader's fingerprints were all over the heist. Of course, Nader would never do the actual hands-on dirty work, but he'd sure as hell facilitate it. "What's the wrinkle?"

"Desmond Fox's name is surfacing on that deal now, too. Seems they both have a yen for the diamonds."

Sam grunted, not all that surprised. "This is turning into a regular bottom-feeder convention."

Desmond Fox and Fredrick Nader were both spawned from the same swamp. Fox had been on the BOI's radar almost as long as Nader. There was no love lost between these two thieves. No honor either. They competed for the same markets, undercut each other at every opportunity. So it stood to reason if they competed over drugs or weapons they'd mix it up over hot ice.

"Of course, we could get lucky and they'll do each other in," Reed pointed out. "Save us all a lot of trouble."

"Don't believe in luck. And I want Nader for myself."

Reed nodded. "So how do you want to play this?"

Sam glanced at Abbie Hughes again, rubbed a thumb over his lower lip.

"We could lean on her," Reed suggested after a moment. "Scare the info out of her."

Sam shook his head. "Let's save that for plan B. Don't want to take a chance that approach would backfire. She might clam up, warn off little brother, and that would be the end of that. We'd lose them both."

No. This called for a more subtle approach.

"You said she's single?"

Reed shoved more coins into the slot. "Divorced."

"Boyfriend?"

"Not from what I've gathered."

"So maybe she needs one."

"Don't look at me." Reed sounded disgusted. "I arranged to run into her the other night, thinking maybe we could get chummy, you know? Got shut down without so much as a hi, how are ya. I gave her every opening and she set up nothing but roadblocks."

"And you're up and around after that kind of hit to your ego?"

"Hey, I can't help it that most women find me irresistible—or that this one has no taste. Speaking of no taste . . . maybe *you're* her type."

Ignoring the dig, Sam glanced toward Abbie Hughes again. "Yeah," he said, prepared to do whatever it took to bring Nader down. "Maybe I am."

Abbie spotted the gay cop cowboy the minute she came back from break. It was hard not to. The guy was incredible looking. While she felt a little kernel of unease that he'd turned up again—where she worked, this time—she wasn't going to let it throw her off her stride.

The Vegas Strip wasn't all that big. Not really. There were only so many places for people to eat, sleep, and gamble. When he drifted off twenty minutes or so later without so much as looking her way, she chalked it up to coincidence. Just as she found it coincidental that the tall man with the dark eyes and short dark hair who'd been playing the slot beside the golden boy ambled over to the blackjack tables.

Big guy. The western-cut white shirt and slim, crisp Wrangler jeans told her he was a real cowboy. The kind who made his living in the saddle, not the kind who just dressed the part. He was confident but quiet with it, she decided, as she dealt all around to her full table then cut another glance the big guy's way.

He stood a few feet back from the tables, arms crossed over a broad chest, long legs planted about a shoulder-width apart, eyes intent on the action on the blackjack table next to hers. On any given night there were a lot of lookers in a casino, so it wasn't unusual that he stood back from the crowd and just watched. What was unusual was that between deals, her gaze kept gravitating back to him.

What was even more curious was that when one of her players scooped up his chips and wandered off, leaving the third-base chair empty, Abbie found herself wishing the tall cowboy would take his place.

What was up with that? And what was up with the little stutter step of her heart when he ambled over, nodded hello and eased his lean hips onto the chair.

"Howdy," she said with what she told herself was a standard, welcoming smile.

He answered with a polite nod as he reached into his hip pocket and dug out his wallet. When she'd paid and collected bets all around, he tossed a hundred-dollar bill onto the table.

Abbie scooped it up, counted out one hundred in chips from the chip tray, then spread them on the green felt tabletop for him to see. After he'd gathered them in and stacked them in front of him, she tucked the hundred into the slot in front of her.

"Place your bets," she said to the table of seven, then dealt the first round faceup from the shoe. When all players had two cards faceup, she announced her own total. "Dealer has thirteen."

Her first-base player asked for a hit, which busted him. When she got to cute, quiet cowboy, he waved his hand over his cards, standing pat with eighteen.

You could tell a lot about a person from their hands. Abbie saw a lot of hands—polished and manicured, dirty and rough, thin and arthritic. The cowboy's hands were big, like he was. His fingers were tan and long with blunt, clean nails, not buffed. Buffed, in her book, said pretentious. His were not. They were capable hands. A workingman's hands, with the occasional scar to show he was more than a gentleman rancher. Plenty of calluses. He dug in.

She liked him for that. Was happy for him when she drew a king, which busted her. "Luck's running your way," she said with a smile as she paid him.

He looked up at her then and for the first time she was hit with the full force of his smile. Shy and sweet, yet she got the distinct impression there was something dark and dangerous about him.

Whoa. Where had that come from? And what the heck was going on with her?

Hundreds—make that thousands—of players sat at her table in any given month. Some were serious, some were fun and funny, some sad. And yeah, some of them deserved a second look. None of them, however, flipped her switches or tripped her triggers like this man was flipping and tripping them right now. It was unsettling as all get out.

"Place your bets," she announced again, then dealt around the table when all players had slid chips into their betting boxes.

Whereas the blond poster boy had been bad-boy gorgeous, there wasn't one thing about this man that suggested boy. Abbie pegged him for midthirties— maybe closer to forty, but it wasn't anything physical that gave her that impression. He was rock solid and sort of rough-and-tumble-looking. Dark brown hair, close cut, dark, *dark* brown eyes, all-seeing. Nice face. Hard face. All edgy angles and bold lines.

Maybe that was where the dangerous part came in. He had a look about him that was both disconcerting and compelling. A presence suggesting experience and intelligence and a core of solid confidence that needed no outward display or action to reinforce it.

He was the quintessential quiet-hero type. Clint Eastwood without the steely squint. Matthew Mc-Conaughey without the long hair and boyish charm— and *with* a shirt on, something McConaughey was generally filmed without. Although, the cowboy *did* have his own brand of charisma going on because sure as the world, he was throwing *her* for a loop.

"Cards?" she asked him now.

"Double down."

Smart player, she thought, and split his pair of eights. She grinned again when he eventually beat the table and her on both cards.

"I think maybe *you're* my luck." He tossed a token in the form of a red chip her way.

"Tip," she said loud enough for her pit boss to hear, showed him the five-dollar chip before she pocketed it. "Thanks," she said smiling at him.

"My pleasure."

He spoke so softly that the only reason she understood what he said was because she was looking right at him. The din of the casino drowned out his words to anyone else at the table as the rest of the players talked and joked or commiserated with each other.

The next words out of his mouth—"What time do you get off?"—stopped her cold.

She averted her gaze. "Place your bets," she told the table at large, thinking, *Hokay. Quiet doesn't necessarily equate to shy.*

The man moved fast. Which both surprised and pleased her because it meant that all this "awareness," for lack of a better word, wasn't one-sided. It also made her a little nervous. Her first instinct was to give him her standard, *Sorry. No fraternizing with the customers.*

But then she got an image of a devil sitting on her shoulder—a red-haired pixie devil with a remarkable resemblance to Crystal. *Don't you dare brush him off. Look at him. Look! At! Him!*

She chanced meeting his eyes again—his expression was expectant but not pressuring—and found herself mouthing, "Midnight."

A hint of a smile tugged at one corner of his mouth. "Where?"

She didn't hesitate nearly long enough. "Here." *God, what was she doing?*

"Cards?" she asked the table.

He gave her the "hit me" signal when she came around to him.

He broke twenty-one, shrugged.

"Sorry," she said, liking the easy way he took the loss. "Better luck next time."

"Counting on it." He stood. "Later," he said for her ears only; then he strolled away from the table.

"Dealer pays sixteen," she said absently as she paid all winners and surreptitiously watched what was arguably one of the finest Wrangler butts she'd ever seen get lost in a sea of gamblers.

5

The rest of Abbie's shift dragged by but, finally, a little past midnight, she'd pulled down fifty-five dollars in tips, squared her cash drawer, checked out, passed through her standard security check, and retrieved her purse from her locker—after she'd checked her hair and freshened her lipstick.

She was way too excited about meeting the cowboy. *Way* too excited. When she walked back into the casino toward her table, she wasn't feeling nearly as sure of her rash decision to meet up with him as she had earlier. Making quick dates with strangers was not her style. Making *dates* was not her style.

Get over it, the devil on her shoulder—sounding amazingly like Crystal again—whispered in her ear.

About one thing, Crystal was right. Abbie *had* been out of circulation for a long time. Maybe it was time to test the waters again. And yeah, it made sense that at some point a guy would come along and finally get to her, make her want to step out of her comfort zone and open herself up to new possibilities.

Yeah. It made sense.

"All but the part about going out with a man whose name you don't even know," she muttered as she neared her table.

She spotted him watching the action where Bill Gates—yeah, that was really his name—had taken over for her. A lot of cowboys played at the Vegas casinos and she hadn't imagined it earlier. None of them filled out their Wranglers the way this man did.

"Hi," she said, before she lost her nerve and bailed on him.

He turned, slowly uncrossed his arms, and smiled, looking pleased. "Hi."

Then he just stood there, as if he were waiting for her to say something. As if he already knew she had something she wanted to say. Which she did.

"Just so we're straight on something." Abbie stared at his throat, not quite able to meet his eyes but liking the fact that she would have actually had to look up a bit to do it. "This is a first for me. Letting someone pick me up at my table."

Okay, now would come the part where he would say something like, *A gorgeous woman like you? Not used to pickups? Come on. You must have to beat them off with a stick.*

Or some such line that was supposed to make her gush all over. She'd heard plenty of them. But she didn't hear one from him. He just watched her with those dark, intense eyes, then nodded. "Okay."

Well, that surprised her. So did his unassuming

gaze. So she hit him with a stop sign he couldn't possibly misunderstand.

"And so you know, you've used up your quota of luck for the night."

His grin was slow and full of amusement. "Not even enough left to find a good cup of coffee?"

Score more points for the cowboy. No disappointed frown. No casting about for excuses to find greener pastures—or in this case, a hotter, more willing date.

She finally relaxed, returned his smile. "I think I can take care of that."

"Name's Sam, by the way." He extended his hand. "Sam Lang."

His introduction was all formal and sweet and if he'd been wearing a hat Abbie was pretty sure it would have been white and he'd have tipped his fingers to the brim.

"Abbie." She returned his handshake, far too aware of the strength and energy radiating from his big callused hand and of an underlying sexuality made all the more unnerving because he seemed so totally unaware of the potent effect he had on her.

"Abbie Hughes," she said, feeling suddenly self-conscious. "Let's go get that coffee. I know just the place. It's a short walk from here."

Abbie took Sam to Benny's, a small mom-and-pop diner a couple blocks off the Strip.

"I used to bus tables here when I was in high school," she told him as they slipped into a booth.

"Sure you're set on coffee? They make a mean choco-late malt."

"Another time, maybe. Tonight, coffee works just fine."

Everything was working just fine, Abbie thought as she sat across from him in a booth. He filled every space he occupied, it seemed. His white shirt against the faded red upholstery emphasized how broad his shoulders were. His big hands cupped around a mug of strong, rich coffee underscored the strength in them. And yet, nothing about his demeanor said he'd ever come on too strong.

"Haven't seen you in the casino before." She was curious about that.

"Haven't been back for very long. This is the first chance I've had to check out the action. Strip's changed, man, a *lot* while I've been gone."

"Gone?"

He nodded. "Grew up on a horse ranch just outside of town." He grunted. "Town's almost grown out there now."

"No way. Are you telling me you're a native?"

"Born and raised."

She grinned. "Me, too. We're a rare breed consider-ing all the transplants."

"Rare's a good word," he agreed, his smile extending his meaning to include her.

Oh, man. She could get into a guy who thought she was rare, as in special.

"And gone's a big word," she prompted.

"College. Then the military. After that private work." He shrugged again. "Time passes and one day a man realizes something's missing."

"Home," she concluded.

"Yeah," he said after a moment. "Roots. They mean more as a man grows older."

He, it seemed, was rare, too. Special. "So . . . you're back on the ranch."

He lifted his mug, drank. "Yep. Taking over for my dad."

That was nice. Keeping things in the family. "I'm sure he's glad to have you home."

He smiled politely at the waitress when she swung back by the table and refilled their mugs. Abbie couldn't help but notice the strong lines of his neck, the defined curve of his jaw as he glanced up and nodded his thanks.

There was nothing about this man that didn't appeal to her.

"What about you?" he asked.

"Not much to tell. Afraid I never made it past the city limits. But it's okay. I like it here. Like the climate, have friends here."

"Family?"

Not like his, she was sure. "My brother."

If he wanted to ask more, he restrained himself. She appreciated that because she wasn't at the point where she was willing to share too much personal information. She'd experienced a little too much disappointment in her life to open herself up to someone who was essentially a stranger. And she had plenty of reason to protect herself.

"So, when you're not dealing blackjack, what do you like to do?"

Get Acquainted 101. It was sweet and something more to like about him. She liked it a lot that he wasn't prying too deep or coming on all strong and macho and, let's face it, sexual. The chemistry was there—had been from the moment they'd become aware of each other at her table tonight—but it was nice that he was taking the time to get to know her, too.

"Well," she fiddled with the handle on her coffee mug, "I'm an accounting student at UNLV, so when I'm not working, I'm either in class or studying."

"All work, no play . . ." He let the line trail off.

"Makes Abbie a dull girl," she filled in for him.

His gaze touched her face. "Not from where I'm sitting."

As flirting went, it was subtle. It was also very effective.

"So you're a cowboy." Suddenly she felt like flirting, too.

"Yes, ma'am."

He grinned when he said it and that made her smile. Again. In fact, she'd smiled a lot tonight. Smiled more than she'd smiled with a man in . . . well, she couldn't remember how long.

"So, other than saying things like 'git along little dogie' and 'yee-haw,' what, exactly, does a cowboy do?"

"Well, we *do* get to say that a lot," he agreed. "But we

also do things like refine breeding lines, break and train the stock to ride. My dad has always done some showing. I might get back into that."

She could see him astride a horse. Big and brawny and bold against a sweeping vista.

"You ever ride, Abbie?"

"Actually, yeah. I have. Not that I'm expert. Had a friend once who had horses. I was enthralled by them."

"It seems to be a girl thing," he said with a sage nod.

Yeah. It was a girl thing, she agreed. All that big, bold beauty—much like the big, bold, and beautiful man smiling at her.

"What?" she asked, sensing he had something on his mind.

"Blackjack dealer. Student. Lover of horses. You still haven't told me what you like to do for fun."

"I run," she said.

"Run?"

"Five miles a day."

"In the army we called that PT—physical training—but we *didn't* call it fun."

She laughed. "Depends on your perspective, I guess. It's my self time."

He nodded. "Okay. I see that. My self time is on the back of a horse these days."

"I like roller coasters," she added, because she did and because for some reason she wanted him to know she wasn't as dull as dishwater.

"Ah. A thrill seeker," he said with a lift of his eyebrows. "What other kind of thrills turn you on?"

Okay. From any other man, that would have been sexual. And maybe it was, just a little, but his face never gave it away. He was either a very good actor or the most forthcoming man she'd ever met.

"The Space Needle. But it's been years since I was on it."

"Skydiving?" he suggested, almost as a dare.

"Not yet. But I'd like to."

He sat back in the booth, considered her through narrowed eyes. "What are you doing tomorrow night?"

"Tomorrow night?" She probably should have at least consulted her calendar, made some kind of a show of considering what her answer would be. His lack of pretense just wouldn't allow it. "Nothing. I work the early shift."

"Spend it with me."

Her heart did a little stutter step. "Doing?"

Something as close to devilish as she'd seen darkened his eyes. "How about I surprise you?"

All he'd ever done since she'd met him was surprise her. Just like she surprised herself again when without hesitation she took the leap. "Got to love a good surprise."

"No freaking way!" Crystal couldn't hide her shock when Abbie called her the next morning before class. "You? On a date? With a man?"

"It wasn't a date. It was coffee." Good coffee. Good company. She'd smiled a lot. For a while, she'd even

quit thinking and worrying about Cory, who still hadn't
called or e-mailed.

"It was a major breakthrough, that's what it was,"
Crystal insisted. "Details. Now. Start with what he
looks like."

Abbie walked into her bedroom and reached for
her jeans. She wedged her phone between her ear
and shoulder and wiggled into them. "He looks like a
cowboy."

"Well, can I hear a yee-haw, sista?" Crystal crowed.
"So what kind of cowboy? 'Big hat, no cattle' cowboy or
the 'real deal' cowboy? And please do *not* tell me he
rides rodeo."

Abbie laughed. There were working, breathing, living the life "real deal" cowboys. There were rodeo cowboys who didn't have much more than their rigging bag
and a beat-up pickup and several broken bones to their
name. And then there were the "big hat, no cattle"
cowboys. Men who played at being something they
weren't.

It came as no surprise to Abbie that Sam Lang was
exactly who he appeared to be. He wasn't full of himself. Wasn't on any mission to impress. She'd really
liked that.

"Real deal," she said, working her arms out of the
sleeves of her nightshirt.

"How real?" Crystal wanted to know.

"Born on a working horse ranch outside of Vegas."

"Get out."

"Went to college, did some time in the military, then some sort of private sector work, and now he's moved back home to take over the ranch for his dad, who's ready to retire."

"Solid, stable citizen. Caring son. I'm liking this guy."

Abbie was liking him, too. So much that she had to keep reminding herself to chill.

"So . . . when are you seeing him again?"

"Tonight. After work." Okay. So that wasn't exactly "chilling," but she'd wanted to say yes so she had.

"I am so proud," Crystal whimpered, playing thrilled mother.

Abbie laughed. "It's not that big of a deal."

"Sweetie, this is bigger than Botox. My little girl. Going on a date."

Abbie rolled her eyes.

"Where are you going? What are you wearing? Underwear. Oh, God. *Pleeeease* tell me you own something other than white, cotton, covers-your-entire-ass underwear."

Abbie sank down on the bed, grinning. "I didn't say I was sleeping with him, so my underwear is not an issue. I said I'm going on a date with him. And I don't know where we're going. He said he wanted to surprise me."

"A date. How sixties is that?" Crystal wanted to know.

"I think it's kind of sweet. Look. I've got to run or I'll be late for class."

"You made my day, Abs. This sounds promising. Really promising."

"I repeat. It's just a date."

"It's an act of God, that's what it is."

"Bye, Crystal." Abbie flipped her phone shut.

"Just a date," she repeated to herself as she finished dressing for class.

Just a date with just a man who just happened to be a really nice guy who just happened to turn her on like a strobe light.

She checked her watch. Saw that she was running about five minutes ahead of time and decided to check her e-mails. Still nothing from Cory. While it was like Cory to take off for days at a time, it wasn't like him not to keep in touch, even though she knew it was hard for him to read and type.

"He's a big boy," she reminded herself. Just because he was dyslexic didn't mean he was disabled, although it sure made life hard from him. She'd always been proud of him for making do. He could take care of himself—something that was hard for her to remember because for the longest time, she'd been the one taking care of him. Abbie felt more like his mother than his sister. That was because she was the one who had protected both Cory and herself from their father.

No good would come from dwelling on how rough they'd had it as kids. Especially Cory. He always took the brunt of Dexter Hughes's tirades. Their father had dealt out more than physical punishment and Cory was still searching for his path because of it.

Abbie immediately drew herself away from those memories. What was past was past. Since she still had a little time—and because she was basically a careful person who didn't believe in "too good to be true"—she did what she'd promised herself she wouldn't do. She Googled Sam Lang plus Rancho Royale, which, he'd told her, was the name of his ranch.

It was the smart thing to do, she assured herself. The safe thing. Even if it was intrusive, in this world, a person couldn't be too careful.

"Well, damn," she muttered when she got a hit. An old newspaper article—one of a dozen local-interest pieces the *Vegas Sun* ran every year—profiled Tom Lang and his family. A son, Samuel, and a daughter, Terri.

Sam hadn't mentioned that he had a sister. Abbie quickly scanned the article and felt a sudden clutch at her heart when she hit on another link to Sam Lang. At first she thought it was unrelated. Then she saw the name Tom Lang.

"Jesus. Oh, sweet Jesus," she whispered when an obituary came up.

She read through the obit, her eyes filling as it chronicled the short life of Terri Cooper, daughter of Tom and Vivian Lang. The photograph showed a vital, vibrant, smiling woman.

"She is survived by her parents, one brother, Sam Lang, and a daughter, Tina Cooper."

"How?" she wondered. Then she found it.

A car bomb had killed Sam's sister and her husband only three months ago. Right here in Vegas. In fact, Abbie remembered reading about it. She'd never made the connection with Sam until now because of Terri's married name.

Heart hammering, she read the article. Found an update. The case remained unsolved. Speculation was it was a mob hit but a case of mistaken identity because the Langs were model citizens.

Abbie was numb with shock when she forced herself to power down and head for class. She breathed deep, grabbed her keys, and then set her security system. Another push of a remote closed and locked the gates surrounding her property as she backed out of the garage.

No wonder Sam hadn't mentioned his sister, she thought as she zipped down the street. The pain he must be experiencing. The loss he must feel.

You don't know him well enough to get this invested in his life, she told herself staunchly.

But she knew. She was already invested. The proof was in her uncharacteristic desire to trust him. Her first instinct, in fact, had been to trust him and that was something new for her.

So yeah, she was invested. She couldn't hurt this badly for him if she wasn't.

6

"How'd it go with the Hughes woman?" Reed asked when he called.

Sam stared out his office window as his father drove by in the pickup, hauling a load of hay on a rack behind it.

"It went," he told Reed.

"Need to move on this, Sam," Reed reminded him.

Time was the enemy where Nader was concerned. Abbie Hughes was the key.

"You let me worry about that," he said and hung up.

He was meeting Abbie Hughes for their "date" tonight.

He thought about last night. Sharing coffee. Sharing smiles. Had to remind himself that she wasn't as innocent as she seemed. Tonight, he'd move a step closer to finding out just how deep she'd sunk into the mud with her brother.

Like the man, Sam's pickup was big and sleek and powerful.

"Sorry about the truck," he said when he helped her inside. "Haven't gotten around to buying a car yet."

Abbie smiled and buckled up her seat belt as he settled in behind the wheel. "You get a whole different perspective of the world from up here," she teased.

"Well, there is that," he agreed and made Abbie smile again, like she'd smiled when he'd called her earlier and told her to make sure she wore jeans.

"So, are you going to let me in on where we're going?"

He drove like he moved. Natural and relaxed with understated confidence, which was more appealing than any strut or swagger. His big hand rested on the gearshift knob, steady, sure, sexy as all get out.

"It's a surprise," he reminded her.

She laughed. "Yeah, I got that part."

"Then you'll get the part about if I told you where we were going it wouldn't be a surprise."

"Got me there," she agreed and settled in for the ride.

He was a man of mystery and he seemed to like it that way. She thought about his sister. She'd like to tell him how sorry she was about what had happened, but that would require telling him that she'd been snooping into his life. It wasn't exactly the kind of thing you wanted to reveal on a first date. Plus, he seemed so relaxed and lighthearted. She didn't want to break the mood.

So she decided to let it go. If she got to know him better, the subject was bound to come up. She wanted

to be there for him when it did, she realized, and reminded herself to slow down, breathe deep, and keep
the engine firmly ahead of the caboose.

The lights of the Vegas strip whizzed by as he drove.
Throngs of people packed the sidewalks and wandered
in and out of casinos. Laughter, the distant ring of slots
and the constant buzz of thousands of conversations
drifted on the warm night air.

"Look like fun?" Sam asked with a nod toward the
roller coaster as they approached the New York-New
York casino complex.

"You know, it does. I've never managed to find time
to ride this one."

"Good to know," he said with a sly smile. "Because
tonight's the night."

She jerked her gaze toward his, unable to hide the
delight in her eyes. "Are you serious?"

"As a heart attack," he said, looking and sounding
pleased with himself.

She grinned from him back to the coaster that
looped and wrapped and rose and fell around the
casino. "Cool!"

"You're a screamer," he accused an hour later when
they tumbled out of the coaster—he'd insisted they ride
in the first car.

"Hey. It's allowed," she laughed around a deep
breath as she pulled herself together. "I read it in the
rule book. I didn't see anything about laughing,
though, and you seemed to do that all the way through
the ride."

"Your fault," he said, dropping a hand on her shoulder. "Can't wait to hear you on the Space Needle."

He just kept surprising her. "No."

"'Fraid so, yeah."

She screamed her way through that ride, too. Was still catching her breath when they climbed back into his truck and headed out again.

"This has been fun," she said as he turned onto Convention Center Road. "Serious, serious fun."

"Good. But we're not done yet."

"No more roller coasters," she pleaded, feigning dread.

"No more roller coasters," he promised.

They rode in companionable silence for a while before she turned to look at him. His face was cast in shadows and light from the night and the neon. She was struck again by how ruggedly handsome he was. Just like she was struck by something else. She liked this man. "You're a really good time, you know that?"

"Same goes for you."

"Tonight reminds me of when I was younger." She didn't have a lot of happy memories from her childhood but the ones she did have stuck in her mind. "I used to spend a lot of time with my friend Crystal and her mom and dad when we were kids. They were always up for things like this. We'd go to county fairs; they'd take us on campouts. They even sent us both to a weeklong summer camp. That's where I learned to ride horses, by the way."

He braked for a light, glanced her way. "And weave baskets?"

She grinned. "I'll have you know I was darn good at it."

Yeah. She liked being with him. Being around him not only resurrected the kind of memories that made her feel good about herself, but made her believe that maybe she had a lot of memory making ahead of her.

Okay, so that was a huge leap, but it had been a long, long time since she'd thought about anything but work and school or done anything but worry about finances and Cory.

"Really?" she said when he pulled into a parking lot and she realized what he had in mind. "We're really going to do this?"

"You said you always wanted to skydive."

She made a gulping sound. "I talk big."

"You telling me you're not up for this, Hughes?"

She stared at the building that advertised indoor skydiving, swallowed hard. "Okay, now you're baiting me."

"Is it working?"

She frowned at the building again. "How far do we fall?"

He laughed as he got out of the truck. "All the way to the ground, sunshine. All the way to the ground."

"A. Ma. Zing," Abbie gushed after they'd completed their first dive. They'd both shrugged out of their indoor flight suits and met back up near the entrance. "The real thing must be the biggest rush in the world."

"It's a rush, all right. Especially when you dive out of a plane at fourteen thousand feet in the dark targeting an LZ the size of a pinhead."

"LZ?"

"Sorry. Landing Zone."

"In the dark?"

"More often than not."

"What? Were you a paratrooper or something?"

"Special Forces," he said, but she got the feeling there was much more to the story. "How about a bite to eat?"

Subject change. Okay. She could understand and respect that. She'd met some returning veterans. Hadn't talked to one yet who was eager to share his military experiences.

"Sure. I'm starving. All that adrenaline rush made me hungry."

"How about I pick the place tonight?"

"You're three for three so far. Who am I to question that kind of batting average?"

"You like baseball?"

She laughed when he jumped on her sports analogy. "Figure of speech. Seems a little slow-moving to me."

He smiled again.

"What?"

He shrugged. "Should have known you like your action fast."

Okay. Was that a come-on? Probably. Although she couldn't tell by looking. He drove eyes ahead, expression unreadable.

What if it was a come-on? she wondered. What would she do about it?

She was pretty sure she knew the answer to that and the fact was, it was as exciting as it was scary.

"Why did I not know about this place?" Abbie asked later as they gorged themselves on the juiciest hamburgers, the saltiest fries, and the most amazing chocolate malts that rivaled Benny's for excellence.

"I was just glad to see it's still going," he said, eyeing her French fries.

She sat back, shoved her plate toward him. "Help yourself. I'm stuffed."

"I'm impressed, though. You can pack it away for a girl."

She chuckled. "I think I've just been insulted."

He had the presence of mind to look embarrassed. "Sorry. That didn't come out right."

"But it happens to be the truth, so you're forgiven." She smiled at him then. "Thanks, Sam. Thanks for a really great night."

"You're welcome," he said, his dark eyes locked on hers. "I had a great time, too."

Yeah. It had been an excellent evening. So when he walked her to her door later and left without so much as a buss on her cheek, she wasn't only puzzled, she felt utterly and undeniably bereft.

"What," she muttered as she locked up behind herself, "just happened?"

Muchilena, Honduras
Close to midnight, one day later

Cory swiped a damp palm over the thin stubble covering his jaw. As he stood there, alone in the dark outside
the cantina, he didn't kid himself. He could die here.
Like Derek had died.

He shivered despite the cloying heat. No one would
ever know. All that would be left of Cory Hughes
would be a face on a wall with hundreds of other
missing-person posters.

He leaned his head back against the scarred cantina
wall as a runnel of sweat trickled down his back. Only
one person in the world would give a damn if he ended
up missing or dead. Abbie. His sister would care, even
though all he'd done his entire life was give her grief.

"Swear to God," he whispered heavenward, "if I get
out of this alive, I'm a changed man."

He would make it all up to Abbie. All the worry he'd
caused her, all the guff he'd given her. All the crap he'd
dished out over the years.

From inside the cantina, a blistering *punta*-rock beat
blared out of a tinny-sounding radio and vibrated into
the midnight silence. Muffled and raucous laughter
leaked through an open doorway, punctuated by a
woman's husky squeal.

Somebody was getting lucky. For ten bucks, you
could get damn lucky in this village, where the dogs
outnumbered the men and the men outnumbered the
women three to one.

He dragged his tongue over dry lips. Derek's lifeless eyes haunted him. Nader scared him, made him feel like that helpless, snot-nosed little kid who used to cower in a corner and wait for the old man to kick the crap out of him in a drugged-up rage.

Cory wasn't that kid anymore. He was twenty-two years old. Chicks dug him, he thought, mustering a swaggering pride to beat away his apprehension. They liked his lean, lanky body, his long dark hair and baby blue eyes, liked his smile. It had always made him feel like a man when he could make a woman smile. They smiled best for cash, though.

His heart damn near crashed out of his chest when a stray cat scurried around the corner and leaped into a Dumpster. He swiped a hand over his face, told himself to get a grip.

"Just get through this and you can go as straight as the Vegas Strip," he promised himself, smiled nervously at his little joke, then concentrated on several more deep breaths.

Of course, he'd have to disappear for a while. That would make Abbie cry. Not knowing what had happened to him. He felt bad about that. But he'd feel worse dead.

"Come on, come on, come on," he muttered, jerkily pressing the glow light on his cheap watch and checking the time again.

Where the hell was his contact? Fox's contact, a guy named Juan, was supposed to have been here fifteen minutes ago. Right. Like Cory could trust anyone who wouldn't give their full name and agreed only to a night meet in this alley.

He swiped a damp palm over his face, tried to ignore that it was shaking. That's what was making him so skittish. Fox came with a new set of ground rules—and with a new threat: the wrath of Fredrick Nader.

"Nader doesn't know," he reminded himself. Nader didn't know about Derek's double cross. He might suspect something was off when Derek hadn't shown up with the diamonds, but Nader didn't know that Cory had them now. Not yet.

"*Hola*, gringo."

"Jesus!" Startled, Cory shoved away from the cantina wall. He whipped his head around expecting to see a *ladino* known as Juan. But it wasn't a native Honduran who stared back at him.

It was Rutger Smith.

Oh God.

The night shadows played across the grim, unsmiling eyes of Fredrick Nader's hired muscle. Light from the moon accentuated the shiny baldness of Smith's round head and the mean scar that ran like a scythe from the corner of his left eye to the corner of his mouth.

If there was an emotion buried behind the blank, obsidian eyes that stared into his, it was twisted amusement. If there was blood that flowed in the heart beneath that broad, steroid-inflated chest, it was ice cold. Cory had read a book once about this sadistic killer who liked to watch his victims bleed out while he chopped them up in little pieces. Rutger had always made him think about that book. Rutger always made him think about blood. Lots of it.

"Let's go, Hughes." The tip of the stiletto pressed in against Cory's ribs, then pricked his skin through his T-shirt—just enough to make him yelp. Just enough to make Rutger smile.

Cory swallowed thickly, felt his heart drop to his gut, and knew two things with ultimate certainty. One, he should have trusted his gut and gotten the hell out a long time ago. Two, unless he could convince Nader that he was more valuable to him alive than dead, he was fish food.

7

"All set for tonight?"

Sam glanced up at Reed, then went back to scanning the updates on Nader's activities that Reed had brought with him to the ranch. While Nader hadn't been spotted, his man, Rutger Smith, had turned up in San Pedro Sula. It was a guarantee, then, that Nader wasn't far away.

"All set," he said absently.

"So . . . what's she like?" Reed asked after a moment.

Sam knew Reed was referring to Abbie Hughes. Just like he knew that Reed had been biting his tongue the past couple of days to keep himself from asking about her.

"Like a means to an end."

Nothing but a means to an end, he assured himself because that was the only way he could afford to think about her. It had been four days since he'd taken her out for coffee. Three since they'd gone thrill riding.

He'd taken her to a movie last night. Was seeing her again tonight.

In short, he'd been rushing like a running back, trying to find an in. He'd recognized that she got off on the quiet, sincere cowboy type and he'd played that angle. He hadn't so much as touched her, a feat that had been harder for him to accomplish than it should have been and that he knew both intrigued and puzzled her.

Yeah, it puzzled him, too, just like it pissed him off that he let himself be distracted. Still, the strategy was working. She'd finally asked him to pick her up at her house tonight.

She was starting to trust him, which was exactly what he needed her to do. He wanted her trusting him. Talking to him. About her life. About her family. About her brother. Because he still had a kernel of doubt that she was involved in Nader's business, Sam would much prefer to finesse the information he needed from Abbie Hughes than force it out.

So far, though, he'd gotten nada. And the clock was ticking. Nader wouldn't take a chance of staying in one place too long. The fact that he was still in or near San Pedro Sula suggested only one thing: He was waiting for something. Sam was banking on that "something" being the Tupacka diamonds. It was the only thing that made sense.

Just like it only made sense that Abbie's new car, serious bling, and elaborate security all pointed to her brother throwing some of his action her way. Cory

Hughes could be the weak link in Nader's organization that would finally lead to Nader's downfall.

That's why Sam needed desperately to know what Abbie knew. That's why he was relieved he was finally getting a chance to check out her house. He could get lucky, stumble over something incriminating. If there were stolen goods or drugs in the mix, he could end up using them for leverage to get the info he needed on Cory from Abbie. Nothing spoke to a beautiful woman like the threat of jail time.

If it turned out he found nothing on her, well, one way or the other, he needed to make something happen tonight because Desmond Fox's appearance on the scene wasn't the only new fly in the ointment.

Reed had lobbed the latest news at him yesterday:

"We've lost Hughes."

"Lost him how?"

Reed had shrugged. "Puff of smoke. Flash of light. Gone. Hell. I don't know. He just dropped out of sight."

Which could have meant damn near anything. "Maybe he's smarter than we thought," Sam had suggested. "Maybe he made Mendoza as a tail. Figured he needed to fall off the radar for a while. Then again, he could have pissed someone off, caught himself a bullet."

"Funny you should mention that," Reed had added. "About the same time we lost Hughes, another one of Nader's mules—dude by the name of Derek Styles— also dropped off the grid."

"Something's not right," Sam had agreed.

Which had brought them to tonight. Now with two of Nader's mules missing, it could mean they had run into a buzz saw. All the more reason Sam needed to get something concrete from Abbie or he might miss his shot at Nader again.

"Time's getting short," Reed said now as he prowled Sam's office. "I know it's tough duty, being she's such a *dog* and all," he said, clearly meaning the opposite, "but you might have to take one for the team, get her into bed and fuck the info out of her."

Sam glared at him, came within an inch of shoving a fist in the pretty boy's face. When the haze of anger cleared, he recognized the look in Reed's eyes. He was intentionally trying to goad him.

"Oh, hell." Reed looked like he'd just confirmed his worst suspicions. "I don't believe it. She got to you."

Sam clenched his jaw.

"You like her, don't you?"

Sam glanced up from the report. "What I like is that she has the potential to lead us to Nader."

"But you *like* her," Reed insisted as he dropped into the club chair in Sam's office. He laced his hands over his belly, squinted through narrowed, knowing eyes.

Sam tossed the report on his desk. "What is this? High school? Look. I know what I need from her. And I know what she means to this op. She's a conduit. End of story."

The fact that Reed was right, that Abbie came off as sincere and straightforward and yeah, Sam liked that about her, had no bearing on the op. Or on what lengths he would go to, to get what he needed. If she was in as deep as all indicators said she was, then he'd take her down along with her brother and Nader. No regret. No remorse.

He worked his jaw. Disgusted with himself for wanting to believe the sincerity in her eyes and the innocent act she had perfected. Tonight, he planned to capitalize on the obvious. She was attracted to him. He'd seen it the first night he'd sat down at her blackjack table and nothing had changed his mind since. If that's what it took, then he'd exploit the instant chemistry and use it to his advantage.

Tonight was do or die. If he didn't get the information he wanted by playing nice, then the game was going to get dirty.

"What time are the boys coming in?"

Reed checked his watch. "Their flight lands in two hours."

Luke "Doc Holliday" Colter, former Navy SEAL and the BOI team medic, and Wyatt "Papa Bear" Savage, general operator and former CIA, were flying in from Buenos Aires to help with the sting—if it came to that—then join Sam on the trip to Honduras to flush out Nader.

"You sure you're going to be okay with this?" Reed asked.

No, Sam wasn't entirely okay with it, but he was left with little choice. "Yeah," he said. "I'm okay with it. We'll use the boys as a last resort. You wait for my nod."

"Just work it. You'll have her eating out of your hand," Reed said.

"Yeah. I'm a regular Joe Cool," Sam grumbled, telling himself it wasn't guilt hammering at him over using Abbie. He glanced at Reed. "So, you finished pimping me?"

Reed gave him a long assessing look. "Yeah, I think I've pretty well covered it."

"Then get lost."

"Getting lost," Reed said with a sharp salute and headed for the door. "This is good, Sam," he said, suddenly serious. "What you're doing. Whatever you have to do. It's right. And it's righteous.

"It's right," Reed repeated when Sam said nothing. Then he left, closing Sam's office door behind him.

Sam leaned back in his chair, stared into space, tried to buy into Reed's words.

Tried to make what he'd said true.

But this had nothing to do with right or righteousness. God knows he'd tried to convince himself that it did. Had tried to believe that what he was doing had to be done.

Done for his father, who wanted retribution. For his mother, whose heart would never fully heal. For little Tina, who still cried at night for her mommy and daddy yet soldiered on with her brave little eyes and her mother's spirit.

Yeah. Sam had tried to convince himself this was for Terri and B.J.

He stood. Walked to the window. The truth was in the reflection that stared back at him in the glass. In the hollow eyes. In the brooding rage.

This was about him.

About wanting to sleep one night—*one fucking night*—without seeing Terri's car explode in flames.

About waking up in the dark, drenched with sweat, his jaws clenched against a scream and the suffocating weight of guilt pressing on his chest like a tank.

It was about finding a way to live with himself knowing that his sister would be alive, that Tina would have a mother and a father, that his parents would still have their daughter, if Sam hadn't let the violence of his life bleed into theirs.

If he hadn't fucked up.

If he hadn't blown chance after chance to take Nader out of commission.

If he'd done his goddamn job.

So, no. This wasn't about them. This was about him. The one thought that mobilized him was knowing he had a chance to make Nader pay.

Which brought him to Abbie Hughes.

He checked his watch and headed for the shower.

Did he have any doubt about Abbie Hughes's involvement? Yeah. He did.

Did it matter? No, he told himself, lifting his face to the hot, pounding spray. It didn't matter.

All that mattered was getting to Nader. And guilty or not, Abbie Hughes was going to get hurt in the process.

• • •

"You look great."

Abbie smiled up into Sam Lang's serious brown eyes as he stood at her front door, long and strong and smelling clean and amazing—some subtle, sexy blend of sandalwood and sage.

As usual, his shirt was white and backlit against the dark of night outside; it made his shoulders look even broader. The silver chain holding his army dog tags winked out of the open collar of the shirt he'd tucked into the narrow waist of crisply creased jeans that he wore with a natural ease. If Calvin K and his cronies got a look at him, they'd be salivating over the idea of Sam posing for a GQ cover.

Just looking at him had Abbie experiencing that jolt of anticipation, excitement, and arousal that had knocked her off kilter the first time she'd seen him and that she'd hoped would lessen with exposure.

But here it was. Their fourth date, and if anything, her reaction to him had escalated.

"Thanks," she said, finally having the presence of mind to speak. She'd worn a dress tonight. It was black with a low, scooped neck. It was also sleeveless and short. It made her waist look small, her boobs look big, and her legs look a million miles long.

It was what Crystal called a "fuck me" dress and it was a first for Abbie. She felt both empowered and manipulative and she hadn't yet reconciled her motive for wearing it with her inherent instincts to proceed with care.

Until she saw the look in Sam's eyes.

Then manipulative and empowered felt just fine. So did a little recklessness.

"You're looking pretty good yourself," she added, stepping back so he could walk into the house.

As excited as she was to see him, she was still a little nervous. This was the first time she'd invited him to her home. She was a cautious woman. A careful woman, a care that had been nurtured by an alcoholic mother and an addict father. She'd learned to lock her bedroom door early on; she'd been locking doors both metaphorically and literally ever since.

So, taking that step and not only letting Sam know where she lived but inviting him over—well, it was huge for her. Huge as in *since her divorce, she'd never invited a man into her home* huge.

Huge, as in *she'd spent enough money at Victoria's Secret this afternoon to make Crystal lie down on the dressing room floor and weep for joy* huge.

"K-Y and condoms," Crystal had said when Abbie had frowned at the unopened sack Crystal held out to her before they parted ways. "You've been out of circulation for so long you're going to need a little help."

"Oh, for God's sake. Just because I'm buying new underwear doesn't mean I'm going to sleep with him."

Crystal had just blinked.

"Okay. So I want to sleep with him," Abbie had admitted, snatching the sack from Crystal's outstretched hand.

"Go forth and multiple orgasm," Crystal ordered.

"Orgasm is not a verb," Abbie had pointed out with a laugh.

"Oh, sweetie, it is if it's done right."

Abbie had the very distinct impression that Sam Lang knew how to do it right. That didn't mean she wasn't anxious about where this night might be heading. It had been a long time for her. Sex had never been casual for Abbie. It wasn't casual now.

She liked this guy. Really liked him. That made it that much more important.

Okay. So she'd only known him for a few days, but if something physical didn't happen between them soon, she was going to burst a vein or something—if worry over Cory didn't do it first.

She didn't want to think about Cory now. Told herself her brother was fine and that when he finally showed his face, she was going to give him a piece of her mind— right after she hugged him until his ribs broke.

"Nice," Sam said, after a taking in her living room. He looked huge and handsome in the pale light from the lamps on her end tables and pleased with what he saw. "Mellow."

Sam, she'd learned, was a man of few words. She found it part of his charm. When he had something to say, she knew he put a lot of thought behind it and his concise comments were generally right on target.

"Thanks again," she said, inordinately satisfied with his reaction. The furniture, like her final lump-sum divorcee settlement, had been a long time coming. She could finally afford to redecorate and buy a few things.

"Get comfortable," she said as she unconsciously touched her fingers to the diamond that warmed between her breasts. "I opened a bottle of wine. Be right back."

She had to make herself walk to the kitchen with slow, deliberate steps. Once there, she cursed under her breath because her hands were shaking when she reached into the cupboard for a pair of glasses.

Get a grip.

She wasn't a kid. She'd been around the block—at least she felt like it after Don. He'd soured her. Soured her good. So yeah, it was damn scary that she was on the verge of opening herself up to whatever she was opening herself up to with Sam. It was even scarier that she wished he would open up to her, too. She kept thinking about his sister. Wondering how he was dealing with it.

Wanting—*God help her*—to help him deal with it. It was one of her biggest character flaws—her "need to save" gene. Of all the men she'd ever met, Sam Lang, solid and strong and self-assured, needed saving the way a lion needed rescue from a mouse.

Obviously, she was in a little bit of trouble with this man . . . and she was wearing the underwear to prove it.

Abbie filled two glasses with her favorite Cabernet, then drew in a bracing breath and headed back to the living room. Sam stood in front of her bookcase, his back to her, staring at a picture of Cory.

Lord, sweet Lord, she would never tire of seeing this man in a pair of jeans.

"My brother, Cory," Abbie said, handing him his wine.

He nodded, turned to her. "Good."

Her heart did a little backflip. She knew exactly what he meant, but she wanted to hear him explain it. "Good?"

One corner of his amazing mouth tipped up. "Didn't see a resemblance. So, yeah. It's good to know that he's your brother."

She sipped her wine, taking her cue from the look in his eyes. It was a look that invited, flirted, made suggestions—at least that's what she wanted to see, so she went with it. "As opposed to?"

He lifted his glass, watched her over the rim, his dark eyes serious suddenly and dangerously attractive in the diluted light. "As opposed to competition," he said before taking a slow, savoring sip.

The kind of slow, savoring sip she wanted him to take of her.

"No." Her voice was barely a whisper. "No competition."

That prompted another slow smile. Another gruffly murmured, "Good."

A man of few words, she thought again. Effective. Very effective because she was feeling very flushed all of a sudden.

"You don't talk about him much. Are you two close?"

He was talking about Cory, she realized, shaking off the haze of sexual awareness that made both her vision and her better judgment fuzzy.

Slow it down.

"Yeah." She averted her gaze to Cory's picture because if she looked at Sam one more second, she was going to jump him. "We are close. He's my kid brother, you know? I look out for him."

"Looks like a big boy to me."

She sipped her wine, saw Cory at four, eyes red from crying, tears staining his face as she pulled him, trembling and bruised, out of the closet. The unexpected memory overwhelmed her. "Our mom . . . well, she wasn't much of a mom. Liked her Jack Daniel's, you know?" She shrugged, touched her index finger to Cory's image. "Our father, on the other hand, liked his blow. And he was mean with it. Especially after Mom passed out for the day. That's when he went after us. Mostly, he'd go after Cory."

Abbie's thoughts drifted back there . . . back when she hadn't always been able to be there for Cory. When she was in school—that's when their dad would get him. Rail on him for being stupid, when it was Cory's undiagnosed dyslexia that gave him problems in class.

She became aware of Sam's silence. "Oh, man." She shook her head, embarrassed. "Sorry. Really. I'm sorry. Not sure what sent me back there. Talk about a mood killer."

She shot him an apologetic smile. Would have looked away if she hadn't seen the expression in his eyes. She saw more than sympathy and not an ounce of rebuke.

"Sounds rough," he said.

She squared her shoulders, shook it off. "Yeah, well, it was a long time ago."

"But not so long that you don't still worry about your brother."

She nodded, needed to look away because it would be so very easy to want to lean into this man and leach all the strength out of him.

"Like you said. He's a big boy."

"You see him often?" he asked after a moment.

"Yeah." She nodded. "He lives in Vegas so, yeah. We're in touch." Usually every day but she hadn't heard from Cory in so long.

Tears threatened. Damn and damn again. This was *not* where she wanted this night to go.

"He deal for one of the casinos, too?"

Okay, she told herself. He was trying to be nice. Attempting to show interest in her brother because he realized Cory was important to her.

"No," she said. "Cory's . . . well, Cory's sort of an entrepreneur."

He smiled as if he understood, then confirmed that he did. "So he's unemployed."

She glanced at him. Hard. "Would you like some more wine?" she asked, feeling a sudden and inexplicable discomfort with the conversation. So much so that while Sam's questions about Cory had given her an opening to ask about his family—specifically about his sister—she decided to let it pass.

She reached for his glass. Realized he was standing

very close. So close, he was in her space. Space she hadn't let a man enter for a very long time.

It startled her. Startled him, too, apparently, because when their fingers brushed, he took a step back, actually looked apologetic.

For whatever reason, that small show of apology made her bold. Just like the electric brush of their fingers had made her hyperaware of the sexual energy crackling between them.

Just like the look in his eyes made her brave and bold and reckless.

"Are you ever going to kiss me, Sam?"

8

Breathless. Her own boldness made her breathless. So did Sam's nearness. His scent. His heat.

She managed to swallow, managed to stand her ground, to seek and discard a dozen arguments for why she shouldn't push this, let alone encourage what was about to happen. At least, she hoped it was about to happen.

They weren't talking about just a kiss. A kiss—their first kiss—would shoot them from zero to all the way gone. She knew it and so did he.

So, yeah, there were a dozen reasons why she should back away.

It was too fast. Too soon. Too hot. Too much. Too scary.

And there was only one compelling reason that made it right.

Him.

"I thought you'd never ask," he said finally.

Then God, oh, God, it was going to happen.

Hopefully sometime within her next heartbeat. Please, God, within her next breath.

But he kept her waiting. Kept her wanting. Kept her wondering what kissing him would be like.

He was very meticulous, Sam Lang. Her fingers were trembling when he lifted her glass from her hand, set it, along with his, on the bookshelf. Very intense when he moved back into her, searched her eyes as if he were seeking the secrets to immortality there.

And he was very deliberate when he touched the back of his curled fingers to her cheek, making her tremble, making her breath catch, making her wish he'd put her out of her misery and just do it.

But he didn't.

Dark, searching eyes caressed her face as he lowered his head to hers. Warm, wine-scented breath fanned her cheek as he feathered the gentlest of touches there, then slowly trailed kisses across her jaw in a teasing, torturous seduction.

"Sam." She gripped his arms because he stole not only her breath but her balance. "You're driving me crazy."

"A lot of that going around," he murmured, before finally, *finally*, covering her mouth with his.

Some things were worth waiting for.

Some things were worth praying for.

Sam Lang's kiss, she decided, was worth dying for.

His lips were amazingly soft, his arms devastatingly strong, his heat wholly consuming. This man of few words spoke volumes without uttering a sound, telling her in a hundred different ways how much he wanted her.

The way his mouth opened over hers, the way his heart pounded against hers and his big body tightened and warmed beneath her hands told her things he never could have said with words.

Her hands found his hair, wanting close, needing closer, desperate for skin against skin.

The promise to make it all happen was there, in his touch, in his taste, in the shudder of his big body and the hard length of him against her belly . . . so it stunned her when he lifted his head.

She made an involuntary sound of protest. Involuntary because she was lost in him, suddenly obsessed and needing his kiss like breath.

"Shh." He pressed her face against his shoulder. "Just . . . shh," he soothed again, his arms tight and fast and strong around her.

She could feel his heart slamming as he held her that way, gulping air, working for an even breath.

"Sam?" A desperate whisper.

"Yeah." He squeezed her tight then loosened his hold. "I know." Another fractured breath. "Maybe . . . hell. I didn't mean for that to get so intense. Maybe we should . . . go to . . . dinner."

Abbie lifted her head, beyond confused. "Do you *want* to go to dinner?"

He pushed out a frustrated laugh, let his head fall back. "You're kidding, right?"

Relief rushed through her. She pushed up to her tiptoes. Kissed his throat, savoring the warm, salty taste of him.

"Abbie—"

"Sam." She cut off what she recognized as a precursor to a warning and smiled into his eyes. "Shut up and kiss me."

She'd wanted a smile from him, too. Didn't get one.

His eyes were far too serious as they searched hers. "This was not my plan when I came here tonight."

"Make a plan. God laughs," she murmured and moved into him again.

Again, he pulled back. "Seriously, Abbie. Maybe . . . maybe we should slow things down."

The erection pressing against her belly told her he was so not on board with that idea. "I don't want to slow down." She kissed him again, open-mouthed, hot and hungry.

He groaned. Gripped her arms. "Make sure this is what you want. Make damn sure because one more kiss like that and I won't be able to stop."

"God," she said, matching his sober scowl, "I hope not."

As Sam laid her down it fleetingly crossed Abbie's mind that she'd never done anything but sleep in this bed. As he slowly undressed her it occurred to her that it had been two years since a man had seen her naked.

Two years since she'd worn underwear with anything but utilitarian use in mind or bought something black lace and satin with the singular intent of watching a man's eyes darken with desire when he saw her wearing it. When he took it off of her.

Two long, lonely years since she'd felt confident enough to want a man in her bed. In her body. Filling her head the way Sam filled her head right now.

The look in his eyes, oh Lord, the look in his eyes as he peeled black lace away from her breasts, made her tingle and burn and arch to meet him when he lowered his head and drew her nipple into his mouth.

His mouth.

His mouth was amazing. Hot. Wet. Wild for her.

And hungry. She felt such hunger in him, a hunger that stoked her own as he kissed her and kissed her, then left her lying there wearing nothing but her black panties and a flush of desire.

She indulged herself in the look of him when he rose to his knees above her and started unbuttoning the cuffs on his shirt. He was so . . . beautiful. There wasn't any other word for it. Not just the package he came wrapped in—the breadth of his chest, the tightly knotted abs and narrow hips, the smooth tanned skin—but the intensity in his eyes, the need in his tightly coiled muscles that told her how hard he was reaching for control.

He jerked open his shirt and she shivered. He was still shoving the sleeves down his arms, his dog tags lying flat and warm against bare skin, when she reached for his belt buckle, lowered his zipper. He froze with one broad shoulder cocked. His ab muscles sucked in tight when the backs of her fingers brushed the light dusting of hair there. There where he was hot and lean and the tip of his penis felt satiny soft and damp against the back of her fingers.

The look in his eyes as they met hers made her daring, made her yearn. The catch in his breath when she slowly lowered his zipper the rest of the way down made her restless and reckless. The low groan of pleasure when she burrowed her fingers under the waistband of his shorts and finally found the long, thick length of him intensified the ache low in her belly.

With reluctance, she released him, impatiently shoved his jeans, shorts and all, down his hips. Then she lay back and watched as he got rid of everything that got in the way of hot skin against hot skin.

Everything but her panties. Her black, lace, barely there panties.

Before tossing his jeans, he reached into a pocket, withdrew a condom, and laid it precisely over her navel. She didn't let herself wonder about the implications of him coming prepared, was only grateful that he had. Thankful that he was prepared and perfect and naked.

Completely, gloriously naked—and yet, she felt exposed suddenly.

Until he smiled.

And when he smiled and pressed a knee into the bed and the warmth of his thigh connected with her hip, she lost that last vestige of inhibition. The physical connection overrode any last-second surge of insecurity. She reached for his hand, laced their fingers together and, watching his face, drew their linked hands down to the small patch of lace covering her mons.

Electric anticipation shot through her when he

rubbed their joined hands against her then urged her to part her legs before disentangling their fingers and cupping her there. Caressing. Enticing. Driving her to a level of arousal that would have been frightening if she hadn't trusted him so completely.

The fact that she *did* trust him amazed her. Opened doors leading to hope and optimism and expectations—all elements she'd given up on after Don. Essential elements that bridged the gap between doubt and her decision to take this leap of faith with Sam.

She was wet and achy and all but begging for a deeper touch when he skimmed a finger under the scrap of black lace and brushed her damp curls.

"Sam." She sighed his name, telling him with the undulation of her hips that his touch was wonderful . . . and not nearly enough.

He enclosed her completely then, the heel of his hand poised on her pubic bone as he finessed her lips apart, found the slick, swollen flesh of her clitoris, and stroked her.

She sucked in a breath, bucked, and scrambled to remove her panties so she could open wider for him, indulge more freely, experience more fully the exquisite rush of sensations she'd denied herself for so very, very long.

"Open it." He handed her the condom. "Cover me."

Her fingers shook, were clumsy with excitement as she struggled with the foil packet. With a sound of exasperation, she finally ripped it open with her teeth. She was half laughing, half whimpering as she reached for

him, rolled on the latex, and made room for him between her thighs.

Where the sensations began again.

Stronger. Sharper. Deeper. And devastating.

So devastating, she cried out when he drove deep
and seated himself there, the muscles of his buttocks
bunching beneath her palms, his biceps knotting as he
held himself above her.

"Don't. Move," he groaned between clenched teeth
when she rocked her hips to meet his. "Just . . . don't
move," he repeated, lowering his head to her throat,
where he nuzzled and kissed her neck before moving
to her mouth. "You feel incredible," he whispered.

"Yeah," she smiled against his mouth. "I do."

He played with her mouth . . . nipping, sipping,
sucking on her lower lip before easing his tongue inside.

She opened for him, met each questing thrust, loving the taste of him, the lack of haste as he slowly
began to rock his hips to the rhythm of his tongue.

In. Out. In. Out.

"So good." He felt so good. His weight. His heat. His
strength, which surrounded her but never overpowered
her, never made her feel dominated or defenseless. Instead, she felt unbelievably powerful as he taught her
things about sensation she'd either forgotten or had
never known.

She let him take her completely. Had never thought
she could trust this way again, trust to follow his lead,
trust his reactions to her touch, trust the rightness of it

all. She marveled in the freedom, then stopped thinking altogether when he increased the speed of his thrusts, and the intensity of his rhythm, and let the night dissolve into nothing but tactile, torrid pleasure.

Time, place, even reality blurred, then suspended while he drove her closer to climax.

Relentlessly.

Ruthlessly.

Until she couldn't delay the inevitable. She let go. Let herself free-fall into an orgasm so sharp and fierce she cried out from the sheer intensity and wonder of it. She gasped for breath, cried out in joy and shock and even a little delicious fear as he took her on the ride of her life. Held him tight when he joined her, burying himself deep one last time as his big body stiffened with his own release.

Her nails bit into his back as their slick bodies tensed and pulsed. Heat sought heat as the release rocked through them like a seventh wave, huge and forceful and dangerously consuming.

She clung to him, held on for life while she fought for breath and clarity, all the while wishing the rush would never end.

When he could breathe, when he could gather some semblance of muscle memory to make his arms move . . . when he could think beyond the lush and giving heat of her body and the rush of sensation, Sam forced himself to roll off of her.

He lay on his back in the deepening darkness. Listened to her breathe. Catching his own breath in the ringing aftermath of something that never should have happened. Something that should have been just sex but felt like a helluva lot more.

His conscience slammed recriminations to the beat of his heart, berating him for what he'd just done.

Jesus. He hadn't meant to go this far.

Had he?

No.

Yes.

Hell, he didn't know.

But it was done. The proof of it lay wasted and spent on the sheets beside him. She was decimated. Physically. Sexually. And, if he didn't miss his guess, emotionally.

He turned his head on the pillow. To find her eyes closed. Her breathing slow, deep, even.

Asleep. She'd fallen asleep. If it wasn't so telling, it'd be funny. It was a man's job to fall asleep after sex. Unless the woman was exhausted. School, job, worrying about her brother. Yeah. She was exhausted.

Fighting the wave of tenderness washing through him, he dragged a hand over his jaw and eased slowly to a sitting position. He glanced over his shoulder when she didn't stir. A delicate little snore purred from between her parted lips.

Another rush of feelings sucker-punched him.

Like the need to get her naked and horizontal had sucker-punched him. Like the need to be inside her had robbed him of reason—but not restraint. No, he'd kept a handle on at least that much control. This woman . . . this woman made him want things in a way that threatened that control. Because he didn't know what he was capable of taking if he let himself go, he'd held back. Kept the leash on needs that still pulsed deep in his groin.

That was the worst part, the very worst part, he realized as he slowly stood; he wanted to start all over again. Wanted to kiss her awake, caress her to awareness, finesse her back to arousal, and take them both to the limit and beyond.

"Take one for the team and fuck the information out of her."

Reed's words rang loud and strong in his head, and not one bit amusing. What had happened in her bed hadn't been about gathering information. It had been spontaneous and demanding and real.

It had also been one of the stupidest things he'd ever done in his life. He'd just wanted information. In absence of something concrete, he'd wanted to get a look at her alarm system, figure out a way to breach it without bringing the entire Vegas PD down on them if he and Reed decided they needed to make an "unannounced" return visit. But one thing had led to another, then another, and . . .

Disgusted with himself, he found his jeans on the floor and carried them with him toward the door. Pausing with his hand on the doorknob, he cast one more look over his shoulder to make sure she was sleeping . . . and got sidetracked in the lush look of her lying there. Her long dark hair spread like silk over the white pillow. The peak of a perfect pink breast was cast in silhouette in the darkened room. The length of a long, supple leg splayed wantonly on the sheets. The gold chain that held her diamond lay warm and close against her skin.

He clenched his jaw. Turned away.

What he wanted from Abbie Hughes wasn't supposed to have anything to do with anything but the bottom line.

And the bottom line was getting Nader.

With grim determination, he closed the bedroom door softly behind him. Then he dragged on his pants and started his search, feeling like the lowest piece of scum on the earth for breaking her trust this way.

Until he walked into her garage.

It was clean, neat, uncluttered. Like Abbie.

A black tarp ran the length of the far wall. He drew it aside and found various-sized boxes stacked three deep and six high. It didn't appear that any of them had been opened. He couldn't make out the return address so he flipped on an overhead light. Checked the postmarks.

Honduras. Every last one of them was postmarked Honduras.

Sam swallowed back both regret and guilt. Neck deep. She was in this neck deep.

His cell phone vibrated in his pocket. He checked the readout. It was Reed.

"What?"

"Can you talk?"

Sam glanced toward the kitchen door, where he'd entered the garage. "Make it fast."

"You know that other missing mule—Derek Styles? Well, he turned up yesterday. Dead. Someone dropped the body at a church."

"Fuck."

"Double it. Something's going down. We need to speed this up or we're going to lose Cory Hughes, too, if we haven't already. And that means Nader will be out of reach again."

Sam didn't need Reed to tell him. He knew all too well that time was slipping away. He didn't need a conscience either, but his worked on him anyway when he made his decision. He'd like more time with Abbie. More time to talk, maybe even determine that she was innocent in all this.

But they were out of time and he was fooling himself about her innocence. New car, bling, and Honduras postmarks did not equate to innocent.

"The boys make it in?" he asked Reed.

"Yep. They're locked and loaded. Just waiting for the word from you."

He had the goods; now he just needed to turn the screws and get her to talk. His gut knotted when he thought about how Abbie's face would look when she realized he'd used her.

"Sam?"

"Yeah," he said when Reed prompted him. "Do it."

He stood in the silence for a moment after he disconnected. Then he walked back into the kitchen, found the security panel, and disabled the house alarms. Abbie was still sleeping when he walked back into the bedroom, blissfully unaware that her world was about to come crashing down around her.

He quietly gathered the rest of his clothes from the floor. Cast one long, lingering look at the woman he was about to betray. And felt a surge of longing and regret so strong it made his chest ache.

He could fall for her. Jesus. Was too damn close to falling for her.

Because you're thinking with your dick, he reminded himself angrily and walked out of her bedroom.

He had no business feeling guilt or remorse. He needed to quit thinking about what this would do to her. About the sounds she'd made when she came. The scent of her. The taste of her.

Instead, he needed to focus on what Nader had done to his family. He needed to remember that Abbie Hughes and her brother were, at the least, guilty by association, at the most, accessories to murder.

"Come on, come on," he muttered, hooking a finger in her living room drapes and searching the street for the boys. He wanted this over with. A black SUV pulled up in front of the house a few minutes later.

On a relieved breath, Sam headed for the door. Nodded a grim hello to Colter and Savage as they piled out of the passenger seats wearing FBI jackets and caps, shoulder holsters, and, he was certain, fake badges in their wallets to match the rest of their phony gear.

It had been three months since Sam had seen Luke

"Doc Holliday" Colter, the BOI team's medic, and Wyatt "Papa Bear" Savage. While Holliday was former SEAL and Savage former CIA, both went back to Sam's Task Force Mercy days. Both had forgotten more about weaponry, covert warfare, and guile than most men had ever known.

Sam hadn't seen or talked to either man since Terri's funeral. Hadn't let himself dwell on the fact that he'd missed them until he saw the looks on their faces and understood that the feeling was mutual.

There was no time for sentiment right now as Reed, also wearing FBI gear, slipped out from behind the wheel and joined them outside the garage.

"In here." Sam let them in through the side garage door.

"Holy fuck." Reed whistled long and low when he got a look at the boxes. "Just like Christmas. All we need is some ribbon and tinsel."

"I have a feeling you're going to find all the trimmings you need when you open them up," Sam said.

"And if we don't?" Colter asked.

Sam glanced at Reed, who nodded, indicating he'd come prepared. "Then you know what to do."

Sam let himself into the kitchen and waited there for Abbie to wake up. The last thing they needed was for her to hear them in the garage, think someone had broken into her house, and call the cops.

Then he steeled himself for the look in her eyes when she realized he'd betrayed her.

9

The sheets beside her were cold when Abbie woke up. She stretched, stretched again, feeling sated and relaxed and new.

Crystal was right. And Abbie's memory of sex being highly overrated was dead wrong.

Or maybe it had just been her memory of sex with Don.

Sam had been . . . Her entire body reacted to thoughts of him with a huge, clenching shiver. Sam had been amazing. And thorough. The man had been very, very thorough.

On a lazy sigh, she rolled to her side, stirred the scent of man and sex and satisfaction, and found the dog tags he'd lifted over his head at some point so they wouldn't hit her in the face. *Sexy* and *considerate*, she thought, gathering the tags and the chain in her hand. She drifted on the sensual reminders for a moment, then checked her alarm clock. It was a little past midnight.

"Cripes," she muttered, sat up, and dragged her hair out of her eyes. She'd slept for almost an hour.

She could just hear Crystal. *"You had a man like Sam Lang in your bed—a man who blew the top of your head off with one of the finest orgasms you have ever had—and you fell asleep? Are you crazy???"*

For once, Abbie would have to agree.

She had to be crazy to fall asleep with Sam around.

So yeah, she was a little sleep deprived. Came with the territory. Between work, school, and studying it made for long hours. But to fall asleep. On Sam.

It was embarrassing. And now, he was apparently gone.

"Way to go, twinkle toes," she muttered and, naked, rose from the bed. "A sex siren you are not."

On a whim, she looped the dog tags around her neck, felt a little naughty, a little possessive even, wearing them. Crazy of course, but there it was. She reached for her short silk kimono, wondering if he liked blue. Wondering if she'd snored. Was mortified all over again.

"No wonder he left."

Then she heard a sound. Realized she smelled coffee.

Sweet, she thought, and tying the belt at her waist, she opened her bedroom door. He was still here, helping himself to coffee in her kitchen. She didn't know what to think about that but decided that maybe she liked that he felt comfortable enough to make himself at home. It implied something—something more than sex.

Finger combing her hair and purposefully giving it a

little sleep- and sex-tousled look, she made sure the robe fell open to reveal both her diamond and his dog tags nestled between her breasts. Then she walked barefoot into the kitchen.

Sam was sitting at her table.

"Hi." She smiled when she saw him. Melted a little when she glanced at his hands, remembering how he'd touched her. Loving how he'd touched her.

He glanced up at her, swept her body with a look, his gaze lingering between her breasts.

Instead of a slow, appreciative appraisal of her long bare limbs and sexy smile, he averted his gaze to the cup of coffee sitting in front of him. "You might want to get dressed."

His voice was gruff. His look was all business.

She blinked, more than surprised by a scowl that absolutely did not say, "Come here, darlin', and give me some sugar."

"Wow," she said, confused by the tension she felt in him. "So, guess that answers my question about whether it upset you that I fell asleep."

As attempts for light and breezy went, it fell flat. Her first niggle of concern crept in.

Before she could puzzle out his reaction and the reason for it and her sudden unease, she heard voices coming from her garage.

Her heart jumped. Her gaze flashed to his.

"Someone's in the garage," she whispered urgently.

"I know. Go get dressed," he repeated.

Confusion mushroomed to panic in a single heartbeat. Wrong. Something was very, very wrong. "Sam? What's going on?"

She was already backing out of the room when he stood. Flashed a badge. "FBI," he said. "Just relax. No one's here to hurt you."

If he'd have said, "Jack the Ripper," or "Hillside Slasher" he couldn't have stunned or panicked her more.

"FBI?" She bunched her kimono tighter and higher over her breasts, suddenly feeling exposed and violated. "*FBI?*" she repeated, accusation and more than a little fear making her voice shrill. "I don't understand. What . . . what's going on?"

"Unless you want my men to see you like this," he said, his face void of all emotion, "go get dressed. I'll answer your questions then."

"You will answer my questions now!" Anger and humiliation hit her like a sledgehammer, outdistancing the fear and confusion. "Why is the FBI interested in me?"

The door from her garage opened. A man poked his head inside the kitchen. *Oh my God.* It was the gay cop cowboy.

Even in the FBI jacket and cap he looked like a poster boy. Only the smile was absent—and telling. He wasn't playing now. He was all business. For whatever reason, she appeared to be the endgame. Abbie could see a black nylon shoulder holster when the jacket fell open.

He cut a glance her way, did a double take that had her clutching her kimono even tighter, before he turned back to Sam, hitched his head toward the garage. "You need to see this."

After another fleeting look at her, he disappeared into the garage again.

And just that fast, she knew. "Cory," she said, meeting Sam's eyes as a horrible dread sank through her. "Oh, God. Is this about Cory? Did something happen to him?"

Tears filled her eyes as worry for her brother overshadowed the confusion and disappointment of Sam's betrayal.

"Yeah," Sam said at last. "This is about Cory. Did something happen to him? I don't know. I was hoping you could tell me."

"Tell you? Tell you what?" She was beyond trying to cope with or control her emotions now. She was confused and scared and needed Sam to say something that she could make sense of. "I haven't seen or heard from Cory in days. And I don't understand any of this. FBI? *You're* FBI?"

He glared at her, his eyes hard and angry and impatient. "Dammit, Abbie. For the last time. Go get dressed. We are not going to have this conversation until you do."

She just sort of deflated then. Helplessly shook her head. "Is that what we had before? In my bed? Was that . . . *conversation*, Sam? Or was that an interrogation?"

His jaw clenched and she actually saw a trace of guilt.

"Why didn't you ask?" Her voice was so soft, the silence in the kitchen rang loud around them. "If you had questions about Cory, why didn't you just ask me?"

She swiped a finger over her cheek. Angrily wiped away the tear that had escaped when she finally accepted the truth. "You didn't have to *fuck* me, Sam," she said, her crudeness intentional and full of accusation. "Nail screws would have been just as effective."

And less painful.

She searched his face. Saw nothing.

"I'll wait for you here," he said after a long moment. "Stay away from the phone. And don't even think about trying to leave."

She turned then. Walked to her bedroom, shaking with rage and defeat and a hollow emptiness that took her back to her childhood. Her mother's indifference, her father's hard hand, and later, Don's infidelity—all paled in comparison to the pain Sam Lang had administered with lazy kisses, a gentle caress, and an implied promise that he'd never intended to keep.

"She buy it?" Reed looked up from one of the boxes they'd ripped open when Sam stepped into the garage. Packing material, clay pots and bowls, and primitive statues were strewn all over the garage floor.

Yet all Sam saw was the stunned look on Abbie's face—confused, accusing, hurting.

"Yeah," he said, pulling away from the way she'd looked, the way he'd felt about using her. "She bought it."

Reed was referring to their FBI scam. Just in case,

though, Sam had unplugged her landline and fished her cell phone out of her purse so she couldn't make any calls. The last thing they needed was for half the Vegas PD to swarm the house.

That didn't mean they could afford to drag their feet. The X factor—a nosy neighbor, a passing cruiser—could throw a giant wrench in the works.

"What have you got?"

"Nothing." Wyatt Savage—a big man with a soft southern drawl he'd never quite kicked—glanced up from a stack of open boxes. "Nothing but clay statues, pottery pieces, shit like that. No drugs. No hot rocks. It's all penny-ante stuff."

Sam turned to Holliday. "Progress?"

Colter glanced up from the phone box mounted on a sidewall of the garage. "Almost set." He went back to work installing a tap on her line.

"If Hughes is shipping back illegal goods, I don't think we're going to find them here," Reed said, pulling a velvet pouch out of his pocket. "Not without a little help, at least."

Sam worked his jaw, not liking where this was going but knowing it had to be done. "Plant it," he said. "Wait for my cue." Then he walked back into the kitchen.

He poured himself another cup of coffee and waited for Abbie. He didn't have to wait long. She was dressed in jeans and a pale yellow long-sleeve T-shirt when she walked back into the kitchen. She was covered from head to toe—not even her feet were exposed, as, he suspected, *she* felt exposed.

Her eyes were dry, her posture straight and defensive. The look in her eyes when they met his relayed every emotion Sam would feel if he were in her shoes.

Anger. Betrayal. Confusion. Pain.

And hatred.

Above all, there was hatred.

He rose, poured her some coffee.

"Sit down, Abbie."

"I want to see that ID again." She crossed her arms and stood her ground on the far side of the kitchen table. Ignored the mug he held out to her.

Sam set the coffee on the table and reached into his pocket for his bogus FBI ID and the equally false search warrant Reed had taken care of this afternoon. He held out the badge for her inspection.

She wasn't stupid; she'd figure out the flaws in their con eventually. They had to work fast and keep the pressure on. She may not even be guilty or, for that matter, culpable in her brother's shady dealings, but Sam knew that if she were either, without the FBI ruse, they would get exactly nowhere. He didn't have time to sit and wait for her to talk. He'd wasted enough time already trying to finesse the information out of her. And look where that had gotten him.

"Okay?" he asked as she reluctantly sat down at the table.

"Nothing about this is okay." She shoved the badge across the surface toward him, and his dog tags along with it.

He picked them up. They were still warm from the

heat of her body. He looked from them to her face, blocking the picture of her standing in the doorway, those tags nestled between her breasts.

"We need to know where your brother is." He cut to the chase, wanting to get this over with so he wouldn't have to look at the pain in her eyes.

"I don't know where he is." Her dark hair fell over her face as she stared at the hands she'd linked together on the tabletop. Hands that had driven him to the edge in the dark in her bed.

"When was the last time you heard from him?"

She lifted her head. "What do you want with Cory?" she asked instead of answering him.

"I think you already know."

Her irises darkened from brown to almost black. "This is what I know," she said, her voice brittle. "You're a lying bastard."

Sam closed his eyes. Breathed deep. And smelled her. And sex. "Look. I never meant for that to happen."

She made a sound that was both weary and wise. "Yeah, that's why you came prepared with a condom."

Guilty as charged. "I'm sorry."

"Oh . . . well, I didn't realize you were *sorry*. That makes everything all right, then, doesn't it?"

"Abbie. I understand. You're pissed—"

"You don't understand anything." Her eyes brimmed with tears. She blinked them back by sheer force of will. "I am far from pissed. I am mortified. I feel violated. And you and your 'apology' can rot in hell."

He wished she'd just slug him. Knock him flat on

his ass. Maybe they'd both feel better. At least maybe he'd feel better. Because there was no fixing it, he made himself go on.

"Who does your brother work for?"

She looked away. "I didn't know he worked for anyone."

"What's he doing in Honduras?"

"I don't know."

"Fredrick Nader," he pressed on. "Name mean anything to you?"

She frowned. "Should it?"

"Nader is a known terrorist. He also dabbles in drugs, illegal weapons, and stolen gems."

"And I should care about this, why?"

"You should care about this because he's your brother's employer."

That finally got a reaction other than disdain. Her eyes lasered in on his. "Let's add 'delusional' to 'bastard.' Cory is a lot of things but he's not a thief. And for God's sake, he might not always show the best judgment, but he would never associate with a terrorist."

Sam had to work his damnedest not to offer her reassurances. He gave her a hard look. "I'll ask you again. What's he doing in Honduras?"

She sniffed. "Why don't you tell me, since you have all the answers."

"Okay. Fine. He's working as a low-level mule for Nader."

"A mule?"

"A courier. Delivering packages. Packages containing all sorts of things Uncle Sam frowns on—drugs, laundered money, stolen gems—like the packages he's been mailing to you."

"Those *packages*," she said, contempt dripping from each word, "are full of Mayan knockoffs . . . primitive pottery, native crafts . . . things like that. Cory's been buying them and shipping them to me to store so he'll have an inventory when he comes home and sets up his retail business."

"And you know that because you checked them out?"

She glared at him. "I know because that's what he told me was in them. And unlike with you, I can believe him."

"For the record, I never lied to you."

"No. You just screwed me for fun and profit."

"I never meant for that to happen."

"Yeah. I can see how hard you were fighting it."

Sam pushed away from the table. Walked to the door that led to the garage and opened it. "Reed."

The blond agent followed him back to the kitchen.

"Show her," Sam said.

Reed held one of the Mayan knockoff statues in his hand. It was about the size of a wine bottle. He held it up to the side of his head. Shook it.

"This one's a little heavier than the rest," he said. "What do you think? Should we check it out?"

"Just do it," Sam said.

Reed rapped the soft plaster on the side of her table. The piece broke in half. The inside was hollow.

Sam reached inside, pulled out a tissue wrapped package that Reed had planted there. He tossed it on the table in front of Abbie.

She looked from him to the tissue, her brows knit, her dark eyes questioning.

"Open it," he said.

She slowly shook her head. "What? So you can get my fingerprints on whatever's inside? I don't know what your game is but don't expect me to play nice," she said defiantly.

"I'll do it." Reed unwrapped the tissue paper to reveal a quart-sized plastic bag filled with white powder.

"Now, what do you suppose we have here?" Reed lifted the bag, held it in front of her.

Abbie stared at the bag as if it were poison. Reed sliced the bag open, dipped the tip of his little finger into the powder, then brought it to his nose, Sam could see that she knew what it was. Or what it was supposed to be. She'd told him her father was a drug addict. He figured she recognized blow when she saw it.

"He didn't know," she insisted, her gaze flying from Sam to Reed. "Cory *couldn't* have known. He isn't a dealer. And he wouldn't do this to me."

"Wouldn't do what? Make you an accomplice to illegal drug smuggling?"

She shot up from the table so fast her chair teetered and almost toppled over. "I'm not an accomplice in anything. And I told you. Cory wouldn't *do* this. How many ways can I say it? For that matter, how do I know you didn't plant that bag? You're good at games, right, Sam? Excuse me—you're good at games, aren't you, *Agent Lang*." She made a sound of frustration. "Or is that even your real name?"

"It's my name," he said.

She challenged him with a cold look. "Whatever. I don't understand why you targeted me."

If she was lying, she was damn good, Sam thought, as guilt hammered away at his conviction.

The door to the garage opened. Savage and Colter walked into the kitchen. They were about to level the killing blow.

"The boy's been busy," Colter said, holding a broken statue. "Wanna guess what we found inside this one?"

Abbie went pale when he pulled out a blue velvet pouch covered in plaster dust. He spilled the contents into his hand. An emerald necklace sparkled against his palm. It was one of the best paste re-creations Sam had ever seen. They had Joe Greene—another one of the BOIs—and his connections back in Buenos Aires to thank for that.

"What do you want to bet someone's looking for those little baubles?"

Colter held a thick manila folder marked FBI. He opened it up, thumbed through it, finally found what he was looking for.

"Here we go." He pulled a sheet of paper out of the stack, a photocopied picture of the fake emeralds that had been doctored with a date stamp of six months ago.

"Yep." Savage fully disclosed the photo so Abbie could see it and compare it to the necklace. "That's them."

Sam turned to Abbie, steeled himself against the panicked confusion in her eyes. "You're in a world of hurt here, Abbie. You realize that, right? Tell us what you know so we can help you."

She swallowed. "Your concern is touching."

He ignored the pain that spurred her sarcasm and pressed on. "Drugs. Stolen gems. With all this evidence to back up charges, that innocent act is not going to play well with a jury."

He saw fear as well as pain on her face now.

"Jury? Jesus. You honestly think I had something to do with this?"

Sam glanced at Reed then back at Abbie. "New car. Flashy diamond. Nice digs. You tell me how a student and a dealer at a casino manages all that? And why all the security if you aren't hiding something?"

She went pale. "Do I need a lawyer?" she asked softly.

Sam leaned back, sensing he was close to getting what he wanted, feeling no triumph in the toll this was taking on her. "What you need is to talk to us. Tell us everything you know about your brother and his association with Fredrick Nader. You cooperate, we can cut you a deal. You don't give us what we need, you're facing federal charges for drug trafficking and jewel theft."

He needed to close this deal. Before the shock

wore off and her head cleared. Before she started making phone calls. Started asking questions and found out their FBI act was a fraud. Before she figured out that they were grasping at straws here and that she was all they had to lead them to Nader since Cory had fallen off the grid.

She crossed her arms protectively beneath her breasts. "I keep telling you. I don't know anything."

"This says you do." Sam nodded toward the fake bag of drugs and the paste emeralds. "I don't want to have to take you into custody."

She leveled him a look. "Like you didn't want to have to take me to bed?"

There was so much venom and hurt in her voice, Savage and Reed looked away. And Sam's respect for Abbie Hughes rose another notch. She was tough. It had to hurt like hell to hang out that laundry in front of the other men. It took guts.

"Look," Sam said, going with his gut and counting on the wiretap and the certain knowledge that as soon as they left, she'd make some calls. "Why don't you sleep on it? We'll come back in the morning. But I'll warn you right now, if you lawyer up, which essentially means you clam up, any deal is off the table. I'll see to it you spend the next thirty-plus years behind bars. And don't kid yourself. We've got enough evidence here to make any charge we want to level stick."

She had nothing to say to that.

"You've got until eight tomorrow morning." He nodded toward Reed and Savage to retrieve the "evidence" lying on the kitchen table. "I'll be back then."

He stood, faced her. "Think very hard, Abbie. You can still save yourself if you make the right decision."

"Has it even crossed your mind that I might be telling you the truth? Or are you so used to lying to get what you want, you don't recognize the truth when you hear it?"

Yeah, he was used to lying. What he wasn't used to was feeling guilty about it. "If you're telling the truth, then you've got nothing to hide. If you're lying, then you're in more trouble than you ever bargained for. Either way, your brother is in the thick of this. He's playing with some bad boys, Abbie. If he falls out of favor, Nader won't so much as blink when he kills him. You help me find Cory before that happens and you're helping him."

A single tear trickled down her cheek.

Sam couldn't let that stop him. He walked to the door, aware of her standing stiff and in shock. Her voice, however, thick with heartbreaking disappointment, had him hesitate with his hand on the doorknob.

"So what was I to you in all this? A job perk?"

He hung his head. Breathed deep. Then he made himself turn and face her. "A casualty," he said with all the emotion of a rock. "You were a casualty."

She nodded. Kept nodding as another tear fell. "Well. Good to know it was nothing *personal*."

Like it had been personal for her.

By the time Sam closed the door behind him, all he felt was numb. Forget second guesses, forget regret. Numb worked. Numb overrode the guilt that pummeled his conviction and tried to convince him that the means didn't justify the end. That nothing justified the pain he had caused this woman.

But something did.

Terri's death was all the justification he needed.

10

Abbie watched the door close behind Sam. Stared for long moments after he left.

Then she began shaking.

She planted her elbows on the table, lowered her head into her hands. Fisted her hands in her hair and tried to hold herself together.

Jesus.

Cory—involved in drug trafficking and stolen gem smuggling.

Sam—an FBI agent.

Sam—in her bed. In her body.

"You were a casualty."

She couldn't stall the tears any longer. They hit her like a truck. No matter how she struggled to keep them inside, she couldn't. She wept openly. Wept violently.

For Cory . . . God, what had Cory gotten himself into?

For herself . . . Sam's betrayal cut like glass. Cut her deep.

She was no stranger to pain. Physical. Emotional.

But this. God. She'd been so stupid. She'd been on the verge of falling in love with him.

And he'd been using her. He wanted to send her to prison for something she hadn't done. For something she did not want to believe Cory had done.

She saw the bag of drugs in her mind. The emeralds they said were stolen.

"Cory," she whispered and laid her head on the kitchen table. "Where are you? And what have you done?"

Off the coast of Muchilena, Honduras
Same night

"Truly, there are few areas of Central America worth the C-4 it would take to blow them to dust, don't you agree?"

Tied to a metal chair, blood streaming down his bruised face, Cory Hughes didn't respond.

Fredrick Nader frowned with impatience as he sat in a plush club chair that his steward had carried to the starboard deck. The running lights glittered off the dark water as he observed Hughes's dazed eyes.

"I have, however," Fredrick went on conversationally, "always held a true appreciation for the warm waters off the Isla de Roatán."

Of course, local, low-level government corruption had netted him some rare gem acquisitions over the years and had contributed to his affection for his favorite mooring.

"Have you been there? No? Well, it's a beautiful little island almost true east of La Ceiba," he continued, then nodded at Rutger, who promptly threw a bucket of seawater into Hughes's bruised and bloody face. The boy winced and hissed out a pained breath when the salty brine bit into open wounds.

"In any event, I'd much prefer to be moored near Roatán than here at Muchilena. Very wrong side of the social strata. Too crude for my taste. And while it's been mildly entertaining interrogating you, frankly, your stubborn resistance to answer questions to my satisfaction is starting to bore me."

Fredrick inspected his nails, made a mental note to have Arturo arrange the return of that lovely young manicurist when they next visited Roatán. In addition to a decent manicure, the pretty Maria was a woman of many talents and beautiful breasts.

He got hard thinking about their last encounter. Took pride in the ready response of his prick. He was, after all, sixty-five. Credited his virility to his staunch German lineage and his fastidious determination to keep himself in excellent physical condition.

Hughes raised his head, squinted at him through straggly wet hair and swollen eyes.

"Ah. Good. You're with us again. Let's go over what we already know, all right?"

He rose then, walked over to Hughes, was careful not to step in any blood and stain his white deck shoes.

"Derek Styles stole something from me. Something

I have coveted for years and went to great lengths to obtain. Do you know the legend behind the Tupacka diamonds?"

The beaten man blinked.

"No. I don't suppose you do. Well, allow me. Legend has it that a Spanish conquistador arrived in Honduras and fell in love with the high priestess, Tupacka. He was so besotted by her beauty that he commissioned the diamond necklace as a wedding gift. They were married and the conquistador set sail to take his bride with him back to Spain. Are you still with me?"

Hughes's chin lolled on his chest. His hands were tied behind his back. Fredrick nodded to Rutger, who once again doused the boy with salt water, making him gasp in pain.

"As so often happened during those difficult and dangerous voyages," Fredrick went on, satisfied his audience was once again conscious, "a freak storm came up before their ship cleared the reefs. The vessel went down; all were lost. The only thing of value recovered was the necklace the priestess was wearing when her body washed ashore."

He smiled. "Tragically romantic, is it not? And positively miraculous that the diamonds were recovered to be passed down along with the story over the years and ended up in the National Museum. Until I made arrangements to own them."

He walked directly in front of Hughes. Got right in his face. "I want them back. Styles stole them. You somehow ended up with them. If you want to live to see tomorrow's sunrise, you will tell me where they are.

"Rutger . . . you've been very patient," Fredrick said when the mule remained stubbornly and stupidly silent. "You may get your knife out now and play. Perhaps our young friend will find the slice of your blade more convincing than your fists."

"No. No please . . . don't let him c-cut me. I'll . . . tell you. Tell you."

Fredrick smiled, pleased that they had finally worn him down. "One moment, Rutger. We must hear what the young man has to say. Make it good," he said, all pretense of amusement eclipsed by the acid in his tone. "Your life depends on it."

"What do you want me to do with him?" Rutger asked one hour later.

Fredrick looked up from his glass of port. "Get him off the yacht. Take him to Peña Blanca," he added. He owned a small estancia there near the village. While he hadn't spent time at the ranch lately, he liked its close proximity to both the Guatemalan border, should he have need to flee Honduran authorities, and the El Puente Mayan archaeological site. He did so appreciate the Mayan ruins.

Thick, nearly impenetrable national forest fortressed the estancia to the west. Its location, on the southward slope of Montaña de la Crita provided outlook and defensive advantages.

"Alert the men that a guest is on the way."

By the time Rutger arrived with Hughes in tow, the estancia would be heavily guarded.

Not that Fredrick expected resistance from what was left of Hughes. Not that he expected Hughes to live that much longer. Just long enough to ensure he hadn't lied about the diamonds.

"And the merchandise?" Rutger asked diplomatically. "Do you wish for me to make the trip to Las Vegas and retrieve it personally?"

"Yes. No. Wait. On second thought, I have a much better idea." Why risk Rutger being detained and his passport being confiscated? Rutger was on too many U.S. government watch lists. Damn radical extremists had taken all the fun out of flying.

"Hughes is responsible for this. We'll let him take care of it."

When Cory came to, he was lying facedown on a dirt floor. He rolled painfully from his stomach to his back. He was inside a building. High windows. Hot and dank and dark.

He didn't remember leaving Nader's yacht. He didn't remember anything beyond the pain. The pain told him he was alive. The intensity told him that Nader had finally let Rutger loose with his knife.

His hands were tied in front of him now. His left hand throbbed, ached, burned. Was covered with a thick bandage.

To stop the bleeding.

He remembered then. As he fought for breath, fought for calm, he remembered what he'd told them when he'd seen the moonlight glint off Rutger's knife. He remembered what Rutger had done to him. Why his hand was bandaged.

His hand.

God, oh Jesus God.

"Abbie," he whispered into a silence broken by the wind outside the windows and the swishing, skittering sound of whatever night creature shared the floor of this squalid hovel with him. "Abbie, I'm sorry."

Hot, salty tears ran into his hair, stung when they trickled across his abraded skin. He'd never wanted to involve her in this, but because he was stupid and weak, he'd drawn her into it.

What choice had he had?

What choice?

The only reason he was still alive was because he'd stashed the Tupacka diamonds someplace safe. Because he had, they couldn't afford to kill him. Not until Nader got his diamonds back.

He'd thought it was a safe bet to mail the diamonds back to the States. Not to Abbie. No. Hadn't wanted her caught in the middle.

But then Rutger had brought out his knife, and Cory had told them everything. Now Abbie was in as much danger as he was.

"I'm sorry. I'm sorry. I'm sorry," he wept, and for the first time in his miserable life, he prayed.

"Please, God. Please don't let them hurt her, too."

Las Vegas

Abbie sat up straight. She glanced at the kitchen clock. It was 5:00 a.m. She'd actually fallen asleep at her kitchen table. She couldn't believe she'd slept.

Shut down was probably more like it. She rose abruptly, walked to the counter, and dumped the pot of coffee Sam had made. She didn't want any reminders of him in her house. With shaking hands, she made a fresh pot. Then she stripped and stood under the shower, running it as hot as she could stand it, needing to wash away the scent of him and of sex.

She cried some more.

Then she got mad.

She was still wrapped in her towel when she charged into her bedroom, ripped the sheets off the bed, and threw them into the washer. As the washer filled with water, she stood in front of it, staring at the utility room wall, locked in a battle of images.

Sam, kissing her.

Sam, questioning her.

Sam, lowering his mouth to her breast.

Telling her she could go to prison.

Telling her she felt incredible.

"Enough." She slammed down the lid to the washer and marched out of the small room.

She had bigger problems than Sam Lang's betrayal. Cory was in a world of trouble and she had no idea what to do or how to help him.

At this point, she had no idea what to even think.

Drugs? Stolen emeralds?

It didn't fit. It just didn't fit.

Yeah, she knew Cory struggled. Knew he was too proud to ask her for help—too proud to take it when she offered.

She sipped coffee, thought of him as a little boy. Tears stung again. He'd been so beautiful. So small. So vulnerable. And so damaged. Their father had abused him so badly.

"Why all the security if you aren't hiding something?" Sam had asked.

When you grew up the way she and Cory had, it became very important to know there was a safe place to hide. Locked doors weren't always enough.

They hadn't been enough tonight.

Cory. God, Cory. What was happening?

Yes, Abbie felt responsible for him. And yes, she felt disappointed for him, sometimes disappointed in him. But above all, she loved him. She had to find a way to help him.

She walked to her second bedroom that doubled as her home office and study room, stared at the computer, then booted it up.

"Please, please, please," she whispered as she sat down and waited impatiently for her e-mail to open up. "Please let there be an e-mail from Cory."

She needed to get in touch with him. Beg him to level with her and tell her what was going on.

Her heart pounded as she sat there, waiting for a

handful of new messages to download. A sales notification from an online catalog. A couple of spams her filter didn't catch. Notification that her credit card statement was now available online.

A silly note from Crystal asking how the underwear had panned out.

She swallowed back a rolling nausea triggered by humiliation when she remembered how brazen she'd been when Sam had taken them off of her. She'd been so stupid. She'd actually thought . . . well, it didn't matter what she'd thought. Sam Lang had used her. End of story.

She waited for the last message to download, annoyed because it was taking so long. Probably from Fran. Fran was in one of Abbie's accounting classes at the U and no matter how many times Abbie had told her not to send attachments with jokes, Fran was certain Abbie could not live without seeing the latest chuckle.

She was about to close down her e-mail when the message finally popped up on her screen.

It wasn't from Fran. She didn't recognize the sender's address but the subject line drained all the blood from her face.

All it said was: Cory Hughes. According to the date and time, it had been sent three hours ago.

She couldn't open it up fast enough.

She read the message.

Disbelieving.

Horrified.

Breath caught in her throat, she read it again.

Wishing to God she was wrong. That she'd read it wrong. That she'd wake up and this would all be a bad dream.

But the sound of the wall clock ticking into the silence told her she was awake. The thickness in her throat reminded her she was alive.

With terrified reluctance, she opened the attachment as the e-mail directed her to do. When she finally comprehended who was in the photograph and what had been done to him, the horror began in earnest.

She shot out of the chair, stumbled backward, then ran on rubbery legs for the bathroom.

She fell to her hands and knees.

Retched violently into the toilet.

When she could breathe again, when her abdominal muscles stopped convulsing, she rose on shaking legs. Stared at her reflection in the mirror.

Her face was pale, her eyes wild with terror.

Like Cory's eyes had been wild with terror and pain. Staring back at her from a face that was pummeled and bruised and swollen to the point where she hadn't recognized him at first.

A Spanish-language newspaper lay on a table in front of him—proof of life, she realized—today's date prominent for her to see.

Much of the rest of the newsprint was soaked in blood.

Cory's left hand lay beside the date, fingers splayed wide. Three fingers and a thumb. Blood soaked the newsprint where his little finger used to be.

It lay beside his hand now. Detached. Drained of blood. Lifeless.

Like Cory would be drained of blood and lifeless if she didn't do exactly as she was told.

11

They'd given her fifteen hours, and three of them were already gone. If Abbie wanted to see her brother alive again she was to retrieve a diamond necklace from the Las Vegas post office box where Cory had mailed it, then bring it with her to San Pedro Sula, Honduras.

Fifteen hours. Each hour she delayed beyond that, Cory would lose another finger.

Her stomach rolled again. She swallowed back the nausea. She had to get it together. Not only that, she had to *keep* it together or Cory was going to die.

She printed off the instructions in the e-mail. Read them over and over even though they were crystal clear. Then she paced, wound tight on adrenaline and anxiety, her mind running at warp speed.

She had to think . . . to come up with something . . . a plan that didn't get Cory killed. For that matter, a plan that didn't get them both killed.

If Sam was right, if Cory was involved in something illegal with this man, Fredrick Nader, then while the

ID of the sender was a mystery, it made sense that Nader was the one holding Cory hostage.

She scanned the note again, searching for some-thing—anything—that would give her an edge. Found nothing.

When she arrived in San Pedro Sula, a car would be waiting for her, it said. The driver would be holding a sign with her name on it. He would take her to Cory. She would exchange the diamonds for him and they would be free to go.

Right. They had to think she was either too stupid or too frightened to comprehend that once they had what they wanted, she and Cory were both as good as dead.

Die. Dead. Killed. She could count the times on one hand she'd said those words in her life. Now, every other thought was filled with the stuff of thriller movies and bad dreams. It was all so far removed from anything she'd ever encountered, she felt as if she were drowning in a big glass fishbowl. Swimming for her life.

With the clock ticking—it was close to 6:30 a.m. now—she sat back down at her computer, Googled a travel site, and found an eleven-hour flight from Vegas to San Pedro Sula that left at 10:55 a.m.

She needed to be on that plane. And then what?

No matter how many times she'd worked it through in her mind, she couldn't come up with a way to get ei-ther of them out alive.

She needed help. But the e-mail had been specific about that, too. She was not to contact the police. She was to come to Honduras alone. Still, she knew she needed help.

But she didn't know anyone who would be able to help her.

She looked up from the computer abruptly.

"Yes, you do," she told herself as her heart rate picked up speed.

She *did* know someone. Someone who had a vested interest. Not in her. Not in her brother, but in stolen diamonds. And in Fredrick Nader.

A plan came to her then—unfolded like the pages in a book. She knew exactly what she had to do. She had to use Sam Lang the way he'd used her. Ruthlessly, unapologetically.

It could work, she realized as she thought it through.

It *would* work.

It would probably mean she would end up in prison, but she'd worry about criminal charges later. Right now all that mattered was getting Cory back.

For the first time since this nightmare started, her heart pounded with something other than a helpless, hopeless fear. She ran into the bedroom to find her purse and her cell phone.

Gone, she realized after a frantic search.

Sam. He must have taken them.

So she would have to use the landline, she realized. If Sam Lang hadn't blinked at taking her to bed to get information out of her, he wouldn't hesitate to tap her phones. That meant any call she made would be monitored.

"Bastard."

It couldn't be helped. She picked up the phone and dialed.

"It's . . . six frickin' o'clock in the morning," Crystal grumbled, picking up on the fourth ring. "This better be good."

"Crystal. It's me. Don't ask any questions. As soon as I hang up, boot up your computer and open your e-mail."

"What th—?"

"Please. Just do it." Abbie disconnected.

Sam and his buddies were, no doubt, monitoring her e-mail account too, so she went out on Yahoo and quickly set up a new account under a name only Crystal would recognize. Her hooker name: Jiggles Larue. It was a game they had played one night after a bottle of wine and a lot of laughs. The fake name on the new account wouldn't stop Sam and his FBI pals, but it would slow them down. By the time they found the new account with Abbie's instructions to Crystal, it would be too late for them to stop her. Her plan would be in play and she'd be closer to getting Cory back home or . . . She refused to think about what would happen if it didn't work.

Her fingers flew over the keys as she gave Crystal the short version of what was happening and instructions for what Abbie needed Crystal to do as soon as the post office lobby opened at eight. She ended the note with a caution to make certain she wasn't followed.

She hit Send, waited for what seemed like an eternity, but in fact was only a few minutes before she received Crystal's reply. "Count on me. Be careful."

Thank God for Crystal.

"You too," she typed back and sent off the reply.

Next she replied to Cory's captors, carefully selecting her words. Her heart felt like it would explode as she hit Send, then prayed she'd bought Cory enough time for her to get to him.

On a deep breath, she deleted all messages and the new account, shredded the e-mail she'd printed—all but the picture of Cory—then she picked up the phone again and booked the flight to San Pedro Sula.

With that done, she hurried into her bedroom, dug her passport out of the safe in her closet, and thanked whatever gods of fate had prompted her to have it renewed last year even though she hadn't been out of the States since her honeymoon with Don.

Next, she threw a change of clothes and a few toiletries into a backpack. Then she waited for Sam to show up. If she'd been right about the phone tap, it wouldn't take him long.

A few minutes later, a black SUV pulled up in front of her house and Sam got out. It was nice to know she could count on him for something . . . something other than the truth.

"Is this the part where I'm supposed to say, what took you so long?" Abbie asked when she opened the door to Sam's knock.

She'd been practicing the line in her head. Didn't want to stumble over it, let him know how difficult it was for her to see him again so soon after . . . well, so soon. She stepped aside so he could walk into the living room.

"You're not actually planning to go to Honduras."

It wasn't a question. It was a statement. It was also confirmation that she'd been right about her phone calls being monitored.

"Because I'd be crazy to think you wouldn't find out and try to stop me? I may be gullible, but that doesn't make me stupid. Just like you coming off as a straight shooter doesn't make you one."

A muscle in his jaw worked. It was the only indication that her barb had hit home.

"Cory's being held hostage," she said without preamble.

If he was surprised to hear that Cory had been abducted, he didn't show it.

She walked into her office, intending for him to follow. She'd planned this part out, too, and handed him the photograph she'd printed off, struggling desperately not to look at it. "I received this in an e-mail. Or like the phone tap, do you already have hackers online and this is old news?"

Sam's silence and the grim look on his face as he studied the photo told her he hadn't seen it before now. Which meant he hadn't yet accessed her e-mail. It also meant she still had a small edge until he and his FBI buddies hacked in and intercepted her message to Crystal.

"This is Nader's work," he said, sounding grim. "More specifically, it's the work of his hired muscle, Rutger Smith."

"He wants a necklace," Abbie said. "Something he referred to in the e-mail as the Tupacka diamonds. He says Cory stole them from him and he wants them back."

"I need to see that e-mail."

"That's not going to happen. I deleted it." She didn't want Sam to know the original location of the necklace even though—God willing and with Crystal's help—it wasn't in Cory's post office box any longer. "Look, I don't have time to play any more games with you. Neither does Cory. So here's what's going to happen."

Abbie ignored Sam's hard scowl and drew a bracing breath. "I don't know why Cory had the diamonds in the first place. All I know is that he mailed them back to the States several days ago."

He glanced at her sharply. "To you?"

"No. Not to me. He sent the necklace to a post office box here in Vegas for safekeeping."

He glanced at the photo again. "So, he stole from Nader, knew that if Nader caught him he was as good as dead, so he mailed the diamonds to the States as insurance to keep Nader from killing him."

Except for the theft part, that's the way Abbie had figured it. "Until Nader gets the diamonds back, Cory is still of value to him alive."

"And it's safer for Nader if he has you deliver them instead of coming after them himself."

That made sense to Abbie, too.

"Does Nader know where the diamonds are?"

"He did." She shivered when she thought of the methods they had used to get the information out of Cory. "But not anymore."

She saw the moment Sam realized what she'd done. "The phone call to Crystal. You had her move them."

"*My* insurance," she said. "I let them know that I have the diamonds now. That I've moved them to a new hiding place and if they kill Cory before I get to Honduras to give them the new location they'll never see them again."

"Jesus."

For the first time since she'd met him, she saw Sam Lang rattled.

"You have no idea what kind of scum you're dealing with here."

She glanced at Cory's picture, shuddered again. "Yeah. I do."

"Then you have to know you just signed your own death warrant."

Maybe. Probably. Yeah. She knew that. Except that Sam was her ace in the hole. "What I know is I want my brother back."

"You are *not* going to Honduras," he said, anger rich in each word.

"Because you're charging me with a crime? Hauling me off to jail?" she baited, sounding braver than she felt.

"Fine. Arrest me. That's not going to get you what you want."

They both knew that he wanted Nader. Cory was small potatoes. Abbie had figured that out already. It was the big prize Sam was after.

"You think they're going to go easy on you because you're a woman?" He held the photo in front of her face when she remained stubbornly silent. "Look at it. Look at it!" he demanded when she averted her gaze. "These guys play for real. You're as dead as Cory if you go down there. Hell, if he hasn't already, Nader's probably sent a man to watch your house. Someone could be watching it right now, waiting for you to go to the post office and retrieve the necklace."

"Then it's a good thing I sent Crystal after it," she said, defiant. "Look. You think I'm not scared? Well, I'm scared, okay? I know what I'm up against."

"Then prove it. Tell me where the diamonds are, Abbie. No promises, but if you do that for me, I'll do what I can to get your brother back."

"Oh, I'm counting on that," she said slowly. "You *are* going to help me get Cory back. And once he's safe, you can have the damn diamonds."

He glared at her. Let out a breath. "Last I knew, you weren't in any position to bargain."

"See, that's where I think you're wrong. The way I figure it, the only reason the FBI is after Cory is to get to Nader. I mean, my brother is . . . how did you put it? A low-level mule? Low-level? Come on. It's not Cory you want. It's not even me. You want Nader. You want the diamonds. And we both know I'm your best ticket to getting both, just like you're my ticket to saving Cory."

He was really angry now. "I repeat. You do not know what you're messing with here. Nader will stop at nothing to get what he wants."

"Yeah. You'd know all about that, wouldn't you?"

She hated herself for letting the hurt he'd caused her creep into her voice. Refused to believe she actually saw regret in his eyes.

"This is my brother's life we're talking about. I'd think you'd be happy as hell to use me—again," she added just to watch him squirm. "I mean, I'm your best chance to get the bad guy and save the day. That's what you guys with the *white* hats do, right? You save the day. No matter who gets hurt in the process? No matter who you have to use? No matter how you have to use them." Tears stung her eyes. She blinked them back.

"Abbie."

"No." She held up a hand, backed a step away when he reached for her. She couldn't stand for him to touch her. Couldn't stand to think about how she might react. "No, it's all right. It's the way the game is played. I understand that now. I was just a . . . how did you put it? A casualty. Nothing personal."

A long silence passed. She had him over a barrel. He knew it and so did she. That didn't stop her from wishing he'd been what she thought he was.

And it didn't stop him from trying, one more time, to get what he wanted from her. "How do I know you really have the diamonds?"

Her computer dinged just then, telling her she had mail. God bless Crystal. Her timing was perfect.

"You know why clichés are used so often? Because they work. Like now. A picture is worth a thousand words," she said and opened up the e-mail. Just as she had instructed, Crystal had taken her camera with her to the post office and accessed the box with the combination Cory had given Nader. Then Crystal had snapped a digital photo of the necklace and e-mailed it to Abbie along with proof of today's date in the form of another newspaper.

"Holy God," Abbie said, when she saw the necklace for the first time. The diamonds—hundreds of them—were set in an elaborate mounting that started in a choker, then spread outward and downward like a delicate cape of solid stones and gold.

She could almost understand why someone would be willing to kill for this.

"Tell me what Crystal did with them."

Sam's voice startled her. She dragged her attention away from the photograph after she hit the print button. "That would sort of defeat my purpose now, wouldn't it? As long as you don't know where they are, I've got what us Vegas types call a pat hand."

His gaze never leaving her face, Sam tugged his cell phone off his belt and punched in a single digit.

"Did you pick her up yet?" he asked without preamble.

He listened, then hung up. "Seems your friend has disappeared."

Abbie retrieved the sheet from her printer. She

fanned it slightly so the ink would dry and blessed Crystal again for being so good at what she did. "Yeah, she does that sometimes."

"Four hours," Abbie had told Crystal in the e-mail. "Make yourself scarce for four hours. That's all I need to make sure the plane is in the air and I'm on it. If anyone approaches you after that, just play dumb."

"You're stooping a little low, aren't you? Involving a friend in your mess?"

His accusation hurt. But she was getting used to being hurt by Sam Lang. "That's the difference between you and me. I would never put someone I care about at risk. You're not going to charge her with anything. Just like you don't really care about Cory, you don't care about Crystal either. All you care about is the diamonds. And getting Nader."

She could see by his expression that she'd hit that nail on the proverbial head. "I can give you both. Lead you straight to Nader's door. If you do charge Crystal with anything when this is over, I'll testify that I threatened and coerced her into helping me. And trust me, I can be very convincing. You know all about being convincing, don't you, Sam?"

She grabbed her backpack. Called his bluff. "With or without you, I'm going after my brother. Lock up behind you. I've got a plane to catch."

It wasn't until she was in her assigned aisle seat, her backpack stored on the floor in front of her, that Abbie let herself think about the reckless danger of her plan.

And it wasn't until the cabin attendant came over and told her she'd been upgraded to first class that she knew her strategy had worked.

She leaned out into the aisle so she could see up to the first-class cabin. Sam Lang stood there glaring, waiting for her to join him.

12

Pissed. Sam was totally, majorly, *royally* pissed.

He worked his damnedest not to clench his hands into fists as Abbie Hughes, head held high, looking poised and perfect in a yellow knit top and jeans, walked down the narrow coach-class aisle toward him.

He didn't know what he wanted to do more: Haul her off the damn plane or haul her off to bed. The first would get her out of trouble. The second would get him deeper into it.

He didn't get it. Didn't get one thing about his reaction to this woman—and the control she pushed to the limit.

Part of him wanted to punish her. Part wanted to protect her. But one hundred percent was on board with wanting her.

So yeah, he was pissed that she could fuck with his head like this. He was pissed because he hadn't needed another player in this game to get to Nader. It was never supposed to come to this. Sam had only needed Abbie for information, yet she'd managed to manipulate herself into a key position on the team. *His* team.

Dangling her as bait to flush Nader out of his lair had never been a part of the plan either. Her involvement was going to pose ten times more complications than Sam needed. Her little sleight of hand had placed her square in the middle of a deadly deception that could get her hurt or killed.

Bottom line, that's what was really eating at him. He didn't want anything happening to her.

He lifted a hand when she reached him, indicating she should take the window seat. The strain he hadn't seen on her face in the predawn light in her house was apparent now. A slight bruising of fatigue darkened to shadows beneath her eyes. Her olive skin was visibly pale.

He remembered that skin in the dark of her bedroom. The softness of it. The taste of it. The scent of her and sex. He couldn't look at her without remembering those long, sleek legs wrapped around him, the silk of her hair tangled in his hands.

What it felt like to be inside her.

Her shoulder accidentally brushed his when she eased past him, then slid across plush leather into the roomy window seat in the first-class cabin. The slight touch prompted an immediate physical response. His entire body clenched involuntarily, leaned toward her—like a missile seeking heat.

He backed away, made sure she was settled, then dropped down into the seat beside her. Cursed under his breath.

One touch. One brief touch and he was panting like a damn dog.

Mistake. Taking her to bed had been a big, big mistake. He wished . . . Hell. It didn't matter what he wished. What was done was done. There were much bigger things at play here than Abbie Hughes's feelings. He had a job to do. Whether he liked it or not, she was going to help facilitate it.

He buckled his seat belt. Closed his eyes. Got it together.

"You know, there's one thing that's been bothering me," she said.

He grunted, rubbed a hand over his face. "One thing? You're heading into a snake pit and you're bothered about *one* thing? I can think of about a hundred things that should be scaring the hell out of you."

"What's the FBI doing mixed up in international drug trafficking?" she asked, ignoring his sarcasm. "Isn't that usually handled by the Drug Enforcement Agency? And while I'm asking, what's the FBI doing working an international gem theft? Didn't know you guys crossed national borders."

Yeah. She was smart. He grudgingly admired her for that. Even though the jury was still out on how deeply she was involved in her brother's dirty dealings, he admired her for a lot of things, and that didn't sit well with him either.

"And why, if this is a federal investigation, are you and your road crew," she notched her chin toward Savage and Colter, who were a little hard not to spot sitting across the aisle from them, "not on a government plane?"

Sam could lie to her, shore up the FBI scam, but in the end, there was no longer any point. "We're not FBI."

She opened her mouth. Closed it. Shook her head. Like she'd given up on expecting any truth from him. "Then who are you? Wait. Never mind. Don't bother." She averted her attention to the window as the jet taxied down the runway. "You'd just lie again anyway."

Sam steeled himself against the urge to explain. To try to make her understand that what had happened between them hadn't been about her brother or Nader or the diamonds. It had just happened. He hadn't meant for things to go that far. Hadn't been able to stop when he should have.

"Look, there are issues at play here that you're better off not knowing," he said instead.

She made a sound that was half laugh, half snort of disgust. "Don't you think it's a little too late in the game to be worried about what I know?"

It was a little late in the game to be worried about a lot of things. Like whether or not there had been another way to get to Nader and leave Abbie out of the mix.

"For all I know, you're just another bad guy on the take," she added when he remained silent. "But you know what? I don't care. All I care about is getting Cory back."

"By putting your own life on the line? Great plan."

She breathed deep, looked away again. "Other than

showing up in San Pedro Sula and climbing into a car with a man who is supposed to take me to my brother, I don't have a plan. That's what I need you for. You're the guy who wants Nader. I'll leave it to you to figure out the best way to use me to get him. Whatever you want, I'll do it. As long as you help me find Cory."

He considered her for a long moment. In addition to being intelligent, she was loyal to a fault. She knew the danger she faced, yet here she was. On a fool's mission to save her no-good brother.

"He's not worth it, you know. He's just not worth it."

Her gaze snapped to his, full of fire and fury. "Would you say the same thing about your sister?"

Sam went utterly still. "What do you know about my sister?"

"More than you know about my brother, so don't begin to presume you know his worth. You'd be wrong. Just like you're wrong about me."

She'd hurt him, Abbie realized. She wanted to feel some satisfaction in that fact, wanted to call it payback. That wasn't her. Never would be.

"I'm sorry about your sister," she said when he lapsed into a tense silence. "I read about it online. Didn't put it together until, well, until recently."

He said nothing. So much nothing it finally dawned on her.

"This is about her, isn't it?" It made sense. He wasn't FBI. Wasn't military. "Nader had something to do with her death."

When he finally turned to her, his face was void of

emotion. "Like I said, there are things in play here that you're better off not knowing."

Then he leaned his head back against the seat and closed his eyes.

End of discussion.

The flight from Vegas to Houston lasted three long hours. Even the roomy first-class cabin felt like a tight fit with Sam sitting so close to her. Not just because he was a big man, but because he had such a big presence. And because the memory of him naked and needing her in her bed wouldn't leave her alone.

His slightest movement made her agonizingly aware of him. The accidental brush of their thighs. The bump of an elbow. The sage and citrus scent of him, barely there, but oh so provocative when he turned his head, or shifted his weight.

The confinement drove her crazy. Abbie couldn't wait to deplane at Houston. She planned to spend a little time alone waiting for the connecting flight forty-five minutes later that would take them to San Pedro Sula.

She needed to regroup. To reassemble her thoughts. So as soon as they landed and got the all clear, she shot out of her seat, slid past Sam—who was *not* FBI—and headed for the exit door.

She was still shrugging into her backpack when a firm hand gripped her arm and stopped her before she left the covered jetway.

"Slow it down. We need to find a quiet place and get a few things ironed out."

So much for alone time and her "new" plan to be unaffected by Sam Lang. His grip on her elbow was firm but not bruising. And like the brush of their shoulders when she'd sat down beside him, the humming awareness that ran through her system was as involuntary as it was electric.

She was still recovering from the shock of it when he brought her up to speed on the two men who'd flown with them.

"Wyatt Savage," Sam said with a nod toward the guy on her left as the four of them walked briskly through the terminal.

Savage, like Sam, was a big man, only where Sam was lean muscle mass on a big, athletic frame, Savage was big as in bear. In football terms, Sam was built like a linebacker. Savage was built like a lineman. With kind eyes that she suspected hid secrets she was better off not knowing.

"Ma'am," Savage said with a trace of the South in his voice that she might have found charming if he hadn't seen her wearing only a short silk kimono and understood that Sam had just been in her bed.

"Luke Colter." Sam nodded to the other guy who was quick to flash her a smile and tip his fingers to a Stetson that wasn't there but that Abbie could easily see him wearing.

"Everyone calls me Doc. Doc Holliday. You got a hangnail or a heart attack or a yen for five-card stud— you come to me, okay?"

Colter was tall and rangy and built more like a bas-

ketball player. He had flirty blue eyes and that easy
smile going for him—and the company of Sam Lang
going against him.

"So where's the pretty boy?" Abbie asked.

Doc chuckled. "Lady's got Reed pegged."

"He's a little busy right now looking for your friend."
Sam herded her toward an empty corner near their de-
parture gate.

Abbie put on the brakes. "I need to use the restroom."

"In a minute." Sam steered her toward a seat in the
corner. The three men sat in a semicircle around her,
effectively establishing a barrier between them and the
handful of travelers waiting at their gate.

Abbie rarely felt intimidated—it was one of the advantages of being five foot eight—but these three men
could make a sumo wrestler cow. It wasn't just their
size. It was their presence. Behind Savage's slow, southern drawl and Doc's quick ready grin, both men had an
edge about them that defined them as something more
than the average guy.

There was crispness to the way they carried themselves, an awareness of their surroundings above and
beyond average situational awareness. Not predatory,
exactly but . . . vigilant, she decided finally. And capable. They all appeared to be capable.

"Military?" she asked, glancing around the circle of
three. Sam had once been in the military. Maybe he still
was. She liked that idea a whole hell of a lot better than

drug cartel on a vengeance quest. "Is that what you are?"

"Once upon a time," Doc said. "I like this woman," he added with a nod toward Sam. "She plays heads-up."

"She's going to have to," Sam said, his face stern, "if she wants to get out of this alive."

A cell phone rang. Since they hadn't returned her phone, everyone but Abbie checked their pockets.

"Yo," Savage answered, stood and walked away from them, his head down, his voice low.

"How am I going to communicate with you without my phone?" she asked.

"Unless you've got a special chip, your phone wouldn't work once we got out of the States anyway."

No. She didn't have a special chip. Either way, she had no means of communicating. Before she could get too worked up over that, Sam drew her attention.

"Tell me what you know about Nader."

"I already have. I don't know anything. I'd never even heard his name until you told me about him."

For the first time, Abbie sensed a hesitance in his expression. Like maybe he was starting to believe her—although it was clear that he didn't want to.

"Okay, fine. For the sake of argument, I'll fill you in with the basics," Sam said in a voice so low Abbie had to lean in close to hear him. "Nader has a dozen legit businesses scattered all over Europe that front for his illegal activities. He has money in everything from electronics to real estate to coffee, dumplings to ethanol. All silver-spoon acquisitions.

"But that wasn't enough to satisfy him," Sam continued. "He fancies himself some sort of gentleman
Mafioso type. His legit businesses bore him so he
started dabbling in the gray areas several years ago.
Now he's a major player in everything from selling
arms to terrorists to drug trafficking—has his fingers in a
lot of sour pies. He's got a network that rivals Al-Qaeda
for sophistication and capital, although it's not as big in
scope. His biggest failing is that while he delegates, he
also likes to physically participate in some of his 'business' deals. Not the dirty work—he leaves that to Rutger
Smith."

"Smith is Nader's personal hit man," Doc clarified,
picking up the briefcase he'd been carrying and setting
it on his thighs. He opened it up, drew out a photo. "So
you'll know him when you see him."

He handed her a photograph that appeared to have
been snapped when Smith wasn't watching.

"Somehow I can't see this guy blending into a
crowd." Abbie congratulated herself when her voice
came out strong, because she'd darned near swallowed
her tongue when she saw Smith's picture.

Talk about supersized. Rutger Smith was big, he was
bald, and he was scary as hell. A scar in the shape of a
crescent moon ran from the corner of his left eye to the
corner of his mouth. Yeah. He was scary. Even more
imposing than his size were his eyes. They looked . . .
soulless.

"Six foot seven, around three hundred twenty
pounds of solid mean," Colter supplied. "Carries a

knife and loves to use it. Has as much regard for human life as he has for a cockroach. But killing's not his specialty. Slicing, dicing, and playing with his catch is."

Abbie closed her eyes, thought of Cory, of what Rutger Smith had done to him.

Doc slid another photograph on top of Smith's image. This man looked to be in his late sixties. Thin white hair, slicked back over a deeply tanned face. Trim, physically fit. Distinguished. He could have been a doctor or a lawyer or a CEO of a Fortune 500 company, dressed to the nines in a white jacket and pants, diamonds winking from his ring fingers, gold choker around his neck visible between the open placket of his shirt. Eyes like a snake.

"Fredrick Nader?" she guessed.

Sam nodded. "Like I said, his biggest weakness is what he considers a strength. Sees himself as a general who leads from the front. Can't seem to help himself when it comes to showing up when a big deal is going down."

"And he takes it personal when someone takes something he feels belongs to him," Doc added.

"Like the Tupacka diamonds," Abbie said quietly.

"Yeah," Sam agreed. "Like the diamonds."

"His penchant for cigars—among other things— brings him to Honduras often. Major cigar operations there," Doc interjected. "Likes to moor his yacht, the *Seennymphe*, off the Isla de Roatán. In addition to his addiction to the *maduro habano*, he also has an obsession for the local women."

Abbie looked up from the photo, amazed by the detailed information they had on Nader. "Not FBI. Not military. But some kind of organization that has access to all this information. Who are you guys?"

"We're the good guys," Doc said with a grin she wanted to believe. "Huge leap of faith, I know, but it might be best to just leave it at that."

Shorthand for, *That's all the info you're going to get.* Abbie had little choice but to accept it.

Savage returned to their circle and flipped his phone shut. "That was Mendoza. He'll meet us at the airport with a car and gear."

"Mendoza? There are more of you?"

"Oh, darlin'." Doc's blue eyes twinkled. "If you only knew."

"Yeah, if only." She squelched an unexpected desire to grin back. Cute guy, nice grin or not, Doc was cut from the same cloth as Sam. She could trust him as far as she could toss a tank.

"We want to fit you with a wire," Sam said.

"A wire?"

"Your instructions were to arrive alone. That means you have to get off that plane alone. Nader's man can't know we're along so we'll need to keep a low profile. We have to have a way to track you."

"Oh. Oh, right. And no. I've never worn one."

But it appeared that she was going to. Just like it finally sank in that while she was headed into territory way beyond her comprehension or experience, to these men, it was status quo.

Her single-minded determination to save Cory had suddenly gone from nebulous idea to stark reality. It had been one thing to think about arriving in Honduras in sweeping, unformed terms. It was another thing entirely to face the absolutes: She was going out there alone. Leaving the relative safety of Lang, Colter, and Savage and riding away with a man under the command of a known terrorist. A terrorist who had had her brother beaten and brutalized and who wouldn't hesitate to kill Cory or her, too, if she so much as breathed wrong.

13

"How does it work?" Abbie asked when she'd gotten herself together.

Doc dug into his briefcase again. Pulled out a short, thin wire with a disc about the size of a small button attached to the end.

"You're going to thread this inside your bra strap. The mic will rest flush against your skin beneath the strap."

Yeah, she thought again. They had to have some connections to have such quick access to this type of sophisticated listening device.

"So," she regarded the device skeptically, "it's a real wire. I always thought that was just a term."

"Works on radio waves," Doc went on, showing her the receiver they would use to pick up the radio emissions and track her. "As long as we stay within a couple of miles, we can hear everything you say, everything anyone within three yards of you says."

"Can I hear you?"

Sam shook his head. "Doesn't work that way. If we

could, we'd fit you with an earpiece but it would be too risky. They'd spot it right away."

"What's going to stop Nader's man from finding this?" she asked as Coulter handed her the device. She read enough thrillers and mysteries to know there was technology to sweep for wires.

"The same thing that's going to stop him from detecting this." He pulled out a square chip—maybe twice the size of a regular postage stamp. "GPS transmitter."

Even Sam looked surprised by the small size. "Nate must have sprung big bucks for that little piece of work."

"Brand-new out of the U.K. Smallest GPS tracking device in the world. Company that produced it asked Nate to test-drive it."

"Test-drive?" Abbie didn't like the sound of this. "This is an experiment?"

"No worries," Doc assured her with a smile. "We used it in the field last week. Worked like a charm."

"So where's the antenna?" Sam asked, examining the chip.

"Internal." Doc turned back to Abbie. "I want you to slip it in your shoe, fit it beneath the foot liner, right under your arch. Less pressure there."

Abbie nodded.

"We'll track you every step of the way, okay? And we can operate both the wire and the GPS with remote switches," Doc explained. "Once you meet up with Nader's man, we'll switch both off, give him time to do his sweep, and then switch it back on when we either have visual confirmation that you're on the move or when a safe amount of time has passed. From then on, it's a question of hanging back until you lead us to Nader."

Not for the first time since she made the decision to put her life on the line, Abbie battled back an ominous feeling of dread. She was really going to do this. She was going to set herself up for God only knew what could happen to her.

"Then what?" She had to concentrate to keep her voice from shaking.

"Then you trust us to know what we're doing." Sam's voice was heavy with conviction. "We'll get you out of there."

Trust. There was that word again. She needed to trust Sam Lang. Like she'd trusted him once before. Look where that had gotten her.

Sam must have read her mind. "You can back out any time, you know. Just say the word."

She met Sam's dark brown eyes. Understood that he didn't want her here. "I'm not backing out."

He held her gaze for a long moment, finally nodded. "Nader's patience is going to be shot," he went on, accepting that she meant what she said. "He'll expect you to give him the information he wants. You're going to do it. No resistance. No hesitation. No heroics, you understand? You straight-out tell him where you hid the diamonds."

"Isn't that the same as signing my own death warrant?"

Doc shook his head. "He's not going to kill the golden goose until he's satisfied he knows where you hid the twenty-four-karat eggs, okay? As long as you hold potential value to him, you stay alive. He knows that if he kills you before he has those diamonds in his hot, thieving fist and it turns out you lied to him, then he's back to square one."

"Just like he knows that if he kills Cory before he gets the diamonds back," Savage interjected, apparently anticipating her next question, "he loses your co-operation."

"Look," Sam said, drawing her attention back to him, "we're going to take him down long before he has a chance to find out one way or another."

"How, exactly, are you going to make that happen?"

"Because it's what we do," Sam said with an assurance that left no room for doubt. "We make things happen."

Yeah, Abbie thought. They made things happen. A few days ago, she was taking classes and dealing blackjack. Life was simple, predictable, and boring. Now she was flying blind toward an international terrorist on a mission to save her brother. It was like playing a role in a video game.

"You can take that restroom break now," Sam said. "And you'd better hurry."

She looked from Sam to the devices, nodded. Then she stood, surprised when her legs were steady, and headed for the women's toilet.

A thread-thin piece of wire and a postage stamp

were going to be her first and only lines of defense if something went wrong.

If something went wrong? God. That was pretty much a given.

Something else became abundantly clear to Abbie as she locked herself in a bathroom stall, slipped out of her shirt and bra, and began the process of threading the wire into her bra strap.

No matter how she felt about Sam Lang, no matter that he'd used her, lied to her, she had to let it all go. Her life, Cory's life, now depended on this man and his "associates" for lack of a better word.

The only thing that mattered was finding Cory and getting them both out of Honduras alive.

La Mesa International Airport
San Pedro Sula, Honduras

"She'll be fine," Doc assured Sam at 10:04 p.m. as they watched Abbie walk off the plane alone in San Pedro Sula. "She's smart. She'll keep her head about her."

Sam breathed deep, gripped his seat's leather armrests, and fought to control an inexplicable surge of panic as Abbie walked through the exit and out of sight.

With nothing but a backpack for self-defense.

Yeah, they'd gone over the plan, such as it was. Over and over and over it. She was to take no chances. Do exactly as they'd told her. Count on them to know how and when to strike. She knew the drill.

Yet he couldn't begin to count the bad feelings he had about this.

He couldn't explain it but somewhere along the line he'd gone from not believing in her innocence, to wanting to believe. Then he'd crossed the final line.

He believed her.

And son of a bitch, if he still didn't want her.

He flew out of the seat, ignored Savage and Doc's startled looks, and bolted after her. He caught up with her just before she left the jetway tunnel.

She spun around like she'd been shot when he snagged her arm. When she realized it was him she sagged against the tunnel wall, found her breath. "You scared me half to death."

"I've changed my mind. You're not doing this."

Confusion furrowed her brows. "What are you talking about? We're here. Nader's waiting."

He cupped her shoulders with both hands. "It's too risky."

After she got over the shock of him touching her, she made a sound of disbelief. "Yeah. I got that part. In spades. But it's been risky from the get-go. So I don't . . . I don't understand." She searched his face, thoroughly baffled. "What's this about? Why do you all of a sudden care about the risk to me? As far as you're concerned, I'm a liar and a thie—"

"Goddammit," he swore. "I was wrong, okay?"

She blinked up at him, startled into silence.

"I was wrong," he repeated, more in control now that he'd quit fighting what his gut had been telling him all along: She was clean. "I made a mistake about

you. I'm not going to compound it by letting you anywhere near that murdering bastard."

Her eyes were liquid and wary but bafflement slowly
transitioned to something softer. Not trust. She wasn't
nearly ready to take that leap.

"Why the change of heart?"

Yeah. That was the million-dollar question all right.
One Sam couldn't answer for either of them. "Pick a
reason. Doesn't matter. Bottom line, I can't let you do
this."

She stared at him for all of a heartbeat. Firmly shook
her head. "He's my brother. I can't *not* do this."

It all came back to Sam then. His father's face.
Beaten, defeated. His father's voice when he'd begged
him to go after Nader.

"You can't not do this."

"Just do what you said you would do." Her quiet
conviction sealed both of their fates. "Just get there in
time."

Sam forced himself to let go of her shoulders, still
fighting the urge to drag her back onto the plane to
safety. But he understood that he'd already lost this battle. Understood because he'd fought this particular
fight himself.

Her eyes were dark and searching when he lifted his
hand to her cheek, involuntarily drawn to her mouth.
He leaned in. Pressed his forehead to hers.

Her fingers wrapped around his wrist. Clung. "Just
get there in time," she repeated on a whisper.

"Count on it."

Then he kissed her.

Hard and fierce. As much claim as desperation. Without a single thought of control.

When he pulled back, her gaze was locked on his. Startled. Stunned. Seeking.

"Be careful," he said, hearing the gruffness in his voice. "Be goddamn careful."

She swallowed. Nodded. Eyes full of a heartbreaking mix of determination, apprehension, and good-bye.

Then she turned and disappeared into the terminal.

Abbie's heart was revved to triple time as she turned her back on Sam and walked away.

She was scared.

She was anxious.

But above it all, she was shaken.

"*I was wrong about you.*"

Too little. Too late. That's what she should have said. *Too late, too late, too late.*

Damn him.

Damn him for kissing her.

Damn him for looking at her like . . . like he'd looked at her that night in her bed.

And damn her own stupid hide for wanting to believe him—again.

She drew a bracing breath. Shook it off. Got her bearings in the busy terminal. This wasn't about her or Sam. This was about Cory. She had to keep her head if—

Oh, God.

She stopped short when she saw a hand-lettered sign with her name on it, held above the crowd by a meaty hand.

This was it. The point of no return.

Then she prayed for strength when she recognized the man holding it.

Nader hadn't just sent a driver. He'd sent Rutger Smith.

Abbie's knees went weak with fear. She fought through a wave of revulsion and shot right on to rage. Every cell in her body shifted from prey to predator mode.

This was the animal who had brutalized her brother. Even more than she feared him, she wanted to make him pay for what he'd done. First, though, she had to get to Cory. The only way that was going to happen was if she kept her head and kept right on walking.

He hadn't seen her yet. The terminal was full of travelers even at ten o'clock on this Central American night where outside heat and humidity seeped into the poorly air-conditioned building. She looked toward the floor, spoke softly. "I spotted my driver," she informed Doc, knowing he and Sam would be listening on the receiver.

Also knowing that if she told Sam it was Smith who Nader had sent to pick her up, he'd come charging into the terminal and drag her away.

She made sure that didn't happen.

"Stay close, okay? Just . . . stay close."

Fight or flight. She'd read about the gut-jarring instinct. Had never experienced it firsthand. But when
her gaze connected with Rutger Smith's, it took everything in her to keep moving forward.

His picture hadn't lied. His eyes, when they locked
in on her, were devoid of anything vaguely resembling
humanity.

"I'm Abbie Hughes," she said, stopping a good three
feet away from him.

Smith swept her with a look so cold and remote, she
felt a chill in spite of the warm, tropical night. "My employer is expecting you. I have a car waiting."

"My brother," she said, when he turned to lead her
out of the terminal. "I need to know about my brother.
Where is he? *How* is he?"

Smith stopped. His soulless black eyes bore into
hers. "You would be well-advised to simply accompany
me. I'm to provide transportation, not answers. You'll
have those soon enough."

"I need to talk to him," she persisted as Sam had instructed her. She wasn't to go anywhere until she had
proof that Cory was alive. "I'm not setting foot outside
this terminal until I know he's alive."

Smith regarded her with impatient disdain, the first
sign that he even possessed an emotion. Abbie knew
she had him over a barrel. Without her cooperation,
Nader didn't get his diamonds. And as long as they remained inside the terminal, she was safe. He couldn't
risk making a scene by trying to drag her away.

Without another word, he pulled a cell phone out of his suit pants pocket.

"*Ponga el gringo,*" he said after a long moment. Then he handed her the phone.

Heart hammering, she gripped it with both hands. "Cory?"

Silence. Then a hesitant and weak, "Abbie?"

Tears stung her eyes. "Cory. Baby. Yeah. It's me. It's Abbie."

She heard a shuffling sound. "Don't . . . don't come here."

"Cory—"

Smith jerked the phone out of her hands. "Satisfied?"

No, she wasn't satisfied. But at least she knew that her brother was still alive. Alive and hurt and scared. Scared like that little boy who used to hide in the closet.

Smith turned and headed for the exit.

Shaking with relief and rage and fear for Cory, Abbie resettled her backpack and, because she had no choice, followed.

Like a lamb, she couldn't help thinking as they headed for the exit doors, *being led to the slaughter.*

14

"She's shaken," Sam said, listening with Doc and Savage to Abbie's voice through the receiver.

"She's fine." Savage stared at him hard.

Doc just cocked a brow.

Sam knew they'd heard the whole conversation between Abbie and Nader's driver through the chatter and bustle of the busy terminal. Just like he knew they'd heard the conversation between Sam and Abbie in the jetway.

Neither Doc nor Savage had said anything. Sam figured they were thinking plenty. He knew what they called him. The quiet man. The ice man. Cool under fire. Professional to a fault. They'd never seen him react with anything other than emotionless efficiency. So they were either too shocked by his reaction to Abbie or too worried about how or *if* his feelings would affect the op to comment.

How he felt wasn't going to affect anything. He wasn't going to let it.

The minute Abbie had cleared the jetway, the three

of them were on the move. They grabbed their go bags from the overhead compartments and sprinted off the plane. Once in the terminal, they headed in the opposite direction of the passenger pickup area. Sam couldn't take the chance of being spotted by Nader's man. He'd crossed paths with too many of Nader's henchmen before—and not over tea and crumpets.

"Ring Mendoza," Sam said, anxious to connect with him and get in position to tail Abbie.

"He's waiting in short-term parking," Savage said after a brief conversation. "Older-model SUV. Gray. Local plates."

Mendoza knew his stuff. They needed to blend in, not stand out, and a big-ass new suburban would stick out like a tux at a biker bar.

"Anything happening?" Sam asked Doc as they backtracked toward the exit.

Doc was monitoring Abbie through a headset now. He shook his head. "Traffic sounds. They're outside. Not a lot of chitchat. Wait." He stopped. Held up a hand. Then quickly switched off the tracker.

"He just asked her to hold her arms out to her side."

Which meant he was sweeping her for a wire. Probably also meant he was patting her down. Sam clenched his jaw, forced himself not to think about the bastard touching her. Or the fact that for now, they couldn't monitor her conversation. She was on her own.

Eyes dead ahead, he walked across the parking lot, searching for Mendoza. Raphael spotted them first. He stood in the open driver's door of a dinged and dented monolith of an SUV that looked like it had been through a war.

Mendoza, as always, looked like he'd just stepped out of a photo shoot. His thick dark hair was cropped military short. His black eyes—a product of his Colombian heritage just like his caramel skin—shone clear and intelligent under the security light. He was ripped and ready. Not as big as, say, Gabe Jones or even Sam, but pound for pound, Raphael "Choirboy" Mendoza was one of the toughest fighters Sam had ever seen in action.

"Nice ride," Doc said with a grin as they reached Mendoza.

"Kind of like you, Holliday." Mendoza grinned back. "Not much to look at but good in a fight.

"How's it going?" He turned to Sam, extended his hand in welcome.

Sam gripped his hand hard. "Thanks for signing on."

"Hey. We're still a team. Always will be." Mendoza's smile faded. "I'm sorry," he said simply.

It was the first time Sam had seen Raphael since Terri's death.

Sam nodded.

"We'll get the bastard," Mendoza added and when the moment became too intense, changed the subject by stating the obvious. "No Reed?"

"Not this trip," Sam said. "Needed someone back on the home front."

Sam hadn't been completely straight with Abbie about Reed's activities back in Vegas. For the most part,

Reed was tailing Abbie's friend, Crystal Debrowski, hoping to get a lead on where she'd stowed the diamonds. He needed Reed in place in the event Nader sent one of his flunkies after the necklace. And he was there as backup for Sam's dad. If Nader sent anyone after his family, they'd have to get past Reed first.

"You're going to need these." Mendoza handed out cell phones all around after the four of them had piled into the SUV. Sam rode shotgun; Savage and Doc settled into the backseat. "Already programmed with each other's numbers."

"What other toys did you bring us?" Savage asked, pocketing his phone.

Mendoza's smile was quick and easy. "All your favorites plus a couple surprises."

Which meant that Raphael had acquired a Kimber Tactical Pro 1911 A1 pistol for Sam as well as an H&K MP-5K. He suspected there was also an M-16 rifle or two in the mix. As far as the surprises, Mendoza knew how to plan for an assault and there wasn't a man in the vehicle who doubted it would come down to that.

Sam was taking no chances this time. And he was taking no prisoners.

El Nuevo Porvenir, twenty kilometers north of Peña Blanca, Honduras

A slow smile spread across Desmond Fox's face as he hung up the phone and settled back, naked on the bed.

It was perfect. Perfect irony. Perfect execution. Nader would never know what hit him because Nader had no idea that Desmond was aware of his Peña Blanca estancia. Likewise, the bastard German had no idea that one of Desmond's own men had infiltrated Nader's little detail holding guard over the man—Nader's unfortunate mule—who held the key to retrieving the Tupacka diamonds.

Mules and moles. Desmond liked the play on words, liked that there were animals among men, doing the dirty work. The thought made him laugh. As did the massacre his men would soon carry out at Peña Blanca.

"I know that laugh, *mi amore*." Juanita of the dark hair and lush breasts rose to all fours over him. Her naked body straddled his, her caramel skin and delicious curves willing and warm and wanting to please.

Beautiful. She was but twenty and already so wise. And so deliciously wanton. Of course, Desmond had schooled her well. At fifty, he knew exactly how to instruct a woman to pleasure him. He touched a hand affectionately to her long hair, then gripped it in his hand. With a slow twist, he dragged her close until her mouth hovered over his. Her breath, scented of sangria and sex, melded with his.

"What is it that you think you know about my laugh?" he asked, guiding her head down toward the pulsing erection jutting against his belly.

"It means someone is going to die," she purred, brushing her lips across the head of his cock, tantalizing, teasing, licking.

"One of the things I so love about you, pretty cat, is that you are as ruthless and bloodthirsty as I am."

"*One* of the things?" Her smile was coquettish and coy as she squeezed her generous breasts together, imprisoning his cock between them.

"One of many," he replied tenderly and gentled his hold on her hair. "Carry on, my darling."

Then he lay back, let Juanita work her magic, and rode the wave of her expert brand of pleasure.

Later, when she lay sleeping, her skillful hand pressed against his chest, her head resting on his shoulder, he congratulated himself on both his choice in women and his cunning.

He reached for a cigarette, flicked open his diamond-studded lighter, and drew deep on the first robust puff. Smoke drifted in the darkened bedroom. He let it soothe him. Retribution was near.

Nader had made a mistake when he'd crossed into Honduras uninvited. The pompous German was in Fox territory now. Central America was his. Honduras was his native country, and he called the shots in this part of the world. Nothing got past his radar or his network.

Which was why, at this moment, his men were about to pay Nader's estancia a little visit.

Nader's infringement would not be tolerated, something Nader would soon understand. Just like he would understand how Desmond Fox dealt with those who destroyed what was his. Juan Montoya, one of his best soldiers, was dead. Dead because Rutger Smith had intercepted him before he'd made the meet to procure the Tupacka diamonds from Nader's runaway mule.

Smith had sliced Montoya from gut to gullet. Left him to bleed out in a squalid back alley, where his body hadn't been found until several days later.

No. Montoya's murder would not go unpunished.

And Fox would see to it that Nader would never see the Tupacka diamonds, let alone own them. He may be a thief and much more, but he was also a patriot. The Tupacka diamonds belonged to Honduras, not to Nader.

His eyes on the ground had told him about the arrival of the American woman, the sister of Nader's mule, and Desmond's ticket to retrieving the necklace.

Nader had sent Smith himself to deliver her from the airport to Peña Blanca. Smith was a bonus Desmond had not expected. If all went as planned, when Smith returned to Nader, it would be in pieces.

He glanced at his Rolex. Phase one should be well under way.

Adrenaline. The wonder drug. Someone ought to figure out how to package it in pill form, Abbie thought as she sat quietly in the backseat of a black Lincoln Town Car with Rutger Smith at the wheel.

He hadn't said a word since she'd climbed into the car and shut out the exhaust fumes that clogged the parking lot in thick sultry waves. Only the whine of the tires on the highway and a light rain that had turned into a downpour the farther they traveled broke the silence.

Despite the fact that she hadn't had any real sleep in

over twenty-four hours, she was wired. Desperation. Anticipation. Fear. All fueled the restless energy that hummed through her body while the Lincoln sped through the city that was full of activity even at this time of night.

While still in the city they'd passed a donkey-pulled cart, dozens of broken-down vehicles, and been passed by tiny white compact cabs squashed full of people. If Abbie had been in a laughing mood, the American fast-food places dotting the roadway lit by streetlights would have made her smile. Pizza seemed to be very popular.

Doc had been right to be prepared for Nader's man to search for a wire. He'd scanned her body with some kind of a sweeping device—after he'd completed a humiliating but all-business physical pat-down.

Her skin still crawled at the memory.

That was over two long hours ago, before they'd headed out of the city on Highway 71.

She wanted this over. She'd also reached her limit of silent forbearance. "How much farther?"

She asked as much for herself as for Sam and his men. At least she was counting on them still listening and still being with her.

Hell, she was more than counting on it. She was betting her life on it.

"She just asked him how much farther," Doc said, relaying Abbie's latest and only voice transmission since they'd reactivated the GPS and wire two long fucking hours ago.

Sam glanced sharply toward Doc in the backseat and let out a breath of relief, the first one that hadn't felt like it had been jammed in his lungs for half a century. "And?"

Doc shook his head. "So far, no response."

Sam turned back to the squeak and slash of worn wipers that fought a losing battle with the deluge of warm, tropical rain pummeling the windshield. Breathing. The rustle of clothes. That's all Doc had heard during the entire trip. They'd been literally and figuratively in the dark. Not knowing if Abbie was drugged, hurt, or worse. Every cell in Sam's body had wanted to tell Mendoza to step on the gas, overtake the damn vehicle, and see what the hell was going on.

But he'd made himself hold it together. Barely.

It didn't help that he'd decided early on that he knew where they were headed. At least, based on the route the driver was taking, he had a pretty good idea.

"They should have just passed La Entrada," Sam said after flipping on the interior light and consulting the map he'd been using to do his own tracking. "They should be turning off the highway soon."

"Just did," Savage confirmed, monitoring the GPS. "Heading north. Dirt road, according to the markings. You were right. Looks like he's taking her to Nader's estancia at Peña Blanca."

There was little Sam didn't know about Nader's activities or holdings. "We're looking at less than ten clicks from the start of the side road. Cut the lights at two, okay?"

Mendoza stopped the soft singing that had earned him the handle Choirboy and grunted. "I live to fly blind."

Sam had filled the BOIs in on the setup on the drive so they all knew what they faced. The main buildings of Nader's estancia consisted of a small adobe ranch house and a gardener's shed. Nader spent little time here. The accommodations were Spartan, near rustic—too crude, Sam suspected, for Nader to tolerate for any length of time. The location, however, was ideal as a spot to say, hide something or someone you didn't want found. It was out of the way and remote. The estancia also butted up against a particularly steep slope of the Montaña de la Crita range that provided protection from the north. A lookout could easily spot an approach from the south.

The SUV rocked as Mendoza, following the Lincoln, turned onto the rutted dirt road and hit mud.

"They stopped," Doc said, listening intently while the rain pummeled the SUV's roof and the motor revved and whined along the slime-slick road. He held up a hand, concentrated on hearing.

"Switch to speaker." Sam willed the SUV to move faster as Mendoza herded it over the rough, slippery road. The SUV's wheels slid into deep ruts, threatening to hang up the undercarriage as Mendoza skillfully maneuvered through the mess.

"What's happening?" Abbie asked, her voice sounding reedy and a little thin.

"You wanted to see your brother? You're going to

see your brother," Smith said. "Now get out of the car."

"No," she said staunchly. "You bring Cory to me."

Silence.

Sam held his breath, waited for Smith's reaction.

"Look, bitch," the driver snarled, impatience and anger heavy in his voice. "You don't call the shots. You do as I say. And you remember, the only reason you and your gutless brother are still breathing is because my employer needs information from you. You want your brother? You tell me where the diamonds are."

"So you can kill us as soon as I tell you? No. It's not going to happen that way," she said, her voice stronger now as she faced the man with a reckless defiance that drove Sam crazy. "What's going to happen is that you're going to get Cory, bring him to the car, then you're going to drive us back to the airport. I'm not telling you the location of the diamonds until then."

Goddammit, Abbie, Sam swore under his breath. He'd asked her to trust them. To go along with whatever they asked her to do and know that they had her back.

The driver had apparently had enough.

A car door opened, then slammed.

He heard Abbie's sharp intake of breath, heard her scramble, punching locks.

He closed his eyes when the sound of glass shattering cracked over the wire.

"Fuck," Doc whispered. "Sounds like he slammed his fist through the window."

They heard the *snick* of a car door being wrenched open.

"Out," the driver ordered.

More silence. Then the sounds of a struggle.

"Now walk," the driver demanded. Savage turned back to the cargo area and started digging weapons out from under a tarp.

Sam heard a grunt of sound.

Abbie cried out.

The bastard had hit her.

Sam heard her hit the ground.

He was dead, Sam vowed. Whoever he was, he was a dead man.

"Get up."

Another cry and Sam could picture the bastard dragging her to her feet.

"Walk," he ordered again.

There was no more talk then. Just the sound of Abbie, breathing hard. Rain in the trees. Soles crunching on the ground. They were walking uphill, Sam realized as her breath grew more labored.

"Can you fucking step on it?" he growled at Mendoza as Doc and Savage fixed full clips into their rifles.

Sam accepted the Kimber Savage handed him along with a Glock for Mendoza. The rifles came next, along with two M-16's and four extra thirty-shot magazines for each of them. The Kevlar vests followed. Like Sam and Mendoza, who herded the SUV down the treacherous road like a Formula One driver, they had their game faces on.

"Come on, Abbie," Doc muttered as he eased into his own vest, then Velcroed it shut. "Tell us what's going on."

The driver's voice came over the wire instead. "Wait here," he ordered Abbie, his voice gruff and scratchy as it vibrated over the speaker. "You run, your brother dies, got it?"

Several long, pulsing seconds passed as Sam waited, and waited.

"He's . . . he's about twenty yards ahead of me now," Abbie finally whispered, trying to keep Nader's driver from hearing her.

"It's Smith," she added, her voice sounding strained. "The driver is Rutger Smith," she repeated with emphasis.

All four men swore. Sam clenched his jaw, cursed again at both Abbie's stupidity and her bravery. She should have let them know right out of the block that Smith had her. Sam would have dragged her out of there before she'd ever left the airport terminal.

She'd known it, too. She'd intentionally kept Sam in the dark to keep him from doing just that.

"It's so dark," she whispered. "He's using a flashlight. Calling out names.

"No one's answering him," she went on, her voice suddenly rife with anxiety. "Something's . . . something's wrong. I'm going up there."

"Jesus, no!" Sam shouted, knowing she couldn't hear him and that she wouldn't listen to him if she could.

Her breath puffed out in harsh, hard pants as she ran up the hillside.

"Oh, God." She sounded frantic now. A high-pitched exclamation of pain. A helpless cry. "Oh, God, oh Jesus God."

Then she screamed. And screamed. And screamed until the roaring in Sam's ears and the growl of the SUV's engine and the pounding rain drowned out everything but the need to get to her.

15

Soaking wet, Abbie stumbled up the hillside in the dark after Smith, zeroing in on the beam of his flashlight. She'd come within ten yards of him when he stopped, disappeared inside the black hole of an open door of a small shed. She stopped, too. Between the rain and the pitch-dark forest, she couldn't see three feet in front of her.

Breathing hard, she waited, jumped when she heard a sharp snap, like the sound of a switch being flipped. The hillside was flooded with light, illuminating a scene straight out of a horror movie.

"Oh, God." She sucked in her breath, heard a sound, more animal than human, realized she had made it. She couldn't stop herself from crying. "Oh, God, oh Jesus God."

Blood. Oh, God, the blood.

Bodies everywhere.

And then she screamed. And kept on screaming, incapable of taking her eyes off the blood and gore.

"Shut up!" Smith growled as he stepped out of the building. He strode over to her, slapped her hard.

Her head snapped back from the force of the blow. She stumbled, fell. Landed on top of something soft and warm and wet. A body.

Still warm. Still warm. The body was still warm.

Horrified, she scrambled away, her hands slick with blood and rain and mud. She pushed to her feet on shaking legs, reeled when her own blood rushed south. She steadied herself, was peripherally aware of the sting on her check where Smith had hit her. Of her head throbbing from the blow. Of her sodden hair hanging heavy and dripping in her face.

Her full focus was riveted in morbid fascination on the bullet-riddled bodies lying where they'd fallen in the mud and the wet grass.

It was a bloodbath.

A massacre.

They'd been running.

Trying to get away.

She touched a trembling hand to her mouth. Felt the stickiness of blood and mud and gagged. Her stomach rumbled, revolted. She fell to her knees, retched violently, then watched, recovering her breath as Smith wedged a foot under the chest of a man who lay facedown in the grass; the back of his head was shot off.

Recognition crossed his face before he moved on to the next body, his expression growing darker and more furious with each man he found as rain soaked his suit, plastering it to his big, bulky body.

"Cory." Her brain finally engaged beyond the horror. She shot to her feet, reeled again from lightheadedness, steadied herself until her balance returned. Oh, God. She had to find him. "Cory!"

Battling revulsion and terror and nausea, she started searching for her brother.

She fell to her knees, was gathering the nerve to turn over a body when she heard Smith speak in Spanish. "*¿Quién hizo esto?*"

She spun around, confused. Thought he was talking to her. But he was kneeling over a body. And then that body moved. She scrambled over beside them.

"*¿Quién hizo esto?*" Smith repeated urgently. Rain dripped off his head into the downed man's face.

Abbie's Spanish was rusty but she understood the question. He wanted to know who had done this.

"*Zorro,*" the dying man wheezed through a gurgling breath. "*Zorro . . . sus hombres. Em . . . emboscada.*"

Zorro. *Fox?* She couldn't have heard him right. He was delirious. But then it hit her what he was trying to say. Not *a* fox but someone *named* Fox. Fox's men had ambushed them, he said.

"*¿Dónde está la mula?*" Smith snarled. "*¿Dónde está Hughes?*"

Where's the mule? Where is Hughes?

Abbie's pulse spiked. She held her breath and waited.

The injured man lifted a bloody hand, gripped Smith's shirt. "*Ayúdeme.*"

Help me.

Smith shoved the hand away, jerked the injured

man up by his shirtfront. "*¿Dónde está Hughes?*"

The man gasped, convulsed, then went limp.

Smith swore, looked beyond her, then grabbed her roughly by the hair. "You bitch! You were told to come alone."

Abbie cried out in pain as he jerked her with him and shot to his feet. He dragged her tightly against him, his beefy forearm wrapped about her throat, choking her.

The prick of a knife bit painfully against her ribs. His belt buckle bruised where it pressed against her back.

She gasped for breath, smelled wet wool and blood and death as she frantically dug her fingers into his forearm desperate to loosen his hold. Her head spun. Her ears rang. She saw a man materialize out of the veil of rain and shadows. Wondered if she was hallucinating.

"Let her go, Smith."

It was Savage. Carrying a rifle. Doc and Mendoza stepped to his side, both heavily armed. Which meant that Sam wasn't far behind.

Thank you, God.

Her relief was short-lived. Smith shifted, replaced his forearm with his knife. The cold, cutting steel of it danced against her throat.

"Back off," he demanded in a voice so wintry it made her shiver in her warm, wet clothes, "or she dies."

Sam crept through the forest. Silent, surefooted, even on the slick forest floor, he kept the pool of light flooding the area around the shack in his sights, worked his way quickly uphill toward Abbie.

Rain ran down his face, soaked his clothes. Mud clung to his boots, would have bogged him down if he hadn't been so single-mindedly focused on getting into position. The M-16 he carried wasn't a sniper rifle. But then the shot he planned to take didn't require accuracy at 2,000 yards. Thirty ought to do it.

The air was so thick and wet it felt like he was drowning in it as he drew closer, darting from tree to tree, finally spotting Smith in the relative open.

Open except for Abbie.

The animal had her. Was using her as a shield as Savage and the boys approached, stopped, waited for Smith to make the next move.

That's right, boys. Nice and easy.

Eyes on the prize, Sam shut out the rain. Shut out the splayed bodies littering the soaked ground. Shut out his own breathing. Shut out the terror and the blood smeared across Abbie's face.

He slowly lowered the rifle sling off his shoulder, dropped to his knees. He steadied the barrel against a solid tree trunk, wrapping the sling around his arm to help stabilize the rifle. Peered through the night vision scope.

Water from his sprint through the woods blurred the sights on the telescopic lens. Heart racing with adrenaline, he forced himself to quickly, carefully, tug the hem of his T-shirt out from under his vest and meticulously dry the lens.

Then he settled in again, positioned the butt of the
stock against his shoulder, sited down the barrel.
Honed in on his target.

Same drill.

The rain didn't exist.

The bodies didn't exist.

Abbie's life didn't hang in the balance.

Only the shot mattered.

He was one with his breath.

One with his craft.

Inhale.

Exhale. Squeeze.

Absorb the shock of the recoil.

Before he even heard the crack of rifle fire, or
Abbie's scream, he saw Smith's head explode and blood
and brain matter splatter and spread across the side of
her face.

Savage and Doc were sprinting toward her before
Smith's big body collapsed and Abbie fell forward. She
landed on all fours, head hanging between her stiff
arms.

Mendoza ran straight for Smith, rifle pointed at his
head, taking no chances that the murdering bastard
was no longer a threat.

Sam lowered his rifle, breathed deep. Only then did
he let himself think about what could have happened if
he'd missed. If he'd fired a hair to the left.

Abbie would be dead now, not Smith.

He walked out of the trees. Straight to her side. He

handed his rifle to Savage and dropped to one knee beside her.

"You're okay," he said softly.

"Abbie." He lifted the hair away from her face when she didn't respond. "Smith is dead."

Finally, she moved. A slow, slight nod of acknowledgment, telling him she was still with him.

Then she started shaking.

Fuck it.

He drew her into his arms. Touched his hand to the blood and the mud and the gore covering her. And held her while she fell apart.

"Without stitches you're gonna have a helluva scar," Sam heard Doc tell Abbie as he walked back to the gardener's shed where they'd moved her under an eave and out of the rain. "Sorry, but we're going to have to make do with butterflies."

Under the glow of Doc's Maglite, Sam inspected the long narrow gash running from Abbie's shoulder to mid upper arm. Smith's knife had sliced her good when he'd fallen. It looked rough, yet Sam was relieved the blade had missed anything vital. Doubly so when Doc assured him that most of the blood staining her clothes wasn't hers.

"I'm just going to clean it up now, okay? The dressing will have to wait until we get back to the SUV and my medic kit."

Which was going to have to be soon. The rain had

let up but they needed to head back or what was left of the road would wash out and they'd be stuck here.

Stuck with a dozen bullet-riddled bodies and no Cory Hughes.

"No," Sam said when Abbie looked up, her eyes questioning. "He's not here."

Sam had searched. So that was the good news; Cory Hughes wasn't among the dead. Unless Mendoza and Savage, who had widened the search around the perimeter of the ambush turned up something, the bad news was, Cory Hughes wasn't anywhere.

"Do you think he ever was here?" Abbie bit back a wince when Doc dabbed an alcohol pad to her arm.

"Sorry." Doc eased up. "It's gonna bite but we need to stall any threat of infection in this humidity."

"It's okay." She looked to Sam for an answer to her question.

Tough, Sam thought. She was much tougher than she looked. Much tougher than the woman who had come unhinged in his arms just five minutes ago.

She'd had plenty of reason to fall apart. Smith had slapped her around. The corner of her mouth was cut and swollen; her cheek was already starting to bruise. She'd stumbled into a bloody massacre, hadn't known if her brother was among the dead, and Smith had held a knife to her throat.

So yeah, she'd had a moment. But not for long. She was quiet but she was solid again. At least she was working her damnedest to get there.

"Someone was being held hostage here," Sam said.

The gardener's shed was full of signs that he didn't need to share with Abbie.

"So . . . whoever did this . . . you think they took him?"

"It's looking that way." Sam squatted down in front of her. "Abbie . . . the rain garbled some of your conversation with Smith so we couldn't hear it all. Did he say anything? Anything that told you he might have a clue who had done this?"

"Actually, there was something," she said as if the memory had just come to her. "A man . . . one of the men . . . he was still alive. Smith asked him who had done this. He said the name Fox. That Fox's *men* had ambushed them."

Doc's face was grim when he glanced at Sam. "Had to figure he'd show up in the mix."

Abbie's eyes cut between Doc's and Sam's. "You know who Fox is?"

"Yeah." Sam nodded. "We know him. He and Nader swim in the same cesspool."

"They work together?"

"Not quite. Desmond Fox and Fredrick Nader hate each other's guts. Fox has been pissed ever since Nader got a toehold in the Central American arms trade a few years ago. Honduras is Fox's home turf. He considers Nader a squatter and a threat."

"What do you want to bet Fox knows about the necklace?" Doc suggested after a moment.

"More like Fox *wants* the necklace because he knows it would piss off Nader," Sam amended after he'd thought it through. "That's gotta be what this was about. The question is, how did he know about Cory?"

"I've got a live one over here!" Mendoza's shout came from behind the shed.

"Hold this." Doc pressed Abbie's hand over the gauze on her arm and headed toward the sound of Mendoza's voice.

Abbie started to rise.

"No." Sam stopped her with a hand on her shoulder. "You don't need to see this."

He could see in her eyes that she wanted to argue, but in the end, she sagged back down on the step. "For once, I'm not going to fight with you."

"First time for everything," he said and got the smile he'd hoped for. Not much of a smile but enough for him to know she was holding up.

"Yeah, well. Don't get used to it."

"Wouldn't dream of it," he said and started walking away.

"Sam."

Her voice stopped him. He turned.

She was looking at him, her poor bruised face tragically sad. "Thanks. Thanks for . . . well. Just thanks."

He knew exactly what she was thanking him for.

"Like I said. It's what I do. And you're welcome."

"Who do you work for?"

They all spoke Spanish but since Mendoza knew the local dialect, he did the questioning as the four of them huddled over the wounded man.

Savage shined his Maglite on the man's chest so Doc could work on him. Blood gurgled from several holes. Automatic-weapons fire. It was a wonder the mercenary was still alive, and Sam had no doubt that it was hired muscle they were dealing with.

"*Por favor. Por favor. ¡Me tiene que ayudar!*"

Sam glanced at Doc, who shook his head, telling Sam there wasn't enough help in the world to save this man. He was dying. He just didn't know it yet.

"Tell him we'll help. But we need information first. Ask him again who he works for."

"*¿Para quién trabaja?*"

The man gasped in pain. "Fox. Desmond Fox."

"Bingo," Savage said as Doc worked futilely to staunch the blood flow.

Although he could pretty much guess, Sam had Mendoza ask anyway. "Find out what happened here."

"*¿Qué pasó aquí?*"

"*Fueron mandados para . . .*" The merc stopped, wheezed, then continued, "*. . . emboscar a los hombres . . . de Nader y capturar . . . el americano.*"

"Apparently Fox sent men to capture Hughes and kill Nader's men."

"So Fox knew Hughes was here." Savage's conclusion prompted Mendoza to ask how Fox knew where Nader was holding Hughes captive.

"*¿Cómo supo Fox que el americano estuvo acá?*"

The man's eyes rolled back in his head. His breathing grew more labored. "*Me . . . infiltré en la guardia . . . hace meses. Para . . . espiar. Para . . . informar.*"

Mendoza glanced up at Sam. "He says Fox sent him to infiltrate Nader's guards months ago."

"So we have us a spy," Savage concluded with a nod. "A mole by any other name is still a rat."

A bloodied hand reached up, clutched at Doc's shirt. "*Por favor . . . por favor. Me muero.*"

That needed no translation. He was begging for his life. He was also barely clinging to it.

"We need to know where Hughes is now," Sam said, suspecting they were going to lose him soon.

Mendoza posed the question.

"*Por favor . . . me va a matar si digo más,*" the dying man responded with difficulty.

"Yeah," Sam said when the man expressed fear that Fox would kill him if he talked. "Make sure he knows we'll kill him first if he doesn't tell us what we need to know and tell us now."

Now, before it was too late—not only for the merc but for Cory Hughes.

"We've gotta boogie." Sam led the pack as the four men returned to Abbie's side.

She was beyond being startled as Sam took her arm, careful of her injury, and helped her to her feet. "What happened? Was he able to tell you anything?"

A cell phone rang in the eerie silence.

"Not me," Mendoza said. "Not you guys, either. I set all the phones I gave you to vibrate."

The phone rang again.

Savage headed for Smith's body. Started checking pockets until he came up with a phone.

It rang in his hand. "What do you want to bet that's Nader wanting a report?"

"Don't answer it," Sam said. "In fact, shut it off. Let the bastard stew until we figure out what happens next."

"What did you find out?" Abbie asked again as Sam guided her down the slippery slope toward the road. The beams of four flashlights illuminated the way.

"We'll talk in the car. Right now, we need to move. Take advantage of this break in the rain."

"Wait." She put on the skids. "You're going to just . . . leave him?"

Sam kept his eyes dead ahead. Kept on walking. "He didn't make it."

She glanced at Doc, who wouldn't meet her eyes. Understood then that they didn't want her to know the details.

That was fine. The truth was, she really didn't want to know either. She just wanted to know about Cory.

She was going to have to wait until Sam was ready to tell her, though, because the pace they set took all of her concentration to keep on her feet.

Sam was a hard man. A dangerous man. They all were. My God. Just look at them. Black rifles slung over their shoulders, pistols shoved in their belts. Light beams and shadows illuminated faces as rigid as stone. Eyes as blank of emotion as the night.

Had they seen things and done things that would make most men squirm? Yeah. Of that Abbie was certain.

Where they good guys? She wanted to think so.

The only thing she knew for certain was that Rutger Smith had been a bad, bad guy. And that his blood and part of his brains still clung to her hair.

She pulled up short when a fresh wave of nausea assailed her. She fought it, lost. Finally bent over and vomited.

Sam didn't say a word. He just held the hair away from her face, waited until she was steady again, then guided her the rest of the way down the slope.

16

Off the coast of Isla de Roatán
Aboard the Seennymphe

Fredrick Nader drew deeply on his *maduro habano,* savoring the rich, robust flavor as he stared off the port bow of the *Seennymphe* at the glimmering coastline of Roatán.

His impatience reaching flash point, he dialed Smith's number again as the water lapped gently against the hull and cigar smoke mingled with the salt scent in the air.

Once again, he was sent directly to Smith's voice mail.

He snapped his phone closed.

Clutched the bow rail.

Something was wrong.

He did not deceive himself. No man could be counted on for ultimate loyalty. Still, he had never figured Rutger Smith would turn on him.

For one thing, Fredrick paid Smith too well. For another, he gave the sadistic freak generous opportunities to play, no questions asked.

Fredrick's first thought, then, was that Smith had run up against unexpected resistance that had disabled him. It was a thought he was inclined to dismiss. Smith was not only a brutal opponent, he was exceedingly competent. Fredrick could not imagine any man gaining the upper hand.

Perhaps it was merely a question of foul weather. His onboard radar had detected heavy rain in the Peña Blanca area. Cell signals were notoriously unreliable in Honduras. Applying pressure to the inept regulatory body governing cellular service was something Fredrick had been considering for a time now. He would draft an offer of monetary assistance soon. It was always advantageous to acquire favors to enrich his coffers.

He breathed deep of the salt and sea air and cigar smoke, caught the sensual notes of a distant salsa beat drifting to the *Seennymphe* from the shore. He thought of sweet Carlota, the lovely manicurist, lying naked and willing in his berth below decks.

Tomorrow he would worry about Smith. No point borrowing trouble. The man had served him well.

So had Carlota. And so she would again.

La Entrada, Honduras

Abbie watched through the rear seat window as Mendoza sprinted through the lingering drizzle, heading toward a small house on a dark side street. It seemed that Mendoza had been in this general area for a few months on the hunt for Nader before the rest of them had arrived. He'd made contact with some of the locals. Money had changed hands.

Now it appeared that bit of groundwork was going to net them a place to stay for the rest of the night. At least that was the hope.

So they waited, the SUV motor running. The air conditioner didn't work so the fan merely pushed hot, damp air through the vents, increasing the steam factor instead of decreasing it. The steam heat was still preferable to the mosquitoes that had come out in droves once the rain stopped, so they sat there with the windows up in the dark of night.

Abbie was running on fumes and adrenaline and even the adrenaline had started letting her down. It shamed her to know that they were taking this break because of her even though the mumbled consensus among the men had been that there was nothing more they could do tonight. The roads were too bad. It was too dark. The rain was due to set in again before dawn. There was nothing for them to do but try to find a place to catch a couple of hours of sleep, grab a meal, then go on the hunt for Cory.

It also shamed her that she'd let down in front of Sam. Nothing spelled weakness like tossing your cookies in front of God—and in this case, Sam Lang. Nothing spelled misery like wet muddy clothes with a generous helping of blood and brain matter thrown in for good measure.

She couldn't think about that.

She could *not* think about that.

So she thought of Raphael Mendoza instead, whom a grinning Doc had introduced her to as the Dale Earnhardt Jr. of Honduras. She gave the gorgeous Latino credit. He'd maneuvered the lumbering SUV expertly down the mud-slick road and somehow managed to keep it and them out of the ditches, singing softly all the way.

She thought back to the conversation on the drive. Savage had joined Mendoza in the front seat; Sam had sandwiched her in the back between him and Doc, who had gone right to work dressing her arm.

"Cory," she'd reminded Sam when he seemed more interested in her arm than sharing information. "Did you find anything out about Cory?"

Yeah. They'd found out plenty. She thought she had it straight now but it had taken a while to sort out Sam's comments.

"Like I said," Sam began, "Fredrick Nader and Desmond Fox are blood enemies. Apparently, Fox had been in the mix on the hunt for the stolen diamonds, only Nader cut him out of the deal when he sent Smith to intercept Cory."

She hadn't said anything but she still didn't understand how Cory had gotten mixed up in this. At this point, it didn't matter why he was involved. What mattered was finding him.

"Fox had a mole infiltrate Nader's camp," Sam had added.

"And you know this how?"

"We know this because he was the guy who survived to tell us. When he relayed information to Fox that Nader had stashed Cory at the estancia, Fox decided to snatch Cory and kill as many of Nader's men as possible in the process."

"Nothing says pissed like a massacre," Savage had added over his shoulder.

"The plan," Doc added as he'd applied antibiotic ointment to her cut, "was that one man would stay behind to intercept you, then take you to Fox and Cory."

"The man you talked to?" she'd surmised.

"Yeah," Sam said. "That man."

Who was now dead. Like so many were dead.

"He stayed behind to wait for you to take you to Fox. He hadn't planned on one of Nader's men surviving the attack. He was searching the bodies—for money, probably—and got a little surprise when one of them was still alive and shot him before he could finish him off."

"So we still don't know where Cory is."

"Actually, we do."

The driver's side door jerked open, which sent Abbie's heart racing.

It was Mendoza. "They'll take us," he said settling back behind the wheel and shifting into gear. "We can park the SUV in that shed over there."

"Best Western, Honduras style," Doc said five minutes later, after they'd hidden the SUV in the ramshackle shed and spread a tarp over it for good measure. They'd grabbed their go bags and Abbie's backpack, and trudged toward a small, rustic house. "What do you think's on Pay Per View?"

Mendoza grinned at Abbie. "We like him despite the fact that he's a cockeyed optimist."

She was too numb and exhausted to appreciate either man's warped sense of humor as she all but staggered toward the open door of the house. A dim light shone through the threshold—a candle, she realized.

"*Señorita*," an older woman greeted her politely. Her black hair was heavily threaded with gray and pulled back into a loose bun. She pointed the way toward the back of the house.

Abbie knew she was supposed to follow. But somehow she couldn't make herself move.

"It's okay," Sam said. "You take the bedroom. We'll sleep in here." He nodded toward the floor of the room that appeared to double as living area and dining area.

Abbie nodded.

And still she stood.

The guys made themselves busy claiming various areas of the worn tile floor and working very hard not to notice that she'd frozen.

"Would you rather I slept outside your door?" Sam asked, his voice gentle.

Tears filled her eyes.

"Come on." Sam took her arm. "Let's go check things out."

She moved only because he propelled her forward. On a peripheral level she almost understood what was happening to her. It was because on a real and visceral level, she kept reliving those moments when Smith had had his knife to her throat, the rifle report, the splatter of blood . . .

"Hey."

Sam's voice brought her back. She blinked. Realized they'd moved to a small room lit by a candle.

"Don't think about it," he said, looking down at her, his eyes filled with a hard, intense concern.

"How do you . . . do it?" she heard herself asking. "How do you deal with all the blood and the gore and the—"

"Don't think about it," he repeated. "That's how you deal with it."

She breathed deep. Nodded.

"What about Cory? How are we going to find him?"

"We know where he is, remember?"

Yes. She remembered. Sam had said that Fox's dying man had told them.

"Then what happens next?"

"What happens next is that you rest. We can talk about Cory's rescue in the morning."

In the morning. There would be a morning. Something she had taken for granted before she'd seen the bloodbath in the forest at Peña Blanca.

"Come on," Sam insisted again. "Let's get you cleaned up."

Don't think about it.

Don't think about it.

Easier said than done but she made herself concentrate on anything—the scuffing sound of their footsteps as they walked down the tiled floor of a short hallway; the primitive conditions of the bathroom; the promise of fresh water and soap, which finally garnered some real interest.

"Do you know how to work this?" she asked, frowning at what she hoped was a shower of sorts.

The fact that Sam knew told her even more about the man. Conjured questions about the places he'd been, the experiences he'd had. Just as quickly, though, she dismissed them.

She didn't want to know. Didn't want to know details or history or any more about Sam Lang because when this was ever over, she was never going to see him again.

"You okay now?" he asked.

Never see him again.

She breathed deep. Nodded.

Watched as he left without another word and shut the door behind him.

Don't think about it.

Less than a quarter mile beyond the small hacienda, their hostess had said, was a small stream. Not so small at the moment. It was rampant and wild and full from the recent downpour. In the dark, Sam stood hip deep in the middle of it, scrubbed away the mud and the muck and the stench of death they'd encountered at Nader's Peña Blanca estancia.

He'd bathed in worse places. Like the rest of the guys, he was just grateful he didn't have to sleep in his own stink and Honduras mud.

Just as he was thankful Señorita Garcia's bathroom offered Abbie the chance to wash away the nightmare she'd endured.

"She'll probably need that dressing changed after her shower," Doc said, when they returned to the hacienda. He started digging around in his medic kit.

"Yeah, you go in there like that," Mendoza said with a grin as he stepped into a pair of clean camo pants, "and you're likely to end up needing a little first aid of your own, Holliday."

Doc grinned, looked down at himself. "I was going to put pants on," he assured the room at large.

Savage snorted as he dried himself off with a clean T-shirt.

"I'll take care of it," Sam said, zipping up his pants. He reached for the antibiotic salve and fresh dressing. "You guys go ahead and crash."

He caught the curious looks before he turned to go. Decided not to tell them all to go fuck themselves. That he was just looking out for their ticket to Nader.

But he'd never lied to these guys. He wasn't going to start now.

So he lied to himself instead. Worked like hell to

convince himself that his only reason for volunteering for corpsman duty was pragmatic.

Yeah, and the world didn't go 'round on Saudi crude.

"Come in," Abbie answered when he rapped a knuckle on her door.

On a deep breath, he opened it, stepped inside.

And felt his heart react again. The same way it reacted when he thought of Tina. Like it could melt like wax in the sun.

She was wearing a T-shirt. White. Short-sleeve. Oversized. She was sitting up, scooted to the very top corner of the small, narrow cot, her back pressed into the corner against the adobe wall. Her legs were drawn up, her arms wrapped around her shins, her forehead lowered onto her knees. Her damp hair fell forward, covering her face and part of her legs.

"That, um . . . advice you gave me," she said, finally lifting her head and meeting his eyes. "Not working so great."

She looked fragile and so fucking beautiful he had to remind himself to breathe.

And, yeah. He could see that his advice wasn't working.

She tried for a smile, ended up looking away, shaking her head. "I . . . I can't get those men out of my head. Their eyes."

Sam knew all about the eyes. Lifeless. Soulless. Haunting. He'd learned early on to never look at them.

"Let's check that arm," he said, knowing there was

nothing he could say to snap those images out of focus for her. Only time could do that. Time and distance.

He sat down on the bed beside her, coaxed her forward with a notch of his chin. After a slight hesitation, she slid closer.

"You might want to . . . you know . . . ," another notch of his chin toward her hips. Her very fine hips, barely covered in a very small pair of very pink panties, which were *very* visible.

"Oh." Her face turned red when she realized her T-shirt had ridden up when she'd slid down the bed.

Well, at least he'd taken her mind off dead men.

Which he wasn't. He was so not dead at the moment and his dick was totally on board with that happy fact.

Self-conscious, she tugged the shirt down. Covered her hips. And the very top of her thighs.

His dick was still on board, and he was as low as tire treads for even swerving in that direction.

Face grim, he wrapped his fingers around her upper arm to steady it, then tugged the damp dressing loose. "How does it feel?"

"It's okay," she said while he inspected Doc's handiwork.

"Hurt?"

Stoic, she shook her head.

Right. That sucker had to hurt like hell. So did the bruise on her cheek.

He let her have that bit of defiance. Admired her for it.

"Couple of the butterflies came loose when you

showered," he said, then went to work replacing them.

Very aware of their proximity. Of the wholesome, scrubbed look of her. Of the contrasts between them.

Her skin was soft and smooth. His hands were rough, his fingers scarred. And not nearly as steady as they should be.

He was too damn aware that he hadn't taken time to throw on a shirt and that he was commando beneath his camo pants. Acutely aware, when she shifted position, that there was nothing under that soft T-shirt of hers but bare breasts and satin skin.

Time to go.

Past time to go.

He affixed a final piece of tape.

"You're good to go," he said, hearing a husky awareness in his voice that he hoped to hell she didn't recognize for what it was.

But when her eyes met his, it was clear she understood. Just like it was clear that she was thinking the same thing he was.

It would be so easy. So easy to lay her down, slip those pink panties down her slender hips and make reality go away. For her. For him. For a precious few minutes that would ease this pulsing ache in his groin and make her forget about dead bodies with dead eyes and men who wanted to kill her.

So easy. And so wrong.

Not for him. Wrong for her.

Haul ass outta here, Lang. Now.

"Get some rest," he said, then stiffened when her hand on his arm stopped him from rising.

"Don't . . . please, don't go." Her soft hand slid around to his chest and lightly caressed him.

He damn near went up in flames, swallowed back a lump the size of a grenade. Held the line. Barely. "You don't want this, Abbie."

"And that matters?" she bit out angrily.

Jesus. He deserved that. What seemed like decades ago in Las Vegas, he'd made her think it didn't matter.

"Yeah," he said through the guilt. "It matters."

Her eyes said it all when they searched his. She didn't believe him. Didn't trust him.

But she wanted to. Yeah, he realized, sobered by that knowledge. If, after what he'd done to her, she still wanted him to be a good guy, then at the very least, he owed her an explanation.

His decision was knee-jerk and irreversible.

"Nader killed my sister," he said, opening himself up to a flood of emotions he'd done his damnedest to suppress.

Before she could react with more than shock, and before he could back out, he barreled ahead. "He was pissed at me. Pissed that I was dogging him, that I was on to him. Making it hard for him to run his dirty business down here. When he couldn't get to me, he did the next best thing. He got to Terri. He had a car bomb planted that killed her and my brother-in-law.

"I'm sorry," he said as tears rolled down her cheeks.

"I'm sorry I tricked you. Sorry I blamed you. Sorry I didn't believe you.

"Most of all, I'm sorry I let you maneuver me into a position where I was convinced I needed to bring you down here."

"We . . . we do a lot of things . . . when we love," she said softly.

Yeah. She loved her brother. That's why she was here. He loved his sister. That's why he was here.

"When this is over," he said making himself stand up, "if you ask me again . . . if you invite me into your bed . . . make sure you want me there."

Then, before he could get tangled in the longing in her eyes, he left her.

Las Vegas

Johnny Reed hated stakeouts. They were exercises in combating boredom. He was parked outside Crystal Debrowski's Vegas apartment building in a cramped, rented compact in the middle of the frickin' night. About an hour ago, he'd surpassed boredom and started sliding straight toward coma.

When his cell phone vibrated, it was a welcome relief. He fished the phone out of his pocket, recognized the area code as being out of country. Sam.

"Yo," he answered.

"What's happening?"

Chatty Cathy Sam was not. "Nothing and a little more nothing. On the good-news front, I've been in constant touch with your dad." The apple hadn't fallen too far from that tree, he thought. Like Sam, Tom Lang was sharp, competent, and about as capable as they came. "All's quiet on that front."

Only Sam's brief silence told Johnny the relief he felt in that knowledge. "And the diamonds?" Sam asked.

"Your guess is as good as mine. I've been on Abbie Hughes's pixie friend like white on rice. She's not giving anything away."

He hadn't really figured she would. He was providing protection for the Debrowski chick as much as he was tailing her.

"Any uninvited company?"

"If Nader sent a tail, he's damn good. And since I'm better than good, I'd say it's a big negative. Figure it's a reach to think that Nader made Crystal Debrowski as an accomplice in Abbie's sleight of hand."

"Still better safe than sorry."

"Always. So how's sunny Honduras?"

Sam grunted. "Think monsoon."

"I was thinking more in terms of Nader. What's happening?"

Johnny listened as Sam gave him a Cliffs Notes version of the action going down.

"Holy shit," he said.

"And then some," Sam agreed. "Watch your six."

"Roger that," Johnny said. "Same goes, okay?"

"Later." Sam hung up.

Johnny dragged a hand over his face, stared into

space, and wished to hell he was in Honduras, where he was pretty certain his services were needed a helluva a lot more than they were here.

"Them's the breaks," he muttered and glanced toward the third floor of the apartment building, fourth window from the right corner.

To keep himself entertained and awake, he thought about Crystal Debrowski with her short, spiky red hair and centerfold bod. And he wondered if a pixie wore anything other than fairy dust to bed.

The prospect kept him awake and alert for the next several hours.

17

Cory was sick.

Wished-he-could-die sick.

In-and-out-of-consciousness sick from the beating Smith had given him . . . when? Days ago? A week? Hell, it felt like a year.

He didn't know where he was.

He only knew that he was not where he had been. Someone had moved him. He remembered gunfire. Lots of it. And then . . . nothing.

He rolled onto his back with a groan. Filthy, stinking straw on the floor. On top of broken bricks. Inside.

Yeah. He was inside. With rats again. He couldn't see them in the dark. But he could smell them. And he could hear them.

The stalking bastards were here. In the corners. Scurrying up the walls. Waiting for him to die. Fuckers wanted to eat him.

"Fuckers!" he yelled wildly, then cried out when pain seized his body.

He convulsed into a ball, tried to protect his ribs because he was six again and his father was beating him.

"Don't," he begged, tears leaking from his eyes. "Daddy, don't . . . I'll be g-good. I . . . promise. Don't . . . don't . . . kick me. Don't . . ."

He bumped his hand. Screamed as pain exploded through it, up his arm, knifed into his head.

Abbie.

He wanted Abbie.

"No . . . no," he panted out the words through a raw and scratchy throat. "Don't come here. Don't . . . don't let 'em get you, too . . ."

A burst of light made him recoil in pain. A flood of water roused him further.

"Wake up, gringo."

Cory gasped, involuntarily battling to capture life-sustaining air. To lick his dry lips and taste the water that had been thrown in his face. Water ran into his mouth. Cooled his fevered skin. Fresh air, hot and sweet and scented of a recent rain filled his lungs.

"Eat. Drink."

He squinted up through burning eyes, saw a man set a wooden cup and bowl on the straw and shove it toward him.

"Your sister, she will be here soon, no? You will live until then."

With a slam of the door, the light was gone.

Silence.

And the smell of food. The scent of water.

The scrabbling of the rats growing closer.

Abbie.

Abbie was coming? Here?

No. No. Oh, God, no. Abbie could not come to this hell.

But he couldn't stop her.

So he had to help her.

Which meant he had to eat.

He felt around on the floor for the bowl—backhanded a rat all the way across the room.

Then he cradled the bowl under his chin, held it with his wrist, forked it into his mouth with the fingers of his good hand.

Finished it.

Drank his water.

Then he hitched his way back against the wall opposite the door.

And waited. Waited for inspiration to strike him. Waited for his stomach to expel the gruel they'd given him.

Waited for them to come back.

And prayed to God he could figure out a way to help Abbie . . . Then he cried. Because he couldn't even help himself.

La Entrada, Honduras

"You been in touch with Reed yet?"

Sam looked up from his breakfast and nodded at Savage. "Last night."

"So what's happening on the home front?"

"If Nader has men in Vegas, Reed still hasn't spotted them." That was the frustrating part. The relief came in knowing that everyone at Rancho Royale was fine.

"And the diamonds?" Mendoza asked.

"Abbie's friend is as tight-lipped as a clam. Reed hasn't been able to get anything out of her and from the sounds of it, he's tailing her like a jet trail."

They all grew quiet for a moment. Sam could sense that something was up.

"You know we've got Nader now," Savage said finally as the four of them chowed down on scrambled *huevos* and tortillas Señorita García had cooked—after they'd made a generous offering to the gods of hospitality. "We don't need Cory Hughes to get to Nader and finish him off."

Sam had been expecting this. He downed a swallow of strong, sweet Honduran coffee, knew that Savage was right. Also knew that Mendoza and Doc were on board with Savage's assessment.

They no longer needed Cory Hughes. A little while ago, Mendoza had used Smith's cell phone and his contact list to find Nader's cell phone number. Then he'd made one quick, discreet call to his contact at the local CIA/NSA and Casper the friendly spook had triangulated Nader's location. The murdering bastard was currently on his yacht, which was, as they sat here, moored off the southern coast of Isla de Roatán.

"The longer we wait," Mendoza added, tucking his

St. Christopher's medal beneath the black T-shirt he'd just pulled over his head, "the more restless Nader's going to get over Smith being out of touch."

"Wouldn't be surprised if he's already sent someone out to Peña Blanca looking for him," Doc agreed around a mouthful of eggs.

Sam said nothing. Nothing he could say. No argument he could wage. They were right. The longer they delayed closing in on Nader, the greater the risk that they'd lose him.

"We need to move on this bro," Savage pressed. "We don't have time for Cory Hughes anymore. Have Mendoza drive Abbie back to San Pedro Sula and put her on a plane. He can catch up with us later."

"We had a deal."

All heads turned at the sound of Abbie's voice.

"We had a deal," she restated, her eyes accusing as she honed in on Sam.

Looking sheepish, Doc, Savage, and Mendoza each snagged a couple of tortillas and headed for the door. "We'll get loaded up," Mendoza said. "Meet you outside."

Then, like rats deserting a ship, they bailed.

So did Señorita García, who'd been puttering around in the kitchen but, sensing the tension, walked outside.

The lingering silence rang like an indictment.

"They're right," Sam said, filling a plate, then holding it out to her. "We're going to lose Nader if we delay much longer."

She ignored the plate of food. "And Cory will be dead if we don't go after him now."

Sam hadn't wanted it to come down to this. Nader was the only reason Sam was in Honduras. His entire purpose was to destroy the man who had destroyed his father. To make certain Nader could never touch him or his again.

He thought of Cory Hughes. Of Savage and Doc and Mendoza, who were all risking their lives so he could take Nader down.

Guilt crushed down like a tank as he stood there, meeting her gaze.

She shook her head, disbelieving. "You bastard. You . . . you talk about trust. You talk about mistakes. You . . . you played the honor card last night as if it was your ticket to redeeming yourself for using me. You pretend to care. You make me want to believe—"

She cut herself off, fought the tears that were welling.

"Look. I'm sorry. I'm sorry about your sister. I'm sorry that she's dead. But you can't help her now. You can only help Cory. Who's alive. Please." She choked on the words. "Please . . . be who you want me to think you are. Help me."

Sam stared at her long and hard. "I really did a number on you, didn't I, if you honestly believe I'd go back on my word now."

The relief he saw flooding her face almost made it worth going against his better judgment and the opinions of the BOIs. Almost.

"Eat," he said gruffly. "You need the fuel. Be ready to go in ten minutes."

Then he headed outside, knowing he was about to ask his brothers to go above and beyond.

Knowing that for him, they would do it. Just like he knew that if anything happened to them and if Nader got away, it would all be on his head.

Near El Nuevo Porvenir and Desmond Fox's camp
"Sonofabitch," Mendoza swore as he quick-shifted from forward to reverse and the rear wheels of the SUV sank deeper and deeper into the rutted road.

"Hold on." Savage shoved open the passenger door, stepped out into the muck. "Fuck. We're buried to the hubs. This sucker isn't going anywhere."

No one was happy. Not the BOIs, who thought Sam was out of his mind for wasting time going after Cory Hughes. Not Sam, because he knew he'd compromised not only their lives but their chances of getting Nader.

And not Abbie, who was scared to death that they'd get to Cory too late to save him.

Only Doc attempted to maintain a level of levity in the midst of chaos. "Holy mud rut, Batman. Where's the Batmobile when you need it?"

"I told you this road would be impassable," Savage grumbled.

"Yeah, well, since when are you ever right?" Sam stepped out of the SUV, slamming the door behind him. He scowled down at the wheels, which were buried in mud.

"Everybody out. Abbie, get behind the wheel. Then gun it to hell when I say go.

"Go!" Sam shouted when all the guys were in place, shoulders to the back of the SUV, determined to muscle it out of the mud.

She gunned it.

The SUV rocked, slid and, to a string of curses and grunts, finally, its belly dragging, shot out of the hole.

Abbie braked, steered the vehicle to the middle of the road, and waited for the guys to catch up with her.

It was about that time that Sam smelled gas.

Then the motor died.

"Sonofabitch," Savage swore as he got down on all fours and peered beneath the undercarriage. "Ripped a hole in the gas tank on a rock or something when we pushed her out. We're without fuel, boys and girl."

Abbie got out, her eyes desperate and wild in her poor bruised face.

Everything she felt was telegraphed in those big brown eyes. *This far? We've come this far?*

Hands on hips, Sam squinted against the glaring morning sun, scanned the countryside, acutely aware of Abbie's worried gaze.

They were in the middle of freaking nowhere. A small farm sat a quarter of a mile or so to the south. "I need the field glasses."

Mendoza reached into the back of the SUV, handed them to him.

"Give me all your cash," Sam said, after seeing what he'd hoped to see.

"I hate to tell you this, but there's not enough lempira in Honduras to buy our way out of this mess," Savage grumbled.

"I had something more like horse trading in mind," Sam said after they'd all ponied up. "Mendoza, come with me. The rest of you wait here."

They took off walking across the field.

"I do not do horses," Savage sputtered an hour later. He glowered from Sam to the shaggy brown mount munching on ditch grass in front of him. "Not in Afghanistan, not in Argentina, and not in fucking Honduras."

"Then it's time to expand your horizons," Doc said, swinging easily up into the saddle.

There might not have been enough lempira to buy them a new gas tank, but Sam had had enough to buy the use of six horses. They weren't exactly Derby material but they were stout and sturdy and they'd get them the rest of the way to El Nuevo Porvenir, where the dying mole had told them Desmond Fox was holed up with Cory Hughes.

According to the mole, Hughes was in bad shape. Sam hadn't shared that news with Abbie, who had surprised him yet again with her stoic determination to do whatever had to be done. He could tell she was a little nervous but she swung up into the saddle without a word.

Abbie didn't need any additional stress about Cory's condition. It wouldn't help anything. Just like Savage's grumbling wouldn't help—except, maybe, to provide Doc and Mendoza with a source of amusement.

"Come on, Papa Bear." Like Doc, Mendoza was getting a very large charge out of Savage's skittishness around the horses. "It's just like riding a loose woman. Oh, wait, probably been so long, you forgot how good that feels."

"Fuck you," Savage muttered, hoisting his big body awkwardly into the saddle. "I hope those nags throw you both on your pointy little heads."

Sam shot them a glare that none of them misunderstood.

"You've got to admit," Doc said, "seeing Savage bent out of shape over *anything* is a damn satisfying experience."

"I'll be satisfied when we get the job done." Sam double-checked the binding on the munitions and weapons they'd unloaded from the back of the SUV and tied onto the packhorse. "Let's ride. I want to get in, get Cory, get out, then move on to Nader."

It could have been a photo ad for tourism in Honduras. A brilliant sun dazzled from a cloudless blue sky. A tropical forest, verdant and lush and teeming with life rimmed a vast expanse of gently rolling hills thick with slender, bending grass. The air smelled of sun and flowers and the aftermath of fresh rain.

Across this endless field of green, five horsemen rode, their silhouettes juxtaposed against the crumbling ruins of what had once been sacred Mayan temples. The horsemen's pace was plodding and sure; their striped ponchos posed a muted contrast to the vibrant blues and greens of nature. They rode with lazy ease, their heads hung low, wide-brimmed hats fashioned of local straw grass shielding their eyes against the sun.

Yeah, Abbie thought, it could have been a snippet of rural life in the Copán Province—or so said the sign on the road they'd left behind—had she not been a part of it. Had she not known that beneath those ponchos, Sam, Doc, Mendoza, and Savage were concealing enough weaponry to jump-start a major coup. Had she not known that lashed beneath the blanket on the pack-horse tied to her own mount was a machine gun and enough ammo to take out several buildings or bad guys.

In addition to the horses, Sam had bartered and bargained for the ponchos and hats. None would make the pages of a men's apparel catalogue. The ponchos were old, dirty, worn, and weary, the hats crushed and frayed. But, as Sam had hoped, wearing them in combination with sitting astride the horses went a long way toward camouflaging four very tall men in a country where the average height was around five foot six. Any locals they might encounter wouldn't give them a second look.

The ponchos and hats also did a decent job of camouflaging Abbie's sex—although, from her perspective, flanked by these men who closed ranks around her both figuratively and literally, she'd never been more aware of her gender.

Just as she was very much aware of the fact that Sam

had gone against the advice and the wishes of his men. Men who were risking their lives for Cory—someone they didn't know, didn't care about, and frankly resented for his role as Nader's mule and as a deterrent to their primary goal: Fredrick Nader.

She couldn't thank them. Wouldn't know how. She strongly suspected they wouldn't want her thanks anyway. But there was one thing she could do. She could be a player in Cory's rescue. She didn't know how yet, but she would not cower in the bushes while they took all the heat.

"According to what the mole said, the estancia should be just over that rise," Mendoza said an hour into their trek. "I'll ride ahead and take a look."

He kneed his horse and loped away up the hill.

Cory was right over that hill. Abbie's heart raced at the prospect that she might actually be seeing him soon and getting him to safety. From what she'd gathered, the man they'd found alive at Peña Blanca last night had revealed the location before he'd died. She also understood that Fox had left that man there waiting for her, his sole job to bring Abbie to Fox's El Nuevo Porvenir hideout, where Fox had had exactly the same game plan in mind as Fredrick Nader. Fox would give up Cory when Abbie gave up the location of the diamonds. Neither Fox nor the mole, however, had planned on the mole getting shot.

"One of the things we've got going for us," Sam said, "is that Fox couldn't know exactly when Smith would arrive with you at Peña Blanca. That bought us these

few hours. He has no idea that his man won't be showing up with you in tow. And he won't be looking for
any resistance. Not from you."

"So if he's expecting me, why don't we just give him
me?" Abbie asked Sam as they dismounted in the
shade at the edge of the forest and waited for Mendoza
to return with a report.

Sam cut her a look that pretty much answered her
question.

"Because just like Nader, Fox plans to kill both of
us," she surmised.

"Give the lady a cigar." Doc, more stoic than usual,
loaded bullets into a metal clip and shoved the clip
into the butt of a very lethal-looking pistol.

Battle. They were preparing for battle. Earlier, when
Abbie had joined them by the SUV before leaving
Señorita García's, they'd all been busy doing the same
thing. The precision and the automatic way they handled the guns, double-checked ammo clips, shrugged
into their heavy vests, painted a vivid, telling picture of
who they were and what they were capable of doing.

"You ever fire a rifle?" Sam had asked her then.

She shook her head, feeling very naive and sheltered
and dependent. None of the feelings settled well.

"Show me how."

Eyebrows rose all around, but no one had said a
word.

"I'm a quick study," she said defensively. "Just show
me."

"She could handle the M-4," Mendoza had suggested picking up the smaller version of the M-16 and handing it to Sam. "Just teach her to point and spray."

So Sam had shown her. With the little time they'd had, he'd taught her the basics.

"Point, aim, squeeze. And never point this sucker at anything or anyone you don't feel comfortable killing."

That had been the short and the sweet of it. Of course, she'd only been able to "dry fire," so she hadn't experienced live rounds.

So now, here she was. Disguised as a local who was disguised as a shooter, who was disguised as someone who wasn't scared half out of her mind with Sam's final piece of wisdom ringing in her head.

"Welcome to the world of bullets and bad guys."

18

Abbie stood by her horse and watched Mendoza ride back toward them. Her hands sweated as she tightened her grip on the reins.

Mendoza's gaze met hers as he dismounted, and bless him, he actually looked sympathetic. He understood how anxious she was for news. He shook his head, indicating he hadn't seen any signs of Cory, before digging a pencil and a scrap of paper out of his pocket. Using his horse's hip as a platform, he spread out the paper and started sketching.

"Okay. What we've got is a small estancia just outside of the village. I'm guessing Fox routed out whoever lives there and just took it over.

"Main house here," he continued, drawing a box in the center of the paper. A slight breeze kept lifting the corner. Abbie reached out, held it down for him. "I see one entrance but figure there's also an exit out the back. One guard stationed by the front door."

"Carrying?" Sam asked.

"An AK."

Sam frowned. "That the only guard?"

"At the house," Mendoza confirmed. "There's an outbuilding here. Could be a well house, toolshed, can't tell, but there are four men stationed here, here, here, and here," he explained, marking all four corners of the building with his pencil.

"Gotta be where they're keeping Cory," Sam surmised.

Mendoza nodded. "I agree. No reason to have all that firepower guarding the building otherwise."

"Gotta be more men around." Doc frowned at the rough map. "According to the mole, there are at least twenty."

"The barn?" Savage suggested.

Mendoza lifted a shoulder. "Could be. Could be more in the house. I spotted at least three perimeter guards patrolling the grounds. Looks like they're in place as the first line of defense."

"Who are they defending against?" Abbie asked, puzzled. "For all Fox knows, I'm coming alone. And I was supposed to arrive with one of his own men."

"The reception's not for you," Sam said. "It's for Nader. Fox fully expects Nader to come after him once he finds out about the ambush at Peña Blanca."

"So he's going to be loaded for bear," Savage said with a nod.

"But he's not planning on going up against the Papa Bear," Doc said with a grin aimed at Savage, who Abbie had heard all three men refer to as Papa Bear.

"By the way, how are those saddle sores coming along?"

Savage flipped Doc the bird but since he was grinning, it was apparent he took no offense. What was also apparent to Abbie was that they were up against overwhelming odds.

"How can we possibly get Cory out of there?" she asked.

All eyes turned to Sam.

"Did I see what I thought I saw in your bag of tricks?" he asked Mendoza.

"Brought a lot of toys, Sam. Narrow it down for me."

"A few well-placed mortar rounds could create a nice diversion."

Mendoza grinned. "Thought you might like those."

"Mortars?" Abbie did a double take. "Now wait. I'm no expert on guns or whatever shoots mortars, but I've seen enough combat footage on TV and in movies to know that there's no way you have something like that tied to the back of that horse."

"Smart lady. No mortars, but what we do have are mortar simulators," Mendoza explained, digging under the blanket and pulling out a black metal bar. Three cylindrical tubes about eight inches long and an inch or so in diameter were welded to the bar in an upward trajectory.

"We're outmanned and outgunned, but we also have the element of surprise on our side. They're not expecting an assault. At least not yet. So right now, they're most likely full and lazy from breakfast," Sam said. "We're going to wake 'em up. Use a little pyrotech-

nic smoke and mirrors to convince the bad guys someone's lobbing mortars at them. Give them reason to believe Nader's arrived in force, means business, and has
the superior firepower."

"More than anything else," Doc added, turning to
Abbie, "mortars scare the hell out of you. You don't
know where they're coming from, what they'll hit, and
the odds are damn good a shell can drop in like unexpected company."

Sam nodded. "If we can get them disorganized and
scared enough, some of them are going to run. That's
when we clear a path to snatch your brother and go."

"Go where?" Abbie couldn't help it. "How do we get
out of here? I mean, Cory may be too injured to ride.
And even if he isn't, I'm assuming these guys have vehicles. Correct me if I'm wrong, but I don't see us out-
running them on horseback."

"Talk to me, Raphael." Sam turned toward Mendoza.

"Two pickups and one damn pricey Suburban are
parked in front of the hacienda. I figure these came
with Fox. One of them is going to leave with us. The
other two are going to be profoundly disabled. If there
are more vehicles with the men in the barn, it won't be
a big deal to shoot out a few tires."

"What about the horses? What happens to them?"

Savage rolled his eyes. Okay. So Abbie knew it was
incongruous to be worried about the horses when there
was a major gun battle minutes away, but she couldn't
help it.

"We slap them on the ass and head 'em toward home," Doc said, taking pity. "Don't worry. They know where the feedbag is. They'll be home long before it's time to strap it on."

"This is the way I see it going down," Sam said, keeping them on task. "Abbie, we'll position you at the top of the ridge to fire the simulators on my signal." Mendoza handed her the field glasses so she could watch for Sam's cue.

"Mendoza, Savage, and I will make up the entry team. Doc, you'll hang back on the ridge with Abbie and the M-249. The machine gun," he clarified for Abbie. "Pick off anything that gets in our way."

Doc grinned. "I just loves me a belt-fed machine gun."

"It'd be nice if we could keep the decibel level down initially when we go in after the perimeter guards. Might buy us a few minutes." He turned to Mendoza. "Any chance—"

"That I brought sound suppressors?" Mendoza cut in. "You had to even ask?" He fished around under the blanket on the packhorse again. When he turned back, his hands were full of long black cylinders. He handed them out.

"And one for me," he added, pulling out his own M-4 and affixing the suppressor to the end of the barrel.

Sam turned back to Abbie. "We're going to leave you with an M-4. You shoot only if you're under direct fire, okay?"

She took the rifle. Nodded. Understood that he was

telling her he didn't want her shooting and hitting one of them.

"Okay," Sam said, with a hard look. "Once we take out the perimeter guards, we'll head straight for the shack. That's when I'll need the mortar fire, okay?"

Abbie nodded.

"That should send feet flying. I'll head for the shack, take out the four guards, and get Cory. Mendoza, you and Savage check the barn for stragglers, disable any other vehicles, then go for one of the pickups."

"What if the trucks are locked?" Abbie asked.

Mendoza just grinned. "That's what they make these metal stocks for," he said, patting the butt of his rifle.

"As soon as you see Savage and Mendoza pull around in front of the shed in the truck, beat feet down the hill. I'll spring your brother, get him on board, we'll pick up you and Doc, and we're out of here."

He made it sound so simple. If you left out the part about real bullets and real bad guys, it probably was.

"Questions?" Sam encompassed everyone with a hard look. "Okay," he said when he was met with silence. "Let's check our watches, set the charges for the simulators, and get this show on the road. Doc—"

"I know. Be ready with my medic kit."

Abbie had absorbed every word with stoic fatalism. Until then. The plan was clean and fast and complete. It was the outcome that was unknown. It was the knowledge that they called Colter Doc for a reason.

There could be blood. Any one of them could get hurt—or worse.

They knew it. Yet they didn't hesitate. They were laying everything on the line for Cory. Whom they didn't know. Didn't care about. Didn't even want to help.

It's what we do, Sam had said.

These men . . . *these men who made things happen,* these capable, accomplished, hard-edged men, were all running head-on into danger because she'd asked them to.

"Don't think about it," Sam said, seeking her out while she stood away from the activity, struggling with the weight of these men's lives.

"What have I done?" She met his eyes. "What have I asked of you?"

"The same thing I would have done if I were in your position. The same thing I would have asked."

She swallowed, tried to settle her pulse.

"Abbie." Sam touched her hand, squeezed. "It's not our first hostage rescue."

No. She didn't suppose it was. Knowing that, however, didn't make things any easier.

"Be careful," she whispered, hearing more than concern in her voice, seeing in his eyes that he heard it too.

He leaned down, kissed her. Lightly. Sweetly.

"Careful is my middle name," he promised against her mouth. "Besides, you and I have unfinished business. I plan to come back and settle it."

It was never easy. And it never felt heroic. What it felt was necessary. If a man lost sight of the reality that it was "kill or be killed," that man ended up dead. Sam had every intention of leaving here alive.

With Mendoza flanking him twenty yards to the left and Savage to his right, they worked their way slowly toward the perimeter guards, belly-crawling through the thigh-high grass, rifles cradled in the crooks of their arms, until they reached their targets. Within ten minutes, and without one round of gunfire, three corrupted souls kept long-standing dates with *el diablo*.

Three down, too many to go.

Sam dragged the dead guard behind a tree, then stripped him of his hat and bandoliers full of ammo. He crisscrossed the bandoliers over his own chest and donned the guard's hat. The attempt to disguise himself as one of Fox's men wouldn't fool anyone for very long. He didn't need long. Neither did Savage or Mendoza, who were doing the same. In this game, split seconds counted. Split seconds made for minuscule delays that allowed for maximum effect. A slow reaction by a puzzled guard gave a necessary edge. Tipped the scales in favor of the good guys, especially when there were few against many.

The short clipped chirp of a sparrow—their prearranged signal—first from the left, then from the right, told Sam the BOIs were ready to move on. He answered back then lifted his hand, thumb up, Abbie's signal to set off the charges.

"Atta girl," he said under his breath when ten seconds later she fired off the simulator. A shrill screech whistled through the air, followed by an explosion that

TAKE NO PRISONERS   259

stomped like, roared like, and looked like mortar blasts
and rocked the open area near the shack where they
suspected Cory was being held. Dirt and debris and
enough hellfire and brimstone to wake the dead flew
thirty feet in the air and just as wide and clouded the
area with dust.

On cue, Sam, Mendoza, and Savage came tearing
out of the tall grass. They ran toward the compound
like their tails were on fire, shooting wildly behind
them as if shooting at a combatant, yelling out a warning that the compound was under attack. "*¡Un ataque!
Socorro! Rápido! Somos atacados!*"

They hoped like hell that in the chaos no one noticed they weren't part of the jackal pack.

Just as the front door to the hacienda burst open and
four more bandolier-wearing bad guys joined the
stunned guard already positioned on the porch, Abbie
launched the second "mortar" attack.

As he sprinted low toward the shack, Sam caught
sight of Mendoza and Savage belly-diving under the
tailgates of the pickups. The staccato burst of automatic-weapon fire followed—unmistakably M-16 and
M-4's. The five surprised guards never laid trigger finger to metal of their AK's.

Five more down. The odds were getting better.

Sam ran toward the shack, shouting wildly. "*¡Proté-
jense! Tomen refugio!*" Take cover.

The four startled guards ducked, stared, finally realized he wasn't one of them, and raised their rifles.

Four short bursts from his M-16 and the poorly prepared, poorly trained guards dropped like sandbags.

He stepped over their bodies and bolted for the door. Wooden. Old. Padlocked.

"Stand back!" he yelled in case Cory could hear him.

Then he put his weight behind his foot and kicked like hell. The old dried wood splintered around the padlock hinge. The door swung inward, slammed against the wall.

"Fuck!" He jumped when a rat scrambled across his foot, then shouldered his way inside.

The sunlight shattered the dank darkness that stank of filth and fear and desperation.

A man lay on his back, legs splayed, head and shoulders bolstered crookedly against the far wall. He'd lifted a hand to shield his eyes from the sunlight. The other hand, wrapped in dirty, bloody bandages, lay cradled against his abdomen.

"Cory," Sam said.

No answer. Rats skittered in the corners.

"I'm a friend of your sister's."

That finally got a reaction. He lowered his hand, squinted up at Sam through feverish, bloodshot eyes. "Abbie? Abbie's here?"

"Yeah. Now come on. We've gotta move out. Can you walk?" Sam hooked his rifle sling over his shoulder, went down on one knee beside Cory, and helped him sit up.

"Get her out of here!" Cory begged. "Don't . . . don't let them get her, too."

"No one's going to get her, but we've got to get you out of here now."

Sam grabbed Cory's good hand, draped it around his neck, and hefted him to his feet. Outside, the sound of AK-47 fire and Doc on the machine gun rang like a hailstorm of bowling balls on a tin roof. If all had gone as planned, Doc and Mendoza had already taken out a few more men in the barn, disabled all the vehicles but one of the trucks, and should be about to spin around the shack and pick up Sam and Cory.

Sam heard the rattle of the M-249—closer now— and realized Doc had moved it farther toward the compound.

"Come on." Supporting Cory's weight, Sam grabbed him by the waist of his pants and walked him toward the open door. Sam glanced outside, left and right. Satisfied there was no fire coming their way, he propped Cory upright against the frame.

"Stay," he ordered and, ducking outside, peered around the corner of the shack.

Fuck. Mendoza was pinned down by a water trough. A spray of bullets *thuwnked* into the water, shooting it skyward like a progressive fountain. Sam searched the perimeter, found the shooter, sighted down the barrel through his holographic scope, and fired. A body tumbled off the barn roof and landed on the dry ground with a lifeless thud.

Mendoza shot to his feet, firing from the hip as he ran toward the closest pickup. He tried the lock, then quickly slammed the butt of his rifle through the driver's-side window when he found it locked.

He jerked open the door and lay down in the seat just as the passenger-side window shattered in a spray of gunfire. Sam searched for the new shooter. Found him in an upper window of the hacienda. One pop and the gunman tumbled forward through the glass window-pane, bounced off the porch roof and landed on the roof of the Suburban.

"Come on, Mendoza," Sam urged, knowing Raphael was working to hotwire the truck.

Through the constant spurts of gunfire, an engine roared to life.

Mission accomplished.

Sam swung his rifle around, crept past Cory, who was still on his feet, and peered around the opposite corner of the shack, where he came face-to-face with the barrel of an AK. He dropped, rolled, and fired, and another one of Fox's hired guns hit the dirt.

He rolled back toward the shack, vaguely aware of a burning sensation in his upper arm. Fuck. He'd been hit. When he reached the porch, he checked his arm. Blood seeped out of the hole in his sleeve. Nothing major.

The rapid-fire burst of Doc's machine gun had him ducking back behind the building. He quickly sur-veyed the real estate between the shack and the barn where Savage crouched in the open doorway, holding off gunmen Sam couldn't see.

About that time, Mendoza roared to a rolling stop in front of the barn, his M-4 firing out the passenger window, laying down cover for Savage who, running backward, sprayed rounds toward the open barn door as he sprinted for the truck. When he reached Mendoza, he launched himself, landing face-first in the pickup bed. Quickly righting himself and steadying the barrel of his M-16 on the sidewalls of the truck bed, he emptied a mag into the barn.

"Get ready," Sam told Cory, knowing Mendoza's next stop would be for them.

With a squeal of tires and laying a rooster tail of dust behind him, Mendoza sped their way, then screeched to a stop at the shed.

Sam tossed Savage his rifle, scooped up Cory in a fireman's carry, and ran the three yards to the truck. Bullets kicked up the dirt at Sam's feet as Savage caught Cory and dragged him into the pickup box.

Sam hiked himself up on the open tailgate, grabbed his M-16 from Savage, and joined him in laying down fire.

"Punch it, Martha!" Savage yelled to Mendoza, who promptly gunned the motor. With the rear of the truck fishtailing wildly, they flew toward the edge of the grounds, where Doc and Abbie would be waiting.

The truck roared across the bumpy ground, hit a rut, and sent Sam flying to the edge of the open tailgate. He scrabbled for a hold, lost it when they hit another chuckhole, and flew out the back.

He hit the ground with a thud that knocked the wind out of him. He was convulsed inward, gasping for breath when he saw a shadow loom over him.

"*Hola, gringo.*"

Still gasping, incapable of moving, Sam squinted against the blazing sun. He couldn't make out a face but the unmistakable sight of the business end of an AK-47 was crystal clear.

"*Y adiós.*"

So, this was where it ended.

Sam thought of Abbie, of the guilt she would bear, as Fox's man hiked the rifle to his shoulder, aimed—

A crack of gunfire rent the air.

And Sam was still alive.

The gunman stood above him, stared, eyes bulged in stunned horror, as a circle of crimson stained his chest.

The AK fell from his hand. He looked down at himself, looked at Sam in disbelief. In slow motion, he crumpled to his knees and fell face forward in the dirt.

Sam finally found the strength to push himself upright. He squinted against the sun that silhouetted the figure slowly walking toward him, the rifle that had saved his life still butted against a slender shoulder, dust swirling all around her.

Abbie.

Before he could yell at her to get down, the pickup barreled up beside him. He rolled to his feet, snagged Abbie's hand, and, running alongside the moving vehicle, jerked open the passenger door. He hauled Abbie up against him, lifted and stuffed her inside, piling in after her as Mendoza put pedal to metal.

Doc emerged from the deep grass not thirty yards ahead. Another rolling stop and Doc leapt into the truck bed with Savage and Cory. On his back, he quickly set up the M-249 between his spread legs and started spraying a trail of lead behind them, effectively dissuading anyone stupid enough to try to follow.

The last thing Sam saw as he looked back at the decimated estancia grounds was Desmond Fox, standing feet spread wide, a rifle hanging from his hand, helpless to do anything but watch as they sped away.

19

In-out—less than fifteen minutes. Fifteen minutes that had seemed like fifteen hours. It always did when bullets were flying.

They weren't flying now. Still, Sam kept a vigilant eye on the rearview mirror for any trailers that Fox might have dispatched to follow them. So far, nothing, but no one was doing any deep breathing—yet. Considering they were all wired and revved on adrenaline, no one had much to say either. No one but Mendoza, who turned the air in the truck cab blue with a litany of Spanish curses as he fought the road, fishtailing and gunning his way back toward Señorita García's hacienda at La Entrada.

The stolen pickup scorched a path down the muddy road, cruised right on past their stranded SUV. The heat of the Honduras sun had dried the roads just enough that they managed to keep from getting stuck—barely.

Abbie kept twisting around in the seat beside Sam, casting worried looks at her brother.

"He'll be okay," Sam assured her gruffly. "He was conscious and with the program when I found him."

She whipped around. "He talked to you?"

"Yeah," Sam said. "He knows you're here. He ordered me to get you out of there."

Her eyes brightened.

"Points for the kid," Sam said, still reluctant to see him through his sister's eyes but knowing she needed that little bit of propping up. Knowing she was going to need a lot more than shoring up when it hit her that she'd killed a man.

"You're bleeding," she said in horror when she noticed his arm.

"I do that sometimes," he said, making light of it and trying to lighten the load for her. "It's a scratch. No more. We were lucky," he added pointedly. "Everyone's present and accounted for and other than a few bruises and minor wounds, we're fit and fine. Well, except maybe Mendoza. You're going to stroke out, man, if you don't take a breath."

Mendoza's response was to switch to cursing in English.

The miles passed. They didn't stop flying until they skidded into Señorita García's drive. Mendoza drove straight into the shed where they'd hidden the SUV last night. The engine hadn't even shut down when Sam jumped out of the passenger seat and, with Mendoza right behind him, started covering the truck with a tarp.

Abbie scrambled toward the back as Savage and Doc slid Cory toward the tailgate.

"He's passed out," Doc said, jumping to the ground beside her. "Let's get him into the house so I can assess his condition."

Sam watched, stoic and concerned for Abbie, as she helped Doc and Savage carry her brother into the hacienda.

"The woman has *cojones*," Mendoza said casually as he finished tucking the tarp around the truck.

"Yeah," Sam agreed quietly. The woman had balls.

The woman had killed to save his life. And when everything caught up with her, she was going to suffer because of it.

"You'd better go have Doc check that out." Mendoza nodded toward Sam's arm.

"In a minute." Doc had his hands full with Cory Hughes. Abbie also needed this time with her brother before Sam sent them both away.

He worked his jaw as he sat down beside Mendoza on an overturned bucket, reached for his M-16, and started tearing it down to clean it.

He'd kept his word. He'd rescued her brother.

Now he had another job to do.

One he couldn't afford to delay any longer. Thank God he no longer needed Abbie to do it.

He finished reassembling the rifle, went to work on the machine gun.

"When do you want to move out?" Mendoza asked

as he took a quick inventory of their remaining ord-
nance.

"The sooner the better. Nader's gotta be damn antsy
by now. I want to get to him before Fox does."

Mendoza grinned. "Yeah, gotta figure Fox tagged
Nader for that little raid we just pulled off. Stands to
reason he's going to be pissed."

Join the club, Sam thought, as Terri's vibrant, smiling face filled his mind.

"Can you finish up here?" he asked.

Mendoza nodded. "Got it covered."

"I'm going to go talk to Hughes. See what intel he
can give us about Nader. Then we need to get him and
Abbie out of here. What have you got on the ground for
contacts?"

"Let me make some calls," Raphael said. "We'll get
'em out of here speedy quick."

Speedy quick.

That's what Sam wanted, to get Abbie out of here
speedy quick. Out of danger. Out of the country. And,
until this was over, out of his head.

"How's he doing?" Sam nodded toward Cory, then
jerked when Doc started cleaning his wound. "Ouch,
dammit. What are you using, steel wool? And wipe that
damn grin off your face."

Doc poured more alcohol on a sterile gauze pad and
swiped it over the grazed skin on Sam's upper arm.
"Not often I get to make the great Sam Lang wince.
Give me a sec to savor the moment."

"Savor on your own time. Just clean it up and slap some salve on it."

"Don't rush the doc," Doc warned. "If I don't get this cleaned up, your arm'll fall off, and then you'll come after me with one of your big manly guns. Almost done, so suck it up there, tough guy."

Sam let out a frustrated breath, accepting not only that Doc was a smart-ass, but that he wouldn't be rushed. "So how's the kid?" he asked again.

"He'll be okay. Starved. Dehydrated. Got a raging infection in that hand. Ugly bit of work, that."

Sam could see by the concern in Abbie's eyes just how ugly it was. He watched her across the room where she sat by her brother.

She looked like she'd been through a war. Which she had. Her cheek, where Smith had hit her, had transitioned from red and swollen to shades of purple and swollen. The new dressing Doc had apparently put on her arm gleamed stark white in contrast to her tanned skin. Her hair fell wild and tangled around her face. Still, she was quite possibly the most beautiful sight Sam had ever seen.

"Shot him full of antibiotics and painkillers," Doc said absently, applying antibiotic salve to Sam's wound. "Cleaned up the amputation. Started pushing fluids. Once they take hold—say another twelve hours or so— he's gonna start to feel human again. In the meantime the morphine's going to keep him pretty mellow."

"Is he coherent? Can he talk?"

"Sort of and sort of. Give it a try. You're done."

Sam frowned down at his arm where Doc had covered the grazed skin with a big-ass white dressing. "Was that really necessary?"

"Hey. I was all out of Bugs Bunny Band-Aids. Deal with it."

Sam pushed himself to his feet, walked over to the sofa where Cory Hughes was now sleeping.

"How's he doing?"

Abbie didn't look up at him. Just shook her head. "He's not a bad kid," she said thoughtfully, as if she'd been waiting for him to say otherwise. "He just—" She stopped, shook her head, never taking her eyes off Cory.

"Our father used to beat him over . . . over anything. Cory had a . . . a tough time in school, you know? Every time the school called expressing concern, or Cory brought home a bad report card, he ended up getting a beating. Never occurred to the bastard to have Cory tested to see if he had a learning disability. If he would have, he'd have known Cory was dyslexic. Not even the teachers put it together until the damage was already done."

She touched a hand to Cory's hair when he stirred. "When he was ten, Cory took a beating so bad he ended up with a broken ankle. The ankle never healed right because, according to Dexter Hughes, Cory wasn't worth the trip to the ER."

"Abbie—"

"No." She cut him off when he would have stopped her. "I want you to know who Cory is. What he came from. What he was up against. He was a beautiful, brave little boy who should have been protected and loved, but never was."

"*You* loved him," Sam said gently.

"I was a kid myself. I wasn't enough."

"Where were social services in all this?"

"Where they always are. Overworked, understaffed, and unaware. We slipped through the cracks. Cory paid the price."

Okay. Sam got it. In spades. There were no black-and-whites in life. For Cory, there appeared to have been a whole lot of gray.

"He told me . . . before he went to sleep just now, he told me that he'd screwed up. That he'd gotten sucked into Nader's organization a few months ago. By the time he figured out what he was involved in, he couldn't find a way out."

Sam could believe that. Nader was slick, sinister, and ruthless. "Did he say how he came by the diamonds?"

She nodded. "There was this other guy. Derek some-one."

"Styles?"

She glanced up. "You know who he is?"

What Sam knew was that Styles was dead and Cory Hughes was damn lucky that he wasn't. "What about Styles?"

"Apparently he worked for Nader, too. Planned to double-cross him. Derek set up a deal to sell the dia-monds to Desmond Fox. Something went wrong and Derek was shot in the process. He came to Cory for help and before Cory could get him to a doctor, he died."

So it was Cory who left Styles at the church. Sam could almost figure out the rest. "Cory was left holding the diamonds."

She nodded. "And stuck between a rock and the proverbial hard place. No matter what he did he was in trouble. So, he decided since he was going to die anyway, he'd just as well make the deal Derek had set up."

"But he was smart enough to mail the diamonds back to Vegas."

"Yes. He arranged to meet Fox, but Smith intercepted him."

"And that's where you came in."

"Yeah. That's where I came in." She looked up at Sam. "What's going to happen to him?"

She was asking about criminal charges. She was asking Sam if he was going to turn Cory in to the authorities.

"Let's worry about that later. Right now, we need to get him back to the States where he can get some medical attention. Doc's good, but his resources are limited."

"What about going after Nader?"

Mendoza burst in the door right then. "We've got a problem."

He'd blown it.

Sam braced a hand on the wall beside the window and stared, unseeing, outside.

Nader was gone. Once again, Sam had missed his

chance to deal with the fucker once and for all. By doing the right thing and going after Cory, he'd done the wrong thing. Now a murdering, thieving, morally bankrupt felon was out of Sam's grasp again.

Mendoza's words played back in his head like a bad movie.

"We've got a problem. I made that call we talked about. Figured I'd double-check Nader's coordinates while I was at it. He's weighed anchor, Sam. He must have gotten antsy waiting to hear from Smith. Figured something was up. Looks like he's heading out to sea."

Then as now, Sam felt like he'd been broadsided by a tank.

"How long ago?"

"Earlier this morning."

Too long ago to have any chance of catching him. Yeah, they could line up a chopper out of San Pedro Sula but it would be too late. They were talking hours before they even reached the Isla de Roatán. Nader would be well beyond the island and out of assault range long before then. Even if they could miraculously catch up with him, Sam knew for a fact that the *Seennymphe* was equipped like a fucking battleship. At sea, it was pretty much unbreachable.

He closed his eyes, lowered his head. Thought of Terri. Thought of little Tina. Of his dad.

Sorry. He was so fucking sorry.

"Can we still reach Nader with Smith's cell phone?"

Abbie. Feeling guilty. Thinking there was something she could do.

"Wouldn't matter if we could. He knows something's up."

"He *suspects* something's up," she amended coming to his side. "But he doesn't know anything."

"She's right," Doc agreed.

Sam turned away from the window, glowered at him.

"Well, she *is*," Doc said defensively. "Even if Nader sent scouts to Peña Blanca and they found his men, he'll figure it was Fox who offed them."

"Nader doesn't know you're here," Abbie pointed out, thanking Doc with a nod. "He only knows about me."

Sam met her earnest eyes. "Let it go, Abbie. It's over."

"It's not over." Conviction rang strong in her voice. "Until Nader is either behind bars or dead, it's *never* going to be over. Not for Cory. Not for me. From everything you've told me about him, it's pretty clear that there's not a place on earth where Cory will be safe from this man. When he's ready, Nader will come after Cory. He'll come after me. I don't want to live with that hanging over my head."

Weary. Sam felt so weary. And concerned. Abbie was one hundred percent right about Nader. He'd wait. Then he'd pounce. He'd come after them. Just like he'd come after Sam's family again if he ever made the connection. "There are programs we can get you into."

She made a sound of disbelief. "Witness protection programs?"

"We have connections. We can make it happen."

"I don't *want* you to make it happen. I want you to

get Nader. Not just for me and Cory. For you. Sam," she touched a hand to his arm. "I think I know how you can do it."

"I've been after this bastard for two years. Lost him more times than I can count. And you think you know how to take him down? Abbie, you're way out of your element here," he bit out.

Silence.

Then, to his amazement, Mendoza and Savage joined Doc on the bandwagon.

"Let's hear her out, Sam," Mendoza said carefully. "Can't hurt to hear her out."

Sam was too stunned to speak. Didn't matter. Abbie had plenty she wanted to say and she said it fast.

"Let me call Nader on Smith's phone. I'll convince him that Cory is dead. That he was killed at Peña Blanca but that I escaped and have been hiding out, waiting for an opportunity to contact him. I'll tell him that if he wants the diamonds, he's dealing with me now and I'll set up a place for us to meet. From everything you've told me about him, he'll be too greedy to pass up the chance. And he won't see me as a threat, just a nuisance."

"What he'll see you as is bait. Which is what you'll be. It's not going to happen."

"I'm not bait," she insisted. "I'm your ace in the hole."

"Consider it, Sam," Savage added. "And consider it fast before Nader has too much time to think about what happened at Peña Blanca."

20

Bridge of the Seennymphe

Fredrick considered himself a renaissance man. He held a great appreciation for the arts, for fine wines, a robust cigar. He drew deeply, appreciatively, on his *maduro habano,* delighted that he would never have to contemplate life without them.

Fine things. Yes, he took pride in his fine things, just as he prided himself on his knowledge of his vessel and that he could gladly do without the computers that his captain so relied on to steer the *Seennymphe.*

So it was with great pleasure that he told his captain to take a break, deactivated the computer-charted course, and manually took over the helm himself. He loved the feel of the wheel in his hands, the crisp cut of the bow slicing through the rolling swells, the power of a well-maintained engine.

What he did not appreciate were interruptions when he manned the bridge himself. He'd come here to escape his anger. Anger with Rutger Smith for getting himself killed. He knew this with certainty now. He'd sent men to check. Smith's bloated remains had been found at the estancia at Peña Blanca.

He had Desmond Fox to thank for that. Fox had obliterated Smith and his contingent of guards, stolen Hughes and, may very well already have the Tupacka diamonds in his possession.

The diamonds had been his! He had coveted and schemed to obtain them for the better part of the past two years. Now they were gone. All because a lowly American mule and his deceitful sister had allowed Fox to move in.

They would all die, of course. No one beat Fredrick Nader. The woman would pay most dearly before she and her brother made the final payment with their lives.

"Excuse me, sir."

Edward. His steward.

"I know you wish not to be disturbed. But you have a call, sir. On the ship to shore. A woman. Caller ID indicates she's using Mr. Smith's cell phone, sir. She insists you will want to speak to her."

Fredrick turned, mildly intrigued. "Does this woman have a name?"

"She identified herself as an Abbie Hughes, sir."

Fredrick felt his sphincter muscle tighten with rage. He reached for the phone, dismissed the steward with a nod, then turned back to the helm.

"Miss Hughes. To what do I owe the pleasure?"

"I have something you want."

Short and to the point. Fredrick could appreciate the ruthless brevity, if not her rudeness.

"Ah, I see that you are a true businesswoman." More likely a simpleton like her brother.

"You don't see anything, you bastard."

Beyond rude. She was an impudent American bitch. Too stupid to realize exactly who she was dealing with.

"I do not see the need for vulgarity," he stated, biting back the desire to hang up on her. She claimed to have something he wanted.

"Look, do you want to talk terms or not? If not, I won't waste any more of your time or mine."

Fredrick clenched his jaw, wanting to reach through the phone line and rip her throat out for her impertinence. He forced himself to command composure.

"How do I know you still have access to the merchandise? For all I know, you could have already sold it."

"To Desmond Fox?"

He felt heat flush his face at the taunting inflection in her tone.

"What about Desmond Fox?"

"Don't play dumb, Nader. You were sloppy. Your mistakes led Fox to Peña Blanca, where your men held my brother captive like an animal. Because of you, my brother is dead. Everyone is dead except me. I was the only one who got out alive. Lucky for you because I'm the only one who can deliver that *merchandise* you're so willing to kill for."

As angry as he was, he needed to play this smart. A rush much like a climax flowed through him, just thinking about possessing the diamonds. Like it or not, he must play this greedy, manipulative woman's game to get them. First, however, she must understand there would be a price to pay.

"Smith was one of my best assets. I consider him a great loss, my dear. That falls on your brother's head."

"And my brother's death falls on yours. You cost me his life. If you want the diamonds, it's going to cost you, too."

"Truly?" He couldn't contain his anger. "You *truly* assume you can dictate terms to *me*? You had best tread carefully, Miss Hughes. And tell me this, if you will. How do I even know you still have the diamonds? You've been out of touch for some time. Where have you been? What's taken you so long to contact me? Could it be you've already been in negotiations with Fox?"

"I've been hiding out, where do you think I've been? I've been burying my brother. Now I'm ready to deal with you. Like it or not, I'm calling the shots now. I say where we meet. I say when. I say how. And I say who."

"Your insolence is intolerable."

"What's intolerable is what happened to Cory. Now do you want the diamonds or not? If not, then we're through here. And I *will* make that contact with Fox. He'll be more than happy to pay my price."

The thought of that cretin laying his hands on something as exquisite as the Tupacka diamonds made Fredrick's skin crawl. "Fine. Let's talk price, then, shall we?" he gritted out.

"Four million. American."

He would have laughed had it not tipped his hand. He'd be willing to pay twice as much. Not that she'd ever see a dime of his money. "Three point five and not a penny more."

"Good-bye, Mr. Nader."

"Wait, wait." He made a *tsk*ing sound, allowing her to think she had played him. "If you're going to dabble in international commerce, you must learn to appreciate the subtleties of a lively negotiation."

"What I appreciate is cash. You know the airstrip near La Jigua?"

La Jigua was mere miles from Peña Blanca. He knew the area intimately. "I believe so, yes."

"Meet me there tonight, sundown."

"I'm afraid that's impossible," he said, stalling for the time he would need to get a team in place on the ground. "I'm a hundred nautical miles from shore. Even after I alter course to return to the mainland, I'll have to arrange ground transportation after I dock."

"So use that pricey little chopper riding on your bow. It's sundown today or the deal is off."

He closed his eyes, struggled to keep a seething rage at bay. She would die slowly, this one. "I'll have to access the cash."

"Then access it. You have seven hours. Come alone. If I see anyone but you, this is the last you'll hear from me."

She hung up.

Dead.

The woman was dead. Disrespectful, demanding bitch.

Smarter and gutsier than her brother, he'd give her

that—but just as corrupt. That, at least, was something he could appreciate about her.

Just as he appreciated that she must have something up her sleeve. Fine. He welcomed the opportunity to outsmart her, see the look on her face just before he killed her.

And he *would* kill her. He didn't need Smith for that. He didn't need anyone.

Energized on the prospect, he gave control of the ship back to the computer. Then he left the bridge in search of the captain to inform him to plot a course back toward La Ceiba where he wished to have the *Seennymphe* moored when he returned with the diamonds. While there, he would acquire more *maduro habanos* to add to his supply. A man could never possess too much of a good thing.

In the meantime, he had several calls to make. Men on the ground to mobilize and direct toward the airstrip at La Jigua.

Come alone? So sorry, my dear. That just wasn't going to happen.

La Entrada

"Hot damn. The lady plays hardball." Savage's expression was filled with reluctant admiration as Abbie hung up the phone.

Sam wasn't fooled by her tough-edged dialogue with Nader. He saw how her hand was shaking.

"*Cojones,*" Mendoza agreed from the window where he watched for the transportation he'd called to take

Cory to San Pedro Sula. He'd also arranged for medical attention until Cory was strong enough to fly back to the States.

"Any chance I can get you to negotiate my next loan?" Doc asked with a grin and gave Abbie's shoulders a congratulatory squeeze.

He'd been playing for a laugh from her and got it.

Sam sensed the strain ease out of her shoulders even before she exhaled a deep, pent-up breath.

His tension, however, ratcheted up several tight twists. He hated this. Hated himself for agreeing to let Abbie dangle herself as bait—and no matter what she said, that's exactly what she was.

Bait to lure a rat.

"Car's here," Mendoza said, then went out to meet the driver and give him instructions on where to take Cory once they arrived in San Pedro Sula. Mendoza had a friend, an ER doc who would let Cory crash at his place and would give him medical care.

"I'll be fine," Cory assured his misty-eyed sister as Doc and Savage flanked him and helped him off the sofa. "Just nail the bastard."

"I'll see you tomorrow. We'll fly home together." Abbie hugged him hard, clung, then finally forced herself to let go.

Sam watched quietly, until Cory's gaze locked in on him. "Don't let anything happen to her," he said.

Twenty-four hours ago, Sam would have dressed him down as a sorry little punk who didn't deserve even an ounce of the concern Abbie lavished on him.

Twenty-four hours ago.

In this hour, however, Sam gave him a nod.

A promise—man to man.

An hour later Sam watched Fox's commandeered pickup disappear down the rutted road toward La Jigua with Mendoza at the wheel and Doc and Savage crammed into the cab beside him. Piled under the tarp in the pickup bed was enough weaponry and ammo to oust Osama out of a cave.

But they weren't hunting terrorists today. They were hunting rats who aided and abetted terrorists. Rats who were sure to come crawling out of the ditches around the airstrip with big guns paid for by the head rat: Fredrick Nader. The BOIs were going to make certain they got to the airstrip before anyone else did.

Sam turned back to the hacienda, found Abbie pacing restlessly in the hot confines of the small house.

"Hey," she said, checking a full-fledged flinch when she heard the door close behind him.

He assessed her with concern. "You okay?"

She nodded. She lied. What she was, was wired and edgy.

"Where are the guys?"

"Taking care of business," Sam said.

"What business?" she asked absently, hugging her arms around herself as she restlessly prowled the small room.

"By now, Nader will have reached out and put the touch on any mercs within a hundred-mile radius of here. They'll be on their way to La Jigua to position themselves for an ambush. The guys are going to form a little welcoming committee."

She nodded—with him but not quite. "So you don't think Nader bought that I'm in this by myself."

"What I think is that Nader is in new territory without Smith to run interference for him. He'll go into overkill mode trying to cover his bases. He won't take any chances. He'll send shooters, show up thinking they're all in place, covering the perimeter. He's going to be unpleasantly surprised."

"Because his hired men will be dead."

Her statement was matter-of-fact. Impassive. Like her expression. From a woman who wore her emotions like some women wore perfume. Lavishly. It was that lack of emotion that worried him.

"Yeah," he agreed walking over to her side. "Dead, or indisposed."

She looked away. "Kill or be killed."

He reached out, touched her arm, careful of the injury from Smith's knife. "Abbie . . . this will be over soon. Then you can put it behind you."

For the first time since he'd walked in and found her this way, something other than indifference filled her eyes. Something very much like desperation.

"Is that what you do? You kill someone, then just walk away? Just forget it ever happened?"

He'd known this morning was going to catch up with her. Known she was going to crash when it did. He knew because he'd had his own crashes. And no. You never just walked away. You never forgot. But she didn't need to hear that now.

"I'd be dead now if you hadn't shot him."

She rounded on him. Eyes wide and tortured, her emotional barricades smashed to smithereens. "You think I don't know that? You think I don't know that it was him or you? It doesn't change the fact that I took a life. He . . . he was someone's son. Maybe some child's father."

"Yeah," Sam agreed. "He might have been. But he also made a bad decision. He chose to be on the wrong side."

"Like Cory chose to be on the wrong side?" Torment transitioned to accusation.

Sam understood. She was floundering. And she was lost. Trying to make sense out of something that was senseless and still keep herself together in the face of yet more danger that lay ahead of her.

"That was not a judgment," he said gently. "Look. Everyone's got a story. Everyone has reasons—sometimes compelling reasons—for choosing the paths they take. Some . . . some are luckier than others. They see the light. They get out. Or someone helps them out. Others have the choice taken away from them."

"Like I took that man's choice when I took his life."

"He put himself in that position, Abbie. Not you. You pulled the trigger, but you didn't kill him. He took care of that himself the minute he hired on with Fox."

She dragged her palms over her face. Breathed

deep. Shook her head like she was trying to clear it of the memories. "So, what happens now?"

What happened now was that Sam dropped the subject. She didn't want to talk about it anymore. The important thing was, she'd let out some of what was eating at her.

"Now we eat some of those *baleadas* Señorita García made for us before she left for the market a while ago. Providing the guys left us any. They were stuffing them in their pockets like they were candy before they headed out."

"You go ahead. I'm not really hungry."

He wasn't having any of that. Sam took her elbow, steered her into the kitchen. "Doesn't matter. You need the protein."

He sat her down at a scarred wooden table. She wrinkled her nose, then sniffed, looking mildly interested. "Looks like a tortilla."

"Whatever floats your boat. Just eat. You're not leaving the table until you do."

"You like giving orders, don't you?" she said, more statement than question as she gingerly picked up the *baleada* that was loaded with beans, cheese, eggs, and guacamole.

"Yeah," he said simply. "I do."

And got the reaction he wanted.

One corner of her mouth tipped before she could think about it. "Must be why you're so good at it."

He nodded around a mouthful of tortilla. "It's a gift."

Another smile. A little wily, marginally amused even, though still guarded.

He liked it. Liked that she was finally feeling comfortable with him. And that he had her thinking about something other than this morning.

"It was from my final divorce settlement," she said after several moments of relaxed silence had passed and half of her *baleada* was gone. "New furniture. New car. The final payment arrived last week."

He said nothing, just nodded.

"And the diamond? From my engagement ring. I had it reset. Don was a lot of things, but he wasn't cheap."

"Just stupid," Sam concluded.

He shrugged when she glanced at him over her lunch, which he was glad to see she had begun to enjoy. "He let you go, didn't he? Spells stupid in my book." Then again, he hadn't exactly been Rhodes scholar material in his prejudgment of her.

He stood, then walked to the ancient refrigerator in the corner, dug around inside until he found a couple of beers. Held one up to her.

When she nodded, he found a bottle opener and joined her at the table again.

"So . . . what's the book on you?" she asked. "Ever been married?"

He downed a swallow of cold beer. "Nope."

When he didn't say any more, she gave him an expectant look. "That's a pretty short book."

He helped himself to another *baleada*. "After my

stint in the military, I joined my old CO in Argentina. Private firm. It's kept me busy."

"Saving the world," she speculated with a pointed look.

He shrugged. "Little pieces of it. Didn't leave much time for . . ." he paused, thought, finally settled on, " . . . relationships. Women tend to run the other way when they understand a man in my business—former business," he amended, "has the life expectancy of a fruit fly."

"But you left it?"

He nodded. Felt the weight of that decision.

She leaned back in her chair. "You miss it?"

He looked past her, wishing he didn't know the answer so well. "Wouldn't matter if I did. I've made commitments."

Those emotions she wore so baldly were back on her face again. "I'm so sorry about your sister."

He closed his eyes. Swallowed. "Yeah. Thanks. You finished?"

He wanted to talk about Terri as much as Abbie wanted to talk about putting a hole the size of a quarter through a man's heart.

She nodded. "Full up."

"Let's get out of this house for a while. Too damn hot."

"And go where?"

He checked his watch. "We've got several hours to kill before Mendoza comes back for us. Grab a towel.

Change of clothes, if you've got one. Shampoo, if you've got that."

"Um, excuse me?"

"I saw the shower, remember?" Sam headed for the door. "It's hardly more than a bucket and a nozzle."

"You stumble onto a spa or something?"

He smiled. "Or something."

21

It felt good to be out of the dark house. Out of the heat and shadows of the adobe walls. Away from the lingering scent of antiseptic and blood and fried tortillas.

The sun burned warm on her shoulders as Abbie walked alongside Sam through the tall grass behind the hacienda.

Much like the land they had ridden through this morning on horseback, here, a quarter of a mile from the house, the hills were gentle, sweeping. Up a rise, down another, and both the hacienda and the little hamlet of La Entrada were no longer visible. Just fields of green, blue skies, warm sun. Idyllic. Or it would have been if she could block the reality of last night and this morning.

Rutger Smith's head blown off.

Blood and brains matted in her hair.

Bodies in the mud.

Bodies in the dirt.

Holding a rifle.

Firing.

Watching a man fall.

Knowing she was the one who had killed him.

Killed him.

Killed.

She'd killed a man.

Yesterday, she would have felt instant, crippling nausea. Today, she felt little more than numb.

"You pulled the trigger, but you didn't kill him. He took care of that himself the minute he hired on with Fox."

Someday. Maybe she could accept that Sam's words made sense. Today, she just wanted to forget it ever happened.

And when they crested yet one more ridge and she realized that this was their destination, she realized that's why he'd brought her here. So she could forget—at least for a little while.

"Oh." She stopped. Breath caught. Stared. In wonder. In awe. In glorious, life-sustaining gratitude. "It's beautiful."

She'd needed beautiful. She'd needed a reminder of all life could be. Vital. Vibrant. Embracing.

"Yeah," Sam agreed. "It was pretty dark when we found the water last night but I could see potential. Had a feeling you'd like it."

"Better than a spa," she said with a smile and headed toward the gently meandering stream nestled in a copse of shady trees at the bottom of the rise. Flowers danced on tall stems, bees buzzed, birds sang.

Idyllic, she thought again. Perfection. A commercial for peace and tranquillity. *Calgon, take me away.*

"Bottom is sand," Sam said when they reached the edge of the bank. "Last night it was running bank full. Looks like it's only about two, two and a half feet deep today now that the runoff from the rain has made its way through."

"*Much* better than a spa," she restated with emphasis and toed off her shoes. Anxious now, she eased down the bank and stood ankle deep in the cool, clear water.

"Heads up."

She glanced up. Sam had foraged around in her pack and had come up with her shampoo. She caught the bottle when he tossed it down to her.

"Take your time. You know your way back, right?"

She shaded her eyes against a sun that burned warm and bright behind him where he stood above her on the bank. "You're leaving?"

He reached up, scratched his jaw. A heavy, dark stubble covered his lower face. Made him look imposing, dangerous . . . and darkly handsome. "Thought you might need a little alone time."

Yeah. For a little over twenty-four hours the testosterone level had been off the charts. His gesture was thoughtful and kind. And telling of the man he was. It had been a long time coming, but she knew the truth now.

"You're a good man, Sam Lang."

Something very much like relief crossed his face.

"Yeah, well." He held up the blanket he'd tugged off her bed and carried out here, tossed it on the grass. "Like I said. Take your time. Take a siesta. Do you good to get some sleep."

He gave her a lingering look with those dark, penetrating eyes. It was a look she recognized. He didn't want to leave.

It didn't take any thought at all to realize she didn't want him to go.

"Stay," she said, holding his gaze. "Stay with me."

The muscles in his throat convulsed as he swallowed. Yet there he stood.

"Stay," she said again, more promise than plea this time, and reached for the hem of her T-shirt.

Sam saw the plea in her eyes. Felt the desire as Abbie tugged her T-shirt up and over her head. Her gaze never leaving his face, she tossed it on the bank.

He understood the bone-deep longing to be something more than alone, to be something more than singular. Understood it in spades. He was thirty-five years old. He'd been alone his entire life. So yeah, he understood. Just like he understood that while alone had once been a choice for him, it wasn't nearly as compelling a prospect as it once was.

"Stay," she whispered again as slender fingers reached behind her back, unhooked the clasp of her bra.

He felt his throat tighten along with his groin when she slid the straps down her arms, tossed the delicate pink satin at his feet.

There she stood—shoulders back, exquisite, proud, beautiful. It was not an attempt to tease. Tease implied playful. Tease implied pretending.

There was no pretending here. She wanted more than that from him. She needed more. Needed his strength and the physical release his body could give her. In her eyes he saw a barely veiled desperation to feel something other than terror and anxiety and the ultimate stopgap: numb.

Wise or woefully stupid, he needed it, too. Suddenly craved it as much as he craved the feel of her hands on his body.

Stone-cold fox.

Reed's words didn't even come close. She was beyond description. Sam had never wanted the way he wanted around this woman.

Her breasts were beautiful and brazenly feminine. Her movements feline and sensual as the sun danced against her hair and the wind moving through the trees shot dappled shadows over her olive skin.

She held a hand up, beckoning.

And he knew he wasn't going anywhere that didn't take him closer to her.

He dragged his shirt over his head, mesmerized by the sight of her shimmying out of her jeans, rolling pink panties down her hips and smiling with an endearing mixture of relief and anticipation when he shucked the rest of his clothes and joined her in the cool, flowing water.

She reached for him, moved quickly into him,

pressed her quivering breasts and tight pink nipples against his chest. Skin against skin, heat against heat, they stood there, water lapping and gurgling around their bare legs.

"You know this is crazy," he whispered against her mouth, loving the feel of her beneath his hands as he skated them down her slender back, cupped her hips and pulled her flush against him.

"More than," she agreed and opened wide, indulging herself in the hunger she'd enticed from some primal place deep inside him.

He loved kissing her. Loved the soft sounds she made. Sounds of pleasure, sounds of surrender and impatience and restless, reckless desire. If he didn't slow things down, he was going to take her. Rough. Hard. Fast. She deserved far more than that.

"We've got time," he said, tucking her head beneath his chin and locking his arms around her. "We've got time. Come 'ere." He led her deeper into the water. "Let's get wet."

"I'm already wet." A sexy smile tipped up one corner of her mouth.

He chuckled. Kissed her hard and quick. "Good to know. We will definitely get back to that. For now, though, indulge me."

"I thought that's what I was about to do."

He didn't know when, exactly, things had changed between them. When the thrust and parry of distrust, the dodge and redirect of vulnerability had shifted to this easy, yet sensually edgy openness. This . . . trust.

"You're a good man, Sam."

Just like he hadn't known how badly he'd needed to hear those words from her until she'd said them. Or how much he'd wanted this kind of intimacy.

No. He didn't know when it had all changed. He was only glad for the transition. This woman was special. This woman, he realized with no lack of amazement, and with a clarity that left no doubt, was his.

His.

"Let me wash your hair, Abbie."

The look she gave him spoke volumes. She was surprised, mystified—and a sweet tenderness filled her eyes.

"You really want to do that?"

"Yeah. I really want to."

He sat down, cross-legged in the sandy bed of the stream and urged her down onto her back in front of him. Anchoring her shoulder blades on his crossed ankles, he guided her head onto the cove between his thighs.

Her dark hair floated over his legs. Water cascaded gently over her shoulders, streamed between her bare breasts, pooled in the indentation of her navel.

He took the shampoo bottle from her hand, squeezed some into his palm then tossed the bottle onto the bank above them.

"Umm," she closed her eyes, and he felt the lingering tension start to drift from her body as he gathered her hair and lathered it up with shampoo. "How much is this deluxe spa treatment going to cost me?"

"We'll work something out," he said around a smile, wholly mystified by the texture and weight of her hair.

And by the look of her long, slim body stretched out wet and naked in front of him.

With deliberate care, he massaged her scalp, then worked his way down to her neck, kneading the aching muscles there, feeling the tension ease with each caress of his thumb.

"Very nice," she murmured. "You're going to get a good tip for this."

"Here's a tip," he said, gliding his hands over her collarbone, moving slowly toward the lovely rise of her breasts. "You are beautiful."

He covered her breasts with his big hands, molded their slick wetness in his palms, stunned anew by the silk and the weight of them and the instant response of her nipples hardening against his palms.

She lifted her arms, clutched his hands, pressed them deeper into her, arched her back in anticipation and pleasure. "Sam."

"Shhh," he leaned forward, kissed her, chuckled when his chin hit her nose and they did a little dance of redirection until they found a fit that worked.

He sucked her lower lip between his teeth as he slowly pulled away.

She stopped him with a hand around his nape, turned her head from side to side, rubbing against his erection. "I want you inside me, Sam."

"In time."

She let out a sound that was part laugh, part growl, and all frustration. "Has anyone ever suggested that you have control issues?"

"Many times," he said, carefully rinsing her hair. He loved the look and feel of it as it floated around her head, tickled his thighs. Loved the look of her as she lay there, eyes closed, sun dancing against the water and reflecting off her wet skin.

"Anyone ever tested that control?"

"Many times," he said again. "But no one more than you."

Her wet lashes fluttered against her cheeks. She smiled up at him. "Oh, I think I like knowing that."

She sat up then, faced him on her knees as the water lapped around her waist. "I think I very much like knowing that."

Then she leaned in, wrapped her arms around his neck, and kissed him. Warm lips. Questing tongue. Delicious sighs.

His control slipped away like water running downstream. He gripped her waist, lifted her, urged her legs around his hips, and settled her down on top of him. The lips of her sex opened against his cock as she rocked her hips against him.

"Inside," she demanded, nipping his lower lip, then plunging her tongue back into his mouth in a desperate plea for penetration.

Too fast, too rough, he thought, struggling to slow himself down, to proceed with finesse. She wasn't having any of it. She reached down between their bodies, encompassed his throbbing cock in her hand. Positioned him, then lowered herself hard and fast.

Penetration was instant. Amazing. Mind-shattering.

She stiffened, cried out, then took his mouth again and begin moving. Hungry. Demanding. Wild and wanton.

He claimed her mouth on a groan, gripped her hips, and rocked her up and down on him in a fast and frenzied rhythm. He swallowed her sultry sighs. Was aware of her frantic breath. The slap of water. The slap of their bodies, primal, perfect, and consuming.

She cried his name, arched her back, ground herself against him, and came on a long, exhalation of breath and a low, slow moan. He held her there, buried thick and deep and pulsing, felt his cum tighten his balls, a sweet pressure building beyond reason. He pumped one last time, gripped her hips tight, knowing he'd leave bruises, unable to do a damn thing about it, and let himself go. Pleasure, rich, electric, and beyond cataloging, ripped through him, annihilated him, transformed him.

"Abbie," he murmured, hugging her hard against him. Just, "Abbie," as she crumpled, boneless and gasping, against his chest.

They stayed that way for a long time. Knotted together like a giant pretzel in the waist-deep water, their toes turning into prunes. Her cheek on his shoulder. His chin on the top of her head. When he felt his leg start to go to sleep from their crisscrossed positions, he reluctantly roused her.

"Come on. Let's wash up and get dry."

Laughing lazily, they wobbled to their feet. Then they

washed each other. It was a new experience for Sam. This tender, relaxed intimacy. He told her as much when they'd waded out of the water and lay down on their backs on the blanket to dry in the shade.

"Me too," she confided, rolling onto her side to face him.

He met her eyes, glanced down at her bandaged arm. "We'll need to get a fresh dressing on that."

"I'm fine."

"Yeah, well, you won't get any arguments from me on that count."

She smiled. Touched a finger to his lips. He opened his mouth, sucked that finger inside.

"Is this real?" she asked, a crease suddenly developing between her brows.

He could have pretended he didn't, but he knew what she meant. He breathed deep, kissed her palm. Crossing his arms beneath his head, he stared at the tree limbs overhead. "I guess we'll find out when we get back."

He was a veteran of too many conflicts—sanctioned and otherwise. Emotions ran high in the heat of battle. In the heat of the moment. What a person felt in the midst of grave danger sometimes didn't translate to the "real world."

He knew what he felt. Knew that wouldn't change. What he didn't know was how she would feel when the fog of danger had lifted.

"I want it to be, Sam. I so want this to be real."

He turned his head, felt a fresh wave of tenderness

and longing at the raw emotion in her deep brown eyes. "Yeah. So do I."

So do I, he thought, pulling her against his side and urging her to get some sleep.

They had to get out of this first. They had to get Nader. If they didn't, there'd be no future for either one of them, real or otherwise.

He watched over her while she slept. Reluctantly roused her an hour later.

They dressed in silence, the easy intimacy gone.

Reality had encroached on paradise.

The black cloud cast by Fredrick Nader hovered over them once again.

"Let's go do this," she said, her emotions under wraps for the confrontation to come.

"No chances. You take no chances, you understand?"

Yeah. He could see in her eyes that she understood his equivalent of an order. What he couldn't see was if she intended to obey it.

22

Sun glinted off the hood of the black Town Car as Fredrick Nader, unaccustomed to driving himself, headed west into the setting sun. His turnoff was just ahead. There the highway ended and the dirt road began. Dust immediately attached in a thin dull film to the windshield and sucked onto the gleaming paint as he continued down the washboard-rough road toward the La Jigua airstrip.

Fredrick much preferred the German craftsmanship of a Mercedes-Benz. The vehicle was richer, cleaner, subtly striking, and superior to the American pretender. On short notice, however, he'd had to make do.

The glorious strains of Mozart's Horn Concerto no. 3 enveloped him, the rich, mellow notes resonating through eight stereo speakers. The Austrian had been brilliant. Too bad he hadn't been German.

And too bad Miss Abbie Hughes would not live to see another sunrise.

His calls had been successful. He'd worked with Caesare Fuentes and his mercenaries before. One call and Fredrick had been assured that a minimum of twelve men, fully armed, and hungry for the balance of their payment, would be in place at the airstrip far in advance of Miss Hughes's expected arrival and that of any mercenaries she may have hired to defend herself. And yes, he fully expected she would bring protection.

Fredrick had ultimate confidence in the men Fuentes would send. But, as insurance, he'd hired another dozen men, also heavily armed. They kept pace out of sight in three Jeeps half a mile behind him, ready to shoot to kill should Fredrick meet up with resistance.

Come alone? The thought was laughable.

One could never be too careful, after all. Likewise, one could never fully trust a woman. Like her brother, she was a stupid, greedy American. Before he was finished with her, she would be screaming for mercy. The thought shot blood to his groin in a rush. No more vicarious thrills. With Smith gone, Fredrick more than relished the idea of taking care of the unsuspecting Miss Hughes himself. Relished it so much, in fact, that he felt remiss for delegating the wet work to Smith in the past.

He let off the gas when the corrugated roof of the neglected airstrip hangar came into view. He cruised cautiously to the access lane, then turned into the drive and pulled to a stop.

But for carrion eaters picking at the carcass of what appeared to be a rotted wild pig at the boundary of the property, he saw no signs of life.

The hangar doors yawned open, the interior lost in shadows. A single-engine Cessna—old and out of commission—was parked on the south side of the hangar, chocks wedged against the wheels, tethers tied to the struts. A thick layer of dust coated its windshield. A sheared prop leaned against a wheel hub.

One lone helicopter sat in the middle of the tarmac. Small. Four-seater. Ridiculously antiquated when compared to his sleek little Eurocopter that had delivered him to San Pedro Sula with swift efficiency.

Fredrick sat behind the wheel of the Town Car, squinted toward the chopper, watched the slow-moving rotor blades, and detected movement in the cockpit.

While he could possibly applaud her ingenuity, he almost felt sorry for Abbie Hughes. She actually thought she could make an aerial escape? Everyone had a price in this part of the world, and he had no doubt that he could buy off the pilot.

He eased within twenty feet of the bird, turned off the motor. Then he readjusted his tie, checked his hair in the rearview mirror, and, even though he knew it was there, patted his jacket pocket for the Walther P38 tucked inside. Another brilliant piece of German craftsmanship.

Adrenaline spiked as he stepped out of the air-conditioned quiet and into the sweltering sunset heat and the whine of the chopper motor. He immediately recoiled and gagged as a wind gust kicked dust in his face and brought the putrid scent of decayed animal flesh.

"She had better be worth it," he muttered beneath his breath and waited for Miss Hughes to come to him.

"Showtime," Savage whispered into his shoulder mic. He lay belly down on the hangar roof beneath a gray tarp meant to camouflage both him and the M-249 machine gun Doc had reluctantly given over to him. "And about damn time. This fucking tin is about to burn my balls off."

"*There's* a picture that'll give me nightmares." Doc returned from inside the hangar where he'd established a defensive position behind the crisscrossed slats of a boarded-up window.

Sam had taken a position behind the wheel strut of the disabled Cessna with full view of Nader and the idling chopper with Abbie and Mendoza inside. He watched Nader's car pull to a stop. Forced a combat calm as the bastard got out from behind the wheel. "Mendoza?"

The main rotor spun slowly. Dust stirred in lazy circles from the prop wash as the turbine engine whined and rumbled.

"Good to go." Mendoza sat behind the joystick of the chopper, his M-4 locked and loaded. The bird was revved and ready to fly if the action got too hot. But for now the chopper was their version of a Trojan horse, only the plan was for Nader to come to it, not the other way around.

Inside the cockpit with Mendoza, Sam knew that Abbie sweltered beneath a Kevlar vest like the rest of them. He also knew that if she so much as set a foot out of the cabin, he'd sprint across the tarmac and haul her back inside himself. He trusted Mendoza to lift the hell out of there if the action got too hot and get her to safety.

It was almost over. The plan was straight up and clean. The boys had handled Nader's advance team of mercs. They were either dead or trussed up like slaughter chickens, piled up behind the hangar.

"Easy as taking your poker money," Doc had reported to Sam after Mendoza had returned to La Entrada, picked up Sam and Abbie, and brought them back to the airstrip.

"So let's keep things easy," Sam had said, and the four of them decided on defensive positions. While Sam hadn't wanted Abbie more than touching distance away from him, he needed to be mobile in case Nader had any other tricks up his sleeve. He also knew that as soon as Nader saw him, Sam would become more of a target than Abbie, which meant she needed to be as far away from him as possible. He didn't want to draw fire her way.

"Whatever you do, Raphael, do *not* let her out of the chopper," Sam whispered into his mic as Nader stood by the front fender of the Lincoln Town Car. Muhammad, waiting for the mountain.

He was going to have a long wait.

Sam watched the cocky sonofabitch. Nader would be shaking in his Italian loafers if he knew what had happened to his men.

"It's exceedingly warm, Miss Hughes," Nader shouted above the engine noise. "Can we get this over with, please?"

"Yeah." Sam stepped out from behind the Cessna, his M-16 butted up against his shoulder, his sites honed in the center of Nader's chest. "Let's get this over with."

"You!" Rattled Nader backed toward the driver's side door.

"Yeah. Me. And it's me you'll deal with this time, not a defenseless woman."

Nader's eyes went wild with fear. With good reason. There was nothing Sam wanted to do more than squeeze the trigger. Empty a thirty-round magazine into the hole where Nader was supposed to have a heart. He sensed Doc behind him, covering his six.

"What's the matter, Nader? Not as much fun manning the front line as it is delegating?" So much for chitchat. It was time to cut to the chase. Time for Nader to know he was about to breathe his last breath.

"How much did it cost you to pay someone to blow up my sister?"

"That . . . that was not my doing."

A red haze filtered over Sam's vision. "Lie again, you slimy maggot. Give me a reason to kill you one bullet at a time."

Hatred sucked at his control, dragging him toward a sinkhole of rage so primal he saw himself committing acts against this man even he would label atrocities.

Every breathing cell wanted to make Nader pay in blood for stealing breath and life from his little sister.

For the guilt that lashed at Sam's conscience like saber slices.

His heart slammed. His hands shook as he sighted down the barrel, his finger pressed against the side of the trigger guard, half an inch away from dropping the hammer. His breath stalled as he watched Nader inch closer to the driver's door. A round through the kneecap would be a good start. Nader would squeal like a pig, squirm in the dirt like a snake. Sam would enjoy every howl of anguish. Relish the thought of leaving him to bake and rot under the sun while vultures picked at his bones.

"Hit the dirt, asshole. Face-first," Sam ordered just as the sound of a fast-moving vehicle registered.

"Company," Doc said. "Jesus H. Christ!" he added as three pickup trucks, loaded with shooters, flew over the hill to the south and barreled down the runway toward them.

"What the fuck?" Doc added as two Jeeps, one of them firing rounds from a belt-fed machine gun kicked up dust, converged from the other direction. "What the hell's going on?"

What was going on was that in thirty more seconds they were going to be trapped.

"Get her out of there!" Sam roared into the mic.

Mendoza was already on it. He revved up the engine to full throttle as the encroaching vehicles moved in fast, sandwiching the chopper between them.

Sam turned back to Nader as he dove inside the Town Car. He pumped a burst into the car but Nader was already cranking the key.

The machine gun rattled from a distance. Savage, on the roof, answered back with the M-249. Abbie and Mendoza were about to get caught in the crossfire. The chopper lifted a couple of inches off the ground, then dropped like a stone.

"Shit," Doc swore. "They took a hit in the tail rotor."

Which meant the bird wasn't going anywhere. Nader hit the gas and Sam saw his chance at taking him down slipping away. In the end, there was only one decision to make.

He had to get to Abbie. She was more important than Nader. Mendoza could make a break for it, but she was a sitting duck.

He shot toward the chopper.

Doc caught up with him, grabbed Sam by the vest and dragged him back toward the hangar. "Are you fucking nuts?" he yelled as he shoved Sam for cover.

Yeah. He was. And Doc was right. Getting killed wasn't going to help Abbie.

From the corner of his eye he saw the Town Car cut a tight circle, gun it for the road. He turned around backward, lifted the M-16 again, sprayed the car with another round of bullets.

The two tires on the driver's side deflated like a failed soufflé. The vehicle swerved, fishtailed, but re-covered as Nader floored it. Limping on two wheels and two hubs, the Lincoln shot out onto the road.

"Sonofabitch," Sam swore as Nader drove away. He ducked behind the open door of the hangar, turned his attention back to the gunman bearing down on the chopper.

"We've got to get them out of there. Savage," he yelled into the mic. "Pick your time, then take out whichever Jeep gets to the chopper first.

"Cover me," he barked at Doc. It was now or never.

"Fuck that." Doc snagged him by the vest again, jerked him back to the cover of the hangar. "You go out there now, you come back a sprinkler. And Gawd-damn—look. Are you seeing what I think *I'm* seeing?"

"What are you talking about?"

"Who the hell's shooting at who?"

Sam glared from Doc to the airstrip. Assessed the action. "Sonofabitch. Are those idiots shooting at each other?"

They were, he realized, putting it together. "Fox. Has to be Fox's men in the trucks."

"And they're putting it to Nader's guns in the Jeeps."

"How the hell did Fox know this was coming down?"

They both ducked as stray rifle fire peppered a line of holes in the metal siding above their heads.

"Hell, Fox had a mole in one of Nader's camps. Wouldn't put it past him to have 'em dug in all over."

Doc was probably right. Mercs hired out for the highest dollar. It was a cutthroat and incestuous community. Loyalty was as foreign a concept as trust.

"I've got to get to Abbie." Sam sized up the chaos. Pickups with shooters firing AK's were circling the Jeeps like wolves. The wolves were barking back. The staccato rattle of Nader's machine gunner ate bites out of the dirt, the chopper, and the racing trucks.

"Savage," Sam yelled.

"Yo."

"I need one of those Jeeps."

"All you had to do was ask."

Behind Sam, Doc's M-16 fired off three burst rounds of 5.56 NATO ammo, the rifle's distinct *pop-pop-pop* discernible, even in the melee, from the heavier thuds of the AK-47 yammering away from the back of the moving truck.

Through the roar of bullets ricocheting and whizzing in the air came the sound of the M-249 rattling through a belt of cartridges as Savage took aim at the closest Jeep.

"And he scores!" Doc hooted as Savage shattered the windshield of the Jeep. Two men tumbled out of the back and ran for cover. The Jeep came to a screeching stop twenty yards from the hangar. Realizing the vehicle had become a bullet magnet, the driver unassed the Jeep and ran like hell.

Sam didn't bother to announce his plans this time. He took off running before Doc could stop him, knowing he'd lay down fire and cover him.

Hunched low, Sam zigzagged a path toward the Jeep while from the hangar roof, Savage swept the ground ahead of him with a barrage of firepower, clearing the way. Sam dove the final two yards to the vehicle, wrenched open the passenger door, and jerked the injured shooter out. He hadn't yet hit the ground when Sam piled inside, slid behind the wheel, and gunned it.

Dirt flew behind spinning tires as he arrowed toward the trapped chopper, hunching low over the steering wheel as bullets flew around him. He skidded to a stop by the cockpit door.

"Thought I was going to miss tee time," Mendoza groused as he helped Abbie out onto the skid. Sam jerked her into the front seat beside him. Mendoza bailed into the back.

"Is there anyone who *wasn't* invited to this party?" Mendoza grumbled, aiming his M-4 and firing a burst toward an approaching truck as Sam laid rubber and shot back toward the hangar.

"Can you guys handle this?" Sam braked to a screeching stop by the hangar so Mendoza could bail out.

"Can a fish fucking swim?" Mendoza joined Doc, who gave Sam a thumbs-up.

Sam hit the gas and took off after Nader.

23

Sam jammed on the gas pedal and roared down the dirt road following Nader's dust trail.

"Buckle up!"

He didn't have to tell Abbie twice. She was white-knuckling it with her grip on the dash beside him.

"And watch out for the glass," he shouted above the wind whipping through what had once been a wind-shield. Glass shards flew, dust swirled around inside the cab as Abbie's hair whipped around her head.

Her hands were shaking as she dutifully reached for the seat belt.

Adrenaline. Fear. Sam knew both reactions well. If he'd felt safe leaving her with the guys, he would have, but the truth was, he wanted her where he could see her.

"What happened back there?"

He squinted against the wind. "Best guess—Fox also had an agenda for Nader."

The seat belt kept her from hitting the roof when they flew over a bump. "That was Fox?"

"Looks that way."

"What about the guys?" She glanced behind them. Sam checked the side mirrors. Pickups had surrounded the remaining Jeeps. "Are they going to be okay?"

"My money's on them." His money was always on them.

Jaw set, he closed in on the dust boiling down the road like a jet trail. Punched harder on the gas.

"I see the car," Abbie said, holding her hair back from her eyes.

"Hold on."

Face grim, Sam roared up behind the Lincoln. "Hold on!" he repeated, then rammed the Lincoln's bumper.

The impact sent a bone-jarring shock through his hands, all the way to his shoulders.

He stomped down on the gas again.

Rammed the Lincoln again. The Lincoln fishtailed, righted itself, and sped on, sparks flying as the car's belly skidded against the dirt on the driver's side where the bare hubs barely kept it afloat.

Beside him, Abbie gasped but, to her credit, didn't scream, curse, or rail at him to back off.

Eyes dead ahead, Sam backed off, put more distance between the vehicles. Satisfied he had a good running start, he punched it one more time.

"Brace yourself."

"Oh, God," Abbie murmured when he pulled up alongside the Town Car, keeping pace at around forty miles per until the Jeep's front wheels were aligned with the Lincoln's rear driver's side wheel.

When they were within inches of each other, Sam steered sharply into the Town Car. The PIT maneuver worked where ramming hadn't. The Lincoln's rear wheels lost traction, started to skid. Sam abruptly braked, nosed the Jeep clear, and fought for control as the Lincoln swerved, spun out, then shot toward the ditch in a cloud of dust and exhaust and rammed, nose first, into the far side.

Where it stopped. Dead still, road dust billowing around it.

Sam tore up to the Lincoln.

"Do not get out of this vehicle," he ordered, grabbing his M-16 and sprinting toward Nader's disabled Town Car.

The driver's door of the Lincoln shot open and Nader stumbled out. Blood covered his face. His left arm hung at a grotesque angle, clearly broken. He leaned against his right side, struggling to stay on his feet.

Sam vowed he was not going to let Nader walk away alive this time. He lifted the rifle. Sighted down the barrel. Positioned his finger on the trigger—and heard the voices roar through his head.

The voice of his sister, screaming in pain, burning to death in a fiery blast. The voice of little Tina crying herself to sleep at night. The voice of his father. *"You can't not do this."*

Nader dropped to his knees. "Don't kill me. Please, I beg you. Please. I'm unarmed. Don't kill me." He was crying now. Pathetic, broken. "I have money. More money than you could ever imagine. I can pay you."

Fuck him. Do it! A new voice this time. His own voice. *Kill him! Don't make your family go through the agony of reliving Terri's death at a trial. Don't take the chance that this sick fuck will buy his way out of what he's done.*

"Please, I beg you, please. Have mercy."

Do it! Do it!

Sam's finger tightened on the trigger. He drew a bead on the spot between Nader's snake eyes.

Yet there he stood. Frozen. Wanting, gut deep, to waste this piece of human garbage and rid the world of his brutal existence.

But something made him hold his fire.

Something human, he realized, that tugged him away from the abyss. Something that delineated him from the likes of men like Nader who could kill in cold blood and sleep like a baby in spite of it.

He killed your sister in cold blood. He deserves to die that way.

He lifted the rifle again.

Watched the pathetic bastard mewl and beg like a damn baby.

Be careful in the company of monsters that you don't become one.

Words Sam had lived by. A warning from Nate Black. His CO. His former boss.

He couldn't do it.

He just couldn't do it. He could not reduce himself

to cold-blooded murder. He could not become a monster like the one sniveling and broken before him.

Swearing under his breath, he eased off the trigger.

He lowered the gun. Covered his face with his hand. Realized his cheeks were wet. Didn't know whether to congratulate or hate himself for having just enough humanity left to stand down.

He lowered his head, breathed deep.

"Sam!"

Abbie's scream snapped his head up, just in time to see Nader push away from the car and lift a gun in his right hand.

Instinct. Muscle memory. The will to survive.

All three took over. Sam raised the M-16, squeezed the trigger. Heard a succession of triple pops as he fired. Kept on firing.

He felt the rifle recoil in his hands even after the gunshots echoed to silence and the brass quit spitting to the *click, click, click* of the empty the rifle. Was aware of Nader's body jump, slump, then fall over before it even registered that he'd pulled the trigger.

Dead.

The bastard was finally dead.

Abbie rushed up beside him. Threw her arms around him.

He wrapped an arm around her, held her tight, breathed deep. It was over.

Or maybe not.

His head came up.

The sound of a fast-approaching vehicle spun him around. A pickup. Full of muscle and guns.

With Desmond Fox himself riding shotgun.

Sam shoved Abbie behind him, stood his ground as the truck slowed, crawled to a stop.

Sam couldn't do a damn thing but stand there, knowing his magazine was empty.

Fox looked from Sam to Nader, where Nader lay dead in the ditch.

He smiled. Turned that sinister smile on Sam. "*Bien hecho.*" Well done.

Still smiling, he ordered his driver to move on. As they rolled by, Fox made a gun with his thumb and forefinger. He pointed it at Sam's head. Pulled an imaginary trigger. "*La próxima vez.*" Next time.

"Jesus." Abbie inched out from behind him as they stood there, watching the truck drive away, followed by the rest of Fox's entourage. "What just happened?"

"Fox just granted me a reprieve."

The death of Nader—Fox's blood enemy—had been the catalyst. The warning that Fox would kill Sam "next time" they met was a gesture of appreciation.

The BOIs pulled up a few minutes later.

"We going after him?" Savage was still juiced on adrenaline from the action on the airstrip and ready to rock and roll.

Sam shook his head. He'd had enough. And the book on Fox told him the only reason Fox wanted the diamonds was because Nader wanted them. As long as the diamonds were returned to Honduras, they wouldn't be hearing from Fox anytime soon.

He pulled Abbie close, hugged her hard against him, and stared at Nader's body over the top of her head.

In that moment, he physically felt the cloud that had been casting a huge, dark shadow over his head start to dissipate.

24

Rancho Royale

"Uncle Sam!" When Tina spotted Sam across the driveway, she took off at a dead run and launched herself at him with the velocity and unerring accuracy of a guided missile.

"Whoa there, cowgirl," he laughed, scooping her into his arms and swinging her in a circle.

"I missed you so much," she declared with the uncensored emotion and innocence of a child. She clung to him, arms locked around his neck, her little legs wrapped around his waist.

"Me, too, sweetie," he murmured, savoring the sweet little-girl scent as he buried his face against her hair.

Over the top of her head, Sam saw his dad.

Tom Lang's face was expressionless, yet asked a hundred questions.

Sam met his dad's eyes, nodded. *It's done.*

His dad compressed his lips. He squared his shoulders, nodded back, his relief and thanks relayed in those minimal yet meaningful gestures.

"So what'd you bring me?" Tina asked on a giggle.

Sam held his dad's gaze for a moment longer, a world of emotions exchanged in that one prolonged look. Then he turned back to Tina, tickled her until she shrieked with laughter.

"What makes you think I brought you anything?" he teased as he set her down, then dug into his go bag for the new boots he'd picked up on a whim at the airport after they'd landed.

"'Cause you love me," she stated with a conviction that filled his chest with a love he couldn't quantify or contain.

"You got that right," he agreed, then laughed out loud when she hugged the boots to her chest.

"Just what I always wanted."

Las Vegas

"How's he doing?"

Abbie shut the guest bedroom door quietly behind her and joined Crystal in the living room. "Today? Not so good."

Abbie was doing her best not to worry about Cory. And Cory was doing his best to convince her that she had nothing to worry about. A tough trick when he'd spent most of the time since they'd come home in bed.

"They're having a hard time knocking out the infection but his temp's down a little today and his color is better."

"What do the doctors say?"

Abbie sank down on her sofa, lifted the glass of wine

Crystal had poured for her, sipped. "To be patient. That he'll be fine. Thanks," she added as an afterthought, lifting the glass so Crystal would know that Abbie appreciated her being here and taking care of her.

"Thank *you*." Crystal lifted her own glass with a grin. "It's your wine. And mighty fine wine, I might add."

Abbie closed her eyes, let her head fall back on the sofa cushion. "I feel like I could sleep for a month."

"All that G.I. Jane stuff wore you down, did it?"

Abbie smiled. Yeah, it had worn her down. So much so that something was long overdue. "Crystal," she said, sobering, "I've never taken the time to thank you."

They'd talked at length since Abbie had gotten back two days ago—mostly on the phone—about what had happened in Honduras, but Crystal had been hungry for details and Abbie had felt obliged to fill her in. Thanking her for what she'd done was way past due.

"For playing hide-and-seek with the gay cop cowboy?" Crystal chuckled. "Piece of cake. I loved leading the pretty boy around by the nose."

Yesterday, Crystal had given Reed the location and the key to a locker at the bus terminal where she'd hidden the diamonds. Sam told her that the necklace was being transported back to Honduras via a special government courier, where it would again be displayed in the National Museum.

"I don't doubt that," Abbie agreed, "but I was referring to what you did for me, no questions asked." Abbie's eyes filled with gratitude. "Cory could be dead right now if you hadn't stuck your neck out for me."

Uncomfortable with genuine displays of affection, Crystal, being Crystal, shrugged it off. "That's what friends are for, babe. Oh, God. I sound just like some sappy greeting card—or an old Dionne Warwick song. Give me a minute. The melody's coming to me."

"Fine." Abbie sat forward. She reached out, covered Crystal's hand with hers. Squeezed. "Brush it off, but I can't. I owe you. Cory owes you. I'm so lucky to have you on my team."

Close to giving in to the mist brimming in her own eyes, Crystal shot off the chair. "I'll bill ya. Better yet, I'll take payment in wine. More?"

Abbie nodded, sank back into the sofa as Crystal walked into the kitchen after the open bottle of Pinot Grigio, content to let her friend step and fetch for her.

She had figured she would sleep like a log when she got back to her own bed. Instead, she'd been restless. Edgy. Plagued with nightmares.

Too many scenarios to count. None she wanted to dwell on. On top of everything else, thoughts of Sam kept her awake. Kept her wondering what was going on with him. With them.

He'd called. Three times yesterday. Twice so far today. Checking on her. Checking on Cory. Making certain she had what she needed. Alluding to their need to "talk." The "talk" they were going to have tonight when he finally came to see her. She'd been trying to stall a bad feeling about that talk. Alternately battled back the worry that he might be planning to tell her good-bye and chastising herself for her insecurity.

"So . . ." Crystal waltzed back into the living room, bottle in hand. "What was it like? Two magical, fun-filled days in sunny, sweltering Honduras dodging bullets and chasing bad guys? With four good guys as bodyguards. They *were* good guys, right?" she added, refilling both of their glasses.

"Yeah," Abbie said, admonishing herself again for looking for problems with Sam where problems didn't exist. "They were good guys."

She thought of Doc—tall, lean, all easy smiles, healing hands. Mendoza—the gorgeous Nascar-wannabe Latino who was constantly humming. And Savage—the big bear of a man who, she suspected, had been as surprised as she'd been that they'd grown to like and respect each other.

All three of them had hugged her good-bye when they'd parted ways in San Pedro Sula. And damn, if she hadn't gotten a little teary-eyed.

"I still haven't grasped who they are. What they do."

Abbie hadn't either. Not exactly. "All I know is that they're based out of Argentina. That Sam used to work with them. I think it's some private contract company—like Blackwater, you know—only what they do is a little off the grid. Kind of 'don't ask, don't tell' stuff. The only thing I know for certain is that I wouldn't want to be on their bad side. These guys know what they're doing."

"And they were after this Nader person even before Cory got involved?"

Abbie nodded. Even though it was Crystal, she chose not to tell her about Sam's connection. His loss was just that. His loss. It was private. While Crystal would sympathize and commiserate, it wasn't Abbie's place to tell the story.

"So, what happens now?" Crystal tucked her feet up under her as she settled deeper into the easy chair.

"I'm hoping that once the Honduran government gets the diamonds back, it will all go away."

"You mean Cory's involvement."

"Yeah. Look. I know he wasn't completely innocent in this, but I also know he got sucked into something, got in over his head and couldn't find a way out."

She knew everything about what had happened now. When Cory was awake, they talked. He'd told her everything over the past couple of days.

"You don't have to defend him to me, Abbie. Cory's basically a good kid. I know that."

Crystal also knew what Cory had been through growing up.

"Anyway, I just want to put it behind us."

Crystal stared at the far wall, nodded. "So. Are you ever going to tell me what happened with Sam down there?"

Abbie swirled her wine, watched the clear, champagne-colored liquid settle, wishing she could shake an uneasy feeling about that "talk" Sam wanted to have.

She thought back to those moments of idyllic paradise they'd carved out in the midst of chaos.

Is this real?

That remained the money question.

"News at ten," she said, aware that Crystal was still waiting. "Maybe I'll know the answer then."

Crystal hadn't been gone fifteen minutes when Abbie heard the guest room door open. She looked up from the sofa to see Cory walk carefully into the living room. "Hey sweetie, how you doing?"

His eyes were hollow; except for the pink the fever put in his cheeks, he was as pale as milk. And thin. Lord, she thought, her heart aching for him, he was so thin.

"I'm okay," he said and, apparently exhausted, sank down on her leather chair.

"And I'm Anne, Queen of Scots," she said with a soft smile. "Can I get you anything?"

He shook his head. "I'm okay. Thanks."

His eyes were sad and serious when he met hers.

"What?" she asked, leaning forward. "You're in pain, aren't you? Maybe it's time for more medi—"

"No." He cut her off sharply, then looked apologetic. "No, sis. I'm okay. A royal screwup, but I'm okay."

Her defense was instant and knee-jerk. "You're not a screwup."

"No? Then why did I almost get you killed because of my mess?"

"You didn't mean for any of it to happen."

"I never mean for anything to happen, but that doesn't stop me from making a mess of my life, does it? And now I've made a mess of yours."

"I'm fine, Cory. Everything is fine."

"Yeah, well, no. It's not. I've done nothing but give you grief my whole life. You don't deserve it. And I don't deserve you."

"So you're saying that if the shoe was on the other foot, you wouldn't help me out?"

"See, that's the difference between you and me. You'd never put yourself in that position. You're too stable, too solid. Too . . . good," he finished finally.

She got down on her knees in front of him, gently covered his poor, bandaged hand with hers. "He did this to you, you know. Our father. But he was wrong, Cory. You're good and you're smart and you're worth one hundred of him."

Tears filled his eyes. "Maybe it's time I start proving you right instead of always managing to prove you wrong."

She brushed the hair back from his forehead. "You don't have to prove anything."

"I do," he said, nodding slowly. "I really, really do. I'm going to make you proud of me, Abbie. I don't know how yet but it's going to happen. You're looking at a new leaf here."

She smiled at that. "New leaf, huh?"

"You know what I mean. I'm going to get my act together."

Abbie had never seen him like this. And she didn't doubt that he meant every word he said.

"I've been thinking . . . maybe I should take some classes."

She nodded, but felt the need to caution him. "Because you think that's what I want you to do or because it's what you want to do?"

"A little of both, maybe. But mostly for me. I'm not getting ahead doing things my way; maybe it's time to try it your way."

"Here's to new leaves then."

He finally smiled, then became very sober again. "I love you, Abbie."

For the first time she could remember, when she looked at him, she didn't see that wounded little boy. She saw a young man. A man who finally understood that his destiny was in his own hands. "Works out great then, because I love you, too."

"I think I might miss that five o'clock shadow," Abbie said when Sam stepped through her front door that night.

What she missed was him. He looked amazing. As always. His face was clean-shaven. His shirt was white, his jeans crisply creased.

Wrangler butts drive me nuts.

Why that little ditty was running through her head, she didn't know.

Or maybe she did.

She was scared. Scared that it *hadn't* been real and

that was what Sam had come here to tell her. Scared because she wanted to fling herself into his arms and kiss him until they were both naked but the look in his eyes stopped her.

"You look tired," he said. "Not sleeping?"

"Not so much, no," she admitted, but stopped short of adding, *and you're the reason why*.

"It'll get better," he said. "How's the arm?"

Okay. They were going to do chitchat. It rang of avoidance. The scare factor inched up the charts.

"The arm is fine."

"How's Cory doing?" he asked as she motioned him to make himself comfortable.

Okay. She gave him props for being concerned and stalled the panic. "He actually had a huge turnaround tonight. I'd about given up on him but amazingly, his fever finally broke. He's in the shower right now."

That much, at least, was a relief. It had been only six hours since Crystal had left and Cory's transformation had been amazing. Abbie had even slipped out of the house for an hour or so, so she could stock the kitchen. She'd fed Cory lasagna tonight—his favorite—and he'd managed to eat and keep it down.

So yeah. That was a relief. Just like their little talk was a relief. This uneasy politeness Sam was displaying was not.

"I need some wine," she said abruptly when the silence and the awkwardness between them got the best of her. "Can I get you some?"

"Sure."

Hokay. Short. Succinct.

What was happening here? More to the point, what *wasn't* happening?

He hadn't reached for her. Hadn't drawn her against him. Hadn't kissed her.

Why wasn't *that* happening?

It was killing her.

Her hands shook as she reached for an unopened bottle of Pinot. She knew she shouldn't have any more wine today. She'd have a headache the size of a truck in the morning and it would be her own damn fault.

Or it would be Sam's fault because try as she might, at this point she couldn't fathom an end to this day that didn't involve her going to bed—alone—eyes red from crying.

"You are such a girl," she muttered and tugged the cork out of the bottle.

"Ask him. Just ask him. Get it over with."

That, of course, was the problem. She was afraid it was over between them.

"So just bite the bullet."

Bite the bullet. Dodge the bullet. Shoot the bullet.

What had once been clichés held deep meaning to her now. She'd done them all.

And she was stalling.

"Hey," she said, surprised to see Cory when she finally gathered the nerve to return to the living room with the wine. "How you doing, sweetie?"

"Sit down, Abbie," Sam said, taking the glasses from her.

That's when she noticed the looks on both men's faces.

Looks that told her she wasn't going to like what came next. Looks that told her she'd better sit down or her knees might give out on her.

"What's going on?"

Cory dropped down on the arm of the sofa beside her. "I'm going to turn myself in to the feds tomorrow."

If Sam hadn't relieved her of the wineglass, she would have dropped it. "What . . . what are you talking about?"

Cory glanced at Sam, who nodded in encouragement. "I screwed up, Abbie. I need to make it right."

"You already have," she countered, feeling panic rise like the blood that flooded her cheeks. "Sweetie, you've been punished enough."

She carefully gathered his bandaged hand into hers. "Everyone's got what they want. You got Nader," she said, turning to Sam. "You recovered the necklace. There's no point to this. There's no need."

"The point is, it's the right thing to do," Cory said soberly. "Sam and I, we talked about it."

"Sam?" She glanced from Cory to Sam, who watched them soberly. "When did you talk to Sam?"

"This afternoon," Sam answered.

"While you were out getting groceries," Cory added. She started shaking, felt her chest tighten as her body reacted to the anger, the disappointment, the blow of yet one more Sam Lang betrayal. "How could you do this? How could you talk him into doing this?"

"I didn't talk him into anything. He's a man, not a boy, Abbie," Sam said carefully. "He's responsible for his own decisions. He's made plenty of wrong ones. Let him make the right one."

"The right one?" She felt the last vestige of hope break down between them. "You mean the one that means he'll end up in prison?"

"I know you don't have any reason to, but will you just trust me on this one? Trust that it will be okay?"

"You are so right." She couldn't keep the accusation from her voice. "I don't have a reason in hell to trust you. That's the biggest blow of all. I *wanted* to. I thought . . . God, I was so stupid. You made me want to believe in . . . in everything," she finished angrily. "And here, all you ever wanted was . . . what? What else *do* you want, Sam? Is this your idea of some kind of poetic justice? You lost your sister? Now I have to lose my brother to make it right?"

Sam's face drained of all color. The pain that filled his eyes before he could check it told her how deep she'd just cut him.

Oh, God. It was a horrible thing to say. But she was scared. Like she'd sensed she should be scared. Scared that something terrible was going to happen.

Something terrible had.

She was going to lose Cory.

As Sam rose slowly and headed for the door, she understood that, once and for all, she'd lost him, too.

The next morning, she felt the loss full bore. She watched with hollow eyes as two men who identified themselves as DEA officers arrived at the house to take Cory away.

"So, you planning on brooding for the rest of your natural life," Reed badgered as he turned into the parking lot of the Federal Building in Vegas, "or you gonna do something about it?"

Sam stared straight through the windshield, not bothering to look at Reed, who'd gone Hollywood with his designer shades and rented convertible. "You know, one of these days, you're going to cross that line."

"The one where you beat the hell outta me?"

"That would be the one."

Reed snorted and cruised the lot searching for a parking spot. "As if you could."

As if he would, Sam thought. As annoying as Reed was, Sam couldn't see himself ever getting pissed enough to take him to task.

"So are you?" Reed persisted.

"Am I what?" Sam didn't attempt to hide his annoyance—not that it stopped Reed.

"Going after Abbie Hughes."

"Got a feeling that bridge has already been burned."

Abbie might forgive him for what he'd done to her, but she'd never forgive him if Cory ended up behind bars.

That was what this morning was about. Not only was the DEA interested in what Cory Hughes had to say about Fredrick Nader's operations, a few more players had pulled on jerseys and helmets and trotted out onto the field. CIA. DIA. DHS. A handful of others. Sam expected all the alphabet agency reps to show up in force. Expected it because he'd put in the calls himself. If Interpol had had a boot on the ground or notice hadn't been so short, they'd have been here, too.

"Yo." Sam glanced up, realized Reed was already out of the car and waiting for him. "You going in or are you gonna stay out here and work on your tan?"

Sam shouldered open the passenger door and headed for the building, relieved when he saw the woman standing on the concrete steps.

"Hello, Sam." Ann Tompkins smiled, hugged him back when he embraced her. "Johnny," she added with a sparkling grin as she reached for his hand over Sam's shoulder.

"Ann. Been a long time."

"Too long," she agreed. "Robert and I have missed you."

"I can understand you missing me, Annie," Reed said with a grin, "but miss Sam? Can't figure that one."

Ann laughed and turned back to Sam. "Let's get this nasty business taken care of, okay?"

"Yeah, let's," Sam managed, not having realized how humbled he would feel by her presence. Or how much relief her calm confidence would inspire in him.

"Thank you," he said, stopping her when she would have turned away.

The words were inadequate at best.

She touched a hand to his cheek. Smiled tenderly. "You're family, Sam. You don't need to thank me."

Then she put on her game face and marched into the building.

25

It was a typical government office, Abbie thought as she sat beside Cory at a long table in the front of a large, windowless room.

Industrial gray paint on the walls. Office furniture circa "several years ago," before budget crunches bit into the workings of the great bureaucracy. The suits lined up around the table were black.

Only Crystal, sitting alone at the back of the room, her wild red hair spiked and shining, her beaded earrings dangling, provided a splash of color in the otherwise black and gray environment.

Abbie wanted this over with, was impatient for it to start. While escorting Cory to a government car earlier this morning, the DEA agent had told Abbie they were waiting for someone else to arrive for "an informal interview."

"He's not being arrested?"

"No, ma'am. Not at this time."

Which implied that he would be at some point.

"I want to come with him."

"You're more than welcome to attend," the agent had said. He gave her his card with the address and told her she could follow them in her own vehicle.

She'd glanced at the card.

"Agent Larson, does my brother need a lawyer?"

"I already told you," Cory had said, ducking into the backseat of the car. "I don't want a lawyer."

Because he couldn't afford one. Abbie knew that was his reason. And because he didn't want her paying for one out of her own limited reserves.

Other than her divorce lawyer, who wasn't even with the firm anymore according to the names on the letter accompanying her settlement payment, Abbie didn't know who to call anyway. But she would find one if necessary. She glanced around the room at the hard faces, waiting in stoic silence. If this interview started smacking of inquest and even a hint of the word *criminal* came up, she was getting Cory representation whether he wanted it or not.

She nodded at Crystal, bless her, who had insisted on coming along for moral support. Then she glanced around the table again. Ordinary-looking men with extraordinary responsibilities and enough government muscle to send Cory to prison for a very long time.

It was scary as hell to be a civilian in the midst of all this federal bureaucracy. So scary that Abbie had already forgotten their names, just as in the blur of nerves and concern for Cory, she'd forget their faces when this was over. They'd all introduced themselves, along with the names of the agencies they represented. DEA: Drug Enforcement Agency. DHS: Department of Homeland Security. DIA: Defense Intelligence Agency. ATF: Alcohol, Tobacco and Firearms. FBI. CIA. Others she'd already lost in the fog of intimidation.

Beside her, Cory looked pale but steady. Steadier than she was, in fact, and not showing one bit of surprise when the door opened and a slim, middle-aged woman walked in followed by Sam Lang and Crystal's gay cop cowboy.

The room was still far from crowded but the addition of these two men suddenly filled up the space with their presence and sucked the air out of her lungs like a vacuum.

Abbie didn't know why it was such a shock, seeing Sam. The pain of it maybe, as much as the surprise.

It seemed, however, that she wasn't the only one in shock.

All around the table, the suits became inordinately still. The quiet mumblings screeched to a halt. Ties were straightened. Throats were cleared. And "what the hell?" looks were exchanged.

The woman walked straight to the head of the conference table and slapped down a briefcase. In that moment, it became very clear to Abbie that whoever she was, her presence had just invoked a major power shift. Regardless of the authority levels around the table, this woman was clearly in charge now.

"Gentlemen," the woman said by way of greeting, "let's cut to the chase, shall we? The Justice Department has declared Cory Hughes a protected witness. As

such, he's been granted full immunity from any and all
potential criminal charges as they relate to his association with one Fredrick Nader, now deceased. In exchange for this immunity, Mr. Hughes has agreed to
provide information critical to national security regarding Nader's network."

Abbie was dumbstruck. She glanced at Cory, who
remained motionless. Glanced at Sam, who relayed
nothing.

"We'll need to clear the room of everyone but the witness now," the woman said, her gaze landing on Abbie
with an encouraging nod. It was a nod that said, *Don't
worry. Everything is going to be fine.*

When she heard the rustle of movement, Abbie realized that Sam and Reed had both stood. It finally galva-
nized her into action. She rose too, squeezed Cory's
shoulder on her way by, and met the two men and
Crystal by the door.

"What just happened?" she asked, turning to Sam
for answers, instinctively knowing that he'd had a hand
in this.

He took her arm, steered her down the hall. "Come
on. Let's go get a cup of coffee and I'll tell you."

"Hey, wait up." Johnny sprinted to catch up with Crystal Debrowski as her sassy little hips sashayed across the
Federal Building parking lot.

Not that he'd expected anything different, but she
kept on walking.

He didn't care. Until Sam came back with their ride—

who knew how long that little "coffee break" with Abbie Hughes was going to take—Johnny had time to kill.

"Come on. Play nice," he said, catching up with Crystal by her car.

"Getting a little tired of you dogging my tail, golden boy."

Yeah, well, Johnny wished he could say the same thing, but the truth was, that sweet little tail had intrigued him for the better part of three days. He'd gotten kind of used to seeing it, and to reacting every time he did.

Hot. The pixie made him hot. Which so did not compute. She was not his type. Not even a little bit.

"One way to stop that," he said, crossing his arms over his chest and blocking her entry by leaning against her driver's side door.

She glowered up at him—all five feet or so of her. "Do tell."

He shot her his money grin. "Quit walking away, darlin'."

She squinted, then laughed like she couldn't believe what was happening. "No. You're not really coming on to me."

Well, yeah, he was. It sort of pissed him off that she thought it was funny. "And if I was?"

She grunted. "You'd be wasting your time and mine."

He frowned when a disturbing thought occurred to him. "You're not one of those girl-on-girl types, are you?"

This time she rolled her eyes. "You are unbelievable, but if that's what it takes to salvage your fragile

ego and get you off my back, then feel free to put whatever spin on it you want."

He felt more relief than insult. Would have been a
shame if she played for the other team, even though he
still hadn't figured out why he gave a rip.

It was a puzzle that was making him crazy.

"You're blocking my way," she pointed out unneces-
sarily, lifting a hand toward her car. "Do you mind?"

"Nah. I don't mind at all." He settled more com-
fortably against the door. "Got all the time in the
world. Beautiful day. I'm in the company of a beautiful woman—"

"Okay." She held up a hand like a stop sign, cutting
him off. "Just stop right there. I don't like you, Reed.
You're too pretty. You're too vain. And you're beyond
annoying."

He tilted his head, frowned. "No, really. Tell me
how you really feel."

She heaved a long-suffering breath. "What's it going
to take to get rid of you?"

"Have dinner with me."

"I'm not hungry."

"Then go to bed with me."

"I'm not *that* desperate."

"But you are desperate. Hey." He held up a hand
when she glared. "It was implied."

Little silver daggers shot out of her eyes.

"Okay. I'm not interested," she amended.

He was having fun. But this approach wasn't working, so he tried another tactic. "You're a good friend. To

show up for Abbie Hughes today. Not to mention going out on a limb for her like you did and hiding those diamonds. You could have gotten in a lot of trouble for that."

"And you care about this why?"

She had him there. "Damned if I know."

She tilted her head, studied him for a moment. Opened her mouth. Closed it. Finally shook her head. "I get off at eight."

He shot away from the car. "Really?"

"Just dinner," she clarified.

Oh. Well. "I knew that."

"Right," she said, sounding disgusted with herself as much as him. "Don't make me regret this."

"No, ma'am." Happy as hell, he stood aside and opened the car door for her. "See you at eight."

"You're buying," she informed him as she settled behind the wheel, cranked the key, and drove away.

"Damn," Johnny muttered, watching her go. "It might not be love, but it sure is fun."

He was still grinning when he checked his watch, then wandered back inside the Federal Building, found a seat in a row of chairs in the hall, and settled back for a little power nap while he waited for Sam to return.

"Her name is Ann Tompkins," Sam said when he and Abbie had settled into a booth across from each other in a diner a couple blocks from the Federal Building. "Ann's with the Justice Department. Deputy Attorney General's office."

Abbie sat back. Her head was still spinning—for a number of reasons. Sam's nearness was one of them. But this thing with Cory . . . she was mystified.

"Justice Department? Attorney General's office?"

Sam nodded. "She flew in last night from D.C." He glanced up at the waitress when she arrived with menus. "Just coffee," he said. "Two."

Abbie leaned forward, elbows on the table. "Why? Why is she doing this for Cory?"

Sam met her gaze, held it. "She's doing it for me. I asked her to intervene."

Abbie blinked. Leaned back. Stared.

Who was this man?

Who was this man that he could ask one of the highest-ranking officials in the United States government to drop what she was doing and fly across the country to help someone she didn't even know?

Abbie had thought she'd known. She'd thought she'd loved him. Thought she'd hated him. Thought she couldn't trust him. With her heart. With her brother's life.

I know you don't have any reason to . . . but will you just trust me on this one? Trust that it will be okay?

He'd asked for her trust. She'd not only refused, she'd lashed out at him using his sister's death as a weapon.

She should have known. And she should have trusted him. After all they'd been through together. After all they'd shared, she should have known he was a man of his word.

"Sam." She reached across the tabletop and covered

his big, scarred hands with hers. "I am so, so sorry for what I said to you yesterday. I'm sorry I didn't—"

"No." He cut her off, rubbed his thumb over the back of her hand. "It's okay. You were scared."

"It's not okay. I was horrible to you. What I said . . . it was inexcusable."

He shook his head, his dark eyes full of understanding. "You were scared," he repeated. "I'd have reacted the same way if I'd been in your shoes. Look, if I could have told you about Ann, about what was in the works, I would have. But it wasn't until the eleventh hour that I found out she'd been able to convince the AG to go for immunity. I didn't want to give you false hope if she couldn't make the threat of criminal charges go away."

"Who are you, Sam Lang?" She had to ask. She had to know as she clung to his hand like she clung to the hope that there might be a future for them after all.

"Long story." He leaned back when the waitress returned and filled their cups.

"I've got time." Time and amends to make.

"You know I was in the military," he began, reaching for her hand again.

She nodded and felt the tension of loss that had been clutched tightly in her chest since he'd walked out her door last night uncoil by slow degrees.

"Spec Ops," he went on. "Delta. That's when I was recruited to join a highly classified multibranch team. Task Force Mercy went places no one else could go. Made things happen no one else was authorized to do. We worked black—way under the radar.

"Anyway, Ann and Robert Tompkins's son, Bryan, was a team member. Helluva soldier," he added, and Abbie could see not only love and admiration in his eyes, but a burden.

"We lost Bry in Sierra Leone." He paused, breathed deep, and she understood, without asking, that Sam had been with Bryan Tompkins when he'd died.

"He was like a brother, you know? Hell, we were all brothers. And after . . . after his death, Ann and Robert invited the team to their home. Made it clear that Bry thought of us as family. Made it known that they thought of us as family, too."

He paused again, shrugged. "It was a little uncomfortable at first. I think they were trying to fill the void. Unconsciously, but, yeah, that's where they were coming from. But their sincerity, their openness . . . it resonated with all of us, you know? Doc, Mendoza, Savage, we all took it to heart. Ann and Robert and their daughter Steph, they eventually became like a second family. For some of the guys—like Reed—it became their only family."

"You've been with those guys that long?"

"Them and many others. Like I said. We were brothers. You didn't go through the things we'd gone through and walk away alone."

"So, that's when you became close with Ann Tompkins."

He nodded. "Yeah. She was a litigator in a high-profile law firm then. A few years ago she was asked to join the DOJ—Department of Justice," he clarified.

"And she can just do this? She can give Cory immunity because you asked her to?"

"Not without a compelling reason, no. Cory has information, Abbie."

"How can that be? He was—how did you put it? A low-level mule."

"Right, but still, he probably knows more about Nader's operation than he thinks. He's seen things, been places inside the organization; he can recognize faces, ID them as belonging to Nader's network.

"Look, Nader's been on the DOJ radar almost as long as bin Laden. Only with bin Laden we know he's behind the nine-eleven attacks. Nader was a sneaky bastard. He was also untouchable by legitimate government—U.S. or otherwise—because we couldn't pin him with anything, even though all fingers pointed his way."

"So that's where you came in? You and this agency you work for now?"

"Worked for," he corrected and again, Abbie detected a regret in his decision to leave the men he considered his brothers. "Yeah. The agency does a lot of contract work for Uncle. The kind of work where if they get tagged, no one in Washington will even admit to knowing the agency exists, let alone that we were on a government-sanctioned op."

Trust. There it was again. Only this time, Sam had trusted Abbie with information that was clearly confidential. The significance of his gesture was not lost on her. Neither was its importance.

"Anyway, with Nader out of the picture, DOJ and all

the alphabet agencies under it figure they've got a window of time where the organization is bound to be in
disarray. That window is now. There will be power
struggles. A lot of jockeying for position. People trying
to prove they've got the ability to take over the reins.
Someone's going to get reckless. Someone's going to
get careless. When they do, with Cory's help, we might
be able to tie them to Nader. And then, what typically
happens will be a domino effect as the big players start
to topple. Once one is tagged, the rest will follow. They
won't be able to rat each other out fast enough.

"That's why Cory is so important," he emphasized.
"And why Ann could authorize immunity for him in
exchange for his testimony."

"But he was willing to testify anyway," Abbie pointed
out.

"Yeah, well, we might have fudged on that a little.
Doesn't matter. Bottom line, with his help, we nail one
guy, tie him to a drug deal or an arms deal, and suddenly, this becomes an on-the-books op to take the organization down. The full force of the U.S. military and
half a dozen European countries can get on board, instead of a handful of guys operating black trying to do
the deed."

While it all made sense, there was something he'd
said that touched her to the core.

*"Yeah, well, we might have fudged on that a little.
Doesn't matter."*

"Fudging does matter," she said, tears filling her

eyes with love for this man. "You went out on a limb for him. That means you went out on a limb for me."

He met her eyes, held her gaze. "I'm about to go out on another one." He drew a deep breath, squeezed her hand so hard it hurt but in a very good way. "I love you, Abbie."

Yeah, she thought, letting the tears fall. She knew. She finally knew.

Dinner. All Crystal had agreed to was dinner. It begged the obvious question, then: So how had she ended up buck naked and tied to her own bed with flex cuffs?

What was she thinking?

She tested the cuffs with a series of angry yanks, swore under her breath when they didn't give, and glared at the ceiling. You couldn't teach stupid. She'd proven that in spades. For her, it just came natural.

"Dessert?"

She jerked her head toward the bedroom door. When she saw him standing there, wearing nothing but that devil-made-me-do-it grin and holding a carton of Ben & Jerry's and a spoon, she almost forgave herself for succumbing to Johnny Duane Reed's line of bull. And when he sauntered back into the room, amazing man parts dangling, six-pack abs flexing, she almost forgot why dessert would be a bigger mistake than dinner.

She looked away, too embarrassed to face him. "Untie me."

He eased a hip onto the bed, leaned across her, and

braced his palm on the mattress beside her shoulder, forcing her to look at him. "Now what would be the fun in that?"

Good God, he was gorgeous. Sex-tousled hair too long and too blond. Bedroom eyes too playful and too blue. Yeah, the golden boy was something. He also had the sexual proclivities of a fallen angel. And when he lowered his head and bussed his amazing lips over her swollen nipple, tickling her sensitive skin with his barely there mustache that matched his barely there beard, she forgot about flex cuffs, stupid mistakes, and the fact that she'd promised herself she'd never let this man near her or her bed.

"Umm," he murmured sucking lingeringly on her nipple before drawing away to smile lazily into her eyes. "About that dessert."

Abbie knelt above Sam in the shadows. Long, dark hair fell across her face. Slim, sleek thighs bracketed his ribs. Deep, husky sighs told him how good this was for her. How right, as she rode him fast and hard, then slow and sweet, taking him so deep inside he became a part of her.

"I love you," she whispered, leaning forward to kiss him, her swollen lips lavish and lush and desperately demanding. "I love you . . ."

He reached up, gently dragged the hair away from her face so he could see her eyes in the semidarkness of encroaching dusk. "Again."

"I love you," she murmured on a moan as she ground

herself against him, enriching the contact, arousing a desire to take her to levels he'd never taken her before.

"Let me," he whispered, gripping her waist in his hands and lifting her. "Let me . . ." He settled her over his mouth, parted her sex with his tongue and indulged.

She cried out when he kissed her there, trembled and fell forward, flattening open palms on the wall above the bed when he sucked. Cried his name when he slid a finger inside her, stroked to the rhythm of his tongue, and tipped her over the edge.

"Sam . . ."

Shivering sighs, fractured breaths, he recorded it all, would always remember the honeyed taste of her release, the silken tremors as she slid boneless to the bed beside him.

He caressed her bare hip with his thumb, loving the sight of her drifting on the backside of pleasure, coming down from the high with a catlike moan of contentment.

Gently shifting her to her back, he entered her, finessed her back to arousal with a slow glide and thrust, a steady build of that amazing, sucking friction that built and swelled and shot him over the edge when her climax convulsed around him like a tight, liquid fist.

"Oh, God," she murmured minutes later, still holding him close, absorbing his weight, her ankles linked around his hips in a staunch refusal to let him leave her body.

"Tell me it's always going to be like this," she whispered fiercely.

"It's always going to be like this," he promised and rolled them to their sides so she could draw a deep breath.

They lay that way for long, lazy moments. He loved watching her face. The heavy lashes lying against her cheeks. The swollen lips that even now, when he was done in and spent, made his cock twitch and swell inside her.

One corner of her mouth drew up in a crooked smile. "Already?"

He laughed. "What can I say? I've always been an overachiever."

She touched a hand to his face; her smile slowly faded. "I'm never going to doubt you again. Know that. I need you to know that."

He knew a lot of things now. Things he'd never known before Abbie.

"I know," he assured her, tucked her face into the curve of his throat and held her.

Held her close. Held her tight. Held her the way he would hold the most precious possession known to man.

Which was exactly what she was.

EPILOGUE

Richmond, Virginia, home of
Robert and Ann Tompkins
Two months later

Boundaries, wedding bands, and babies. Those three words had once spelled confinement to Sam Lang. But as he watched Abbie mix it up at the poker table with Doc, Savage, Reed, and Gabe Jones's wife, Jenna, confinement wasn't what came to mind.

Freedom. Peace. Contentment.

Life.

"Sam, can I top that off for you?"

Sam glanced up at Robert Tompkins, the host for tonight's festivities that included celebrating Ann and Robert's daughter, Stephanie's, birthday and Sam and Abbie's big leap.

Yeah. They'd done it. Love was a drug. High on it and the hope it brought to both of their lives, Sam and Abbie had gotten married a month ago. That the baby was due in a little less than seven months was a constant source of wonder and joy for Sam—and a little slip-up that had provided Reed with fodder for more one-liners than a T-shirt shop.

Sam glanced down at his beer. "I'm good, Robert. Thanks."

"I can see that." He clapped Sam on the back and started making the rounds with the pitcher of beer he'd drawn from the keg behind the bar. Sam took a deep draw from his glass, then elbowed back against the bar and observed the men who he would always consider his brothers, gathered in the Tompkinses' game room.

He'd taken Ann's scolding to heart. It had been too long since they'd all gotten together here in the Tompkinses' Richmond home. That's why Sam had put a shout-out to the BOIs and shamed them into showing up. Not that to a man they weren't all enjoying themselves. They were.

So were Ann and Robert. Watching Robert, laughing and joking with the BOIs, you'd never know he had once been counsel to the President of the United States. Or that Ann, restocking the buffet, had the brass and the balls to pull off what she had for Cory Hughes. Just like you'd never know that they must also still mourn the man who had brought the BOIs together.

Sam glanced up at the portrait of Bryan Tompkins hanging above the fireplace mantel. He lifted his glass in silent salute. Bryan "Babyface" Tompkins had died too young, just like Terri.

Like the Tompkinses, Sam mourned but he carried on. The woman laughing and slapping a celebratory high-five with that wild redhead Gabe Jones had married was the main reason why.

"Did you see that, Gabe?" Jenna yelled across the room. "We just beat Holliday, here, at his own game."

"They cheated," Doc accused, sliding an unlit stogie from one side of his mouth to the other. "You've got to know that they cheated."

"If it makes you feel better to think so," Abbie chimed in and grinned at Sam.

"Jones. Lang. Would you two get over here and control your women?" Colter groused, knowing he'd get the response that was coming.

"Control?" Seated on either side of him, Abbie and Jenna pounced on the word together.

Laughing at the dressing-down they proceeded to heap on Doc, Ann dusted off her hands as she came to Sam's side. "So, when's the baby due?"

"Hopefully not until after it finally sinks in that I'm going to be a father," he said, still awed by the prospect.

If their calculations were accurate, that baby was going to pop out about nine months and fifteen minutes after a very memorable shampoo.

"I've heard of water *births*," Abbie had said after they'd gotten over the shock of the EPT results, "but never water *conceptions*."

"Seems we beat a lot of odds on that trip," Sam had said, holding her close.

As he'd held her close—in his head, in his heart—every day since.

"You're going to be a great daddy," Ann assured him. "I've seen you with Tina. You're wonderful with her, Sam. She adores you."

Things were coming along there. Tina would always miss her mom and dad, but she was tough. Resilient. In no small way, Abbie had played a big part in helping Tina move on. Sam loved her for that and for the effort she made with Tina.

Watching Abbie now, so easy with his friends, remembering how she'd won over not only Tina but his mom and dad, made him realize how lucky he was.

Lucky to be alive. Lucky to have her. Lucky to have these guys.

Gabe Jones joined him at the bar. "You look like the cat that ate the canary."

Ain't that the truth, Sam thought, returning Gabe's grin. He lifted his glass toward the poker table. "Ever wonder what we did to deserve those two?" he asked with a nod toward Abbie and Jenna.

"Must have been all that good, clean living," Gabe said with a grunt as he eased a hip on the bar stool beside Sam.

Sam glanced at his friend, grateful to see him looking so healthy and happy, grateful that he was alive.

"So, how long before you're back on board?"

Gabe had taken a shrapnel hit in his calf in a bombing in Buenos Aires, and a raging infection had finally claimed his leg below the knee.

"Give me another few months," Gabe said after tipping his glass for a deep draw on his beer, "and I'll be back up to speed."

That didn't exactly answer Sam's question but it told him what he needed to know about Gabe's state of

mind. It would take more than the loss of a leg to slow
down the Archangel. Gabe was as tough as they came,
but Sam credited much of his recovery to the woman
currently beating the pants off Holliday at poker.

Gabe set his empty glass on the bar. "So. A baby,
huh?"

Sam grunted. "Helluva deal."

Gabe stood and clapped him on the back. "Better
you than me."

Sam laughed. "Just wait. I've seen the way this works.
Jenna'll get one look at the baby and she'll want one of
her own."

Gabe didn't say anything but Sam got the distinct
impression that the notion didn't settle all that badly on
the big man's shoulders.

"Time to take pity on Holliday," Gabe said and
headed for the poker table.

Sam watched him walk away, then glanced around
the room, listening to the laughter, the good-natured
ribbing.

Mendoza, interestingly, had Steph in a corner, talking in earnest about something that held her rapt attention. Savage and Greene cornered Gabe. Sam knew
they felt the same way he did. God, it was good to see
him again. Healthy, happy, back on board with the BOIs
after all those months of recovery.

Even the head of BOI, Nate Black, had shown up. A
little more introspective than Sam remembered, but
then Nate had always been more cerebral, more sub-
dued than the motley crew he employed.

Speaking of motley crews—Reed and Savage had moved on to the pool table. They were shooting a game of eight ball and trading insults on everything from pedigrees to sexual prowess.

"You can just feel the love, can't you?" Abbie said, grinning as she joined Sam at the bar, cuddling up against his side.

He looped an arm over her shoulders. Kissed the top of her head. "Poker game over?"

"Doc's just too easy to beat," she said, making sure Colter heard her.

"Under control," Doc suggested again with a meaningful nod as he glanced from Abbie to Sam.

"Tell you what." Sam met Doc's easy smile across the room. "You worry about controlling your own woman. Oh, wait. I forgot. You don't have one."

Sam's zinger was met with rounds of, "Whoa-ohs," from the guys who had tagged Sam's comeback as fighting words and were loving it.

"When did you get so smug, Lang?" Doc sputtered as he dealt cards around the table where Gabe and Nate had filled Savage's and Reed's empty seats.

Abbie squeezed him tight. "Yeah . . . when did you get so smug?"

"When I went to Vegas, placed my bet on a game of chance, and won me the purtiest woman in the world."

She rolled her eyes. "Okay, I'd have expected a corny line like that from Reed."

"Should I be wounded or flattered?"

"You should be tired," she said, affecting a sober look,

then whispering so only Sam could hear her. "Very, very tired. So tired, I'm thinking I should take you to bed. You need your rest."

"Oh, it's rest you have in mind, is it?"

She smiled that sultry, sexy smile that had him pushing away from the bar and taking her hand. "Or something."

"Well, it *is* getting late."

"Works for me," she said with a grin. "Now convince them."

"We're going to call it a night, guys. Abbie needs her rest."

"Then you'd better let her go to bed and you stay here," Reed suggested, looking damn pleased with himself.

"At the risk of repeating myself, you outlaws worry about your own women—imaginary or otherwise. You let me worry about mine."

"So much for fooling them," Abbie said as they walked alone down the hall toward the bedroom Ann had shown them when they'd arrived this morning.

"Yeah, well, you can fool some of the people all of the time, all of the people some of the time, but you can't fool—"

"Sam." She cut him off with a kiss when they reached the bedroom door. "When *did* you get so smug?"

He backed her up against the wall. Kissed her with all the love and life she made him feel. "That would have been right about the time I got the girl."

**Pocket Books proudly presents
the next novel in Cindy Gerard's
Black Ops, Inc. series**

WHISPER NO LIES

Coming on December 30, 2008

It was business as usual at Bali Hai Casino on the Vegas Strip, which meant that every nut job and wacko who could arrange bail was on the prowl. Crystal Debrowski figured that in her seven years working casino security she'd pretty much heard every come-on line written in the casino crawlers and lounge lizards handbook. That was because Crystal was what her friend, Abbie Hughes Lang, referred to as a man magnet and yeah, Crystal knew what men saw when they looked at her: Sex on a stick. Pixie features, spiky red hair, and fairy-green eyes. Showgirl breasts and round hips that swayed to a sultry beat when she walked and drew heartbreakers and bizarros from the four corners of the earth.

She'd been lied to, cheated on, hit on, and proposed to. Just when she'd thought she'd heard it all, though, this guy sweetened the pot. Her latest admirer—a Mr. Yao Long, according to the business card sporting an embossed Komodo dragon emblem—had come a long way for a letdown.

Wait until she told Abbie about this joker.

She glanced from Mr. Yao to the man who appeared to be his bodyguard. "I don't believe I caught *your* name."

"Wong Li."

A Jackie Chan look-alike, Wong appeared to do all of his boss's talking for him. Talking that included propositioning Crystal at a one-hundred-dollar-minimum blackjack table where she was filling in for one of her dealers who'd gone on a quick break. Crystal was about ninety-nine percent certain that the gist of Yao's offer ran somewhere in the neighborhood of: Him, lord and master. Her, concubine and sex slave.

"Please tell Mr. Yao thanks, but no thanks," she told Wong.

Because she perpetuated the sex kitten image—a girl had to have some fun, especially if that girl was thirty-one years old and lived in a world where few people took a petite woman seriously—Crystal cut Yao a little slack.

That didn't mean she was going for his insulting proposition. And it didn't mean she liked it. She'd pretty much had it with the opposite sex. Her newly adopted motto was, Men: Can't live with 'em, can't tie 'em to a train track and wait for Amtrak to do the deed. Chalk her disillusionment up to a string of bad relationships.

Johnny Duane Reed was a recent example. That cowboy had heartbreak written all over him and she'd be damned if she knew why every time he blew into town she ended up naked before he ended up gone. Reed always ended up gone.

The latest case in point, however, Mr. Yao Long, did not look happy right now. But then, it was hard to tell for certain. His expression hadn't altered since he'd appeared thirty minutes ago with his bodyguard.

"Did he understand that my answer is no?" Crystal's gaze darted from Wong to Yao as she turned the table back over to the dealer. "Because, I'm thinking that if he did, now would be a really good time for him to leave."

To stress her meaning, she made walking motions with her fingers.

Mr. Yao, all of five feet four inches with salt-and-pepper hair, Armani suit, and Gucci loafers, continued to pierce her with eyes the color of onyx. His expression never wavered.

Was it anger? Disappointment? Gas? she wondered, as a frisson of unease tickled its way down her spine.

"Did *you* understand that my answer is no?" She averted her gaze from Mr. Personality to Wong, hoping to make it clear that it was time for the two of them to say good-bye so she could get back to business.

"Mr. Yao understands your response but respectfully rejects your answer."

She blinked. "He said that?" She hadn't heard a word.

"Mr. Yao is quite taken with you. He expresses regret that you are reluctant to allow him the opportunity to get to know you better but must insist on your cooperation."

"No, seriously. Is he, like, texting you or something because I never saw his lips move." This was so ludicrous it was almost funny. The next words out of Wong's mouth, however, sobered her.

"Miss Debrowski, please understand it would not be wise—"

"Wait." She cut Wong off with a hand in the air as unease shifted to alarm. She didn't wear a name tag and, as gaming manager, practiced anonymity with the fervor of a religious zealot. Yet this man knew who she was. "How do you know my name?"

"Mr. Yao makes it a point to know everything. He is a very important and powerful man in our country."

"Yeah, well, this is *my* country," she informed Wong, searching the sea of gamblers and finally getting the attention of the security muscle on duty this shift. "And in my country, it's neither polite nor acceptable for any man—important or otherwise—to impose his attention where it isn't wanted.

"Max," she said when the twenty-something body-builder walked to her side, pecs and biceps bulging beneath the navy T-shirt with a Bali Hai Security Force logo printed on the breast pocket. "Please escort these gentlemen out. Their business here is concluded."

It wasn't that she couldn't handle the situation, but Max's sheer size was enough to prevent any potential ruckus. She just wanted them gone. The two men spooked her—and Crystal didn't spook easily.

"You will regret this," Wong said softly.

"Already do," she muttered under her breath, relieved when they bowed to Max's muscle and allowed him to walk them across the casino floor to the exit without incident.

"Tip, boss," Sharon Keiler announced, drawing Crystal's attention back to the table action.

She nodded permission for Sharon to pocket the

five-dollar toke, then went on about her business of scanning the action on the casino floor.

She had work to do. Her recent promotion to gaming manager had come at a price. Because she was a woman in a man's world, Crystal had had to work twice as long and twice as hard to earn her current position. She was two weeks into her new post and still learning the ropes. The last thing she could afford to have happen was to let Mr. Wong Li's "you will regret this" parting statement distract her from doing her job.

Everyone wanted to score in Vegas. Everyone had an angle. For every hundred no-luck and good-time gamblers, there was at least one among them intent on upping the odds in their favor. It was her job to spot the cheaters—card counters, past posters, hand muckers, palmers, and techno wizards—whether they were on the casino's payroll or on a weekend junket from Podunk, Missouri.

A war whoop sounded from a bank of Lucky Seven slots. Someone had hit it big. She ambled over that way, prepared to offer the casino's congratulations and assistance with the haul, when that unsettling curl of awareness skittered down her spine again.

She stopped, spun around, and found herself staring straight into eyes as cold as chipped ice. The man was Asian, midforties, impeccably dressed in a black suit and blue silk tie—almost indistinguishable from Wong Li's attire. He held her gaze for a long menacing moment, then turned and melted into the crowd.

"Spooky," she muttered, then resumed walking—and ran headlong into a wall of muscle.

"Excuse me." She backed up—encountered yet another Asian man. Identical suit. Similar tie. Same hard, intense stare.

Again, he impaled her with an ominous look before he turned and walked away.

Damn, if her knees weren't shaking when she forced herself toward the slot that was still dinging and whistling for the crowd that had gathered to see exactly how much money the lucky player had won.

And damned if she'd knuckle under to yet another urge to turn and see if someone else was watching her.

Screw them. No way was she letting them see her sweat because by this time tomorrow, Mr. Yao Long and his ninja squad—and yeah, she figured those guys were with him—would most likely be sailing on a fast boat to China and her life would be back to normal.

Normal. Right. What was she thinking? This was Las Vegas.

Three weeks later Crystal knew she was in deep trouble and she didn't have one single clue how it had come to this.

First the counterfeit chips had shown up on the floor, then one of her sections came up short for the evening shift's take. Tens of thousands of dollars short. Computer security codes were breached by hackers. Dozens of other little, yet vital security glitches—all on her watch—had her pulling her hair out.

So yeah, she became a subject of intense scrutiny. And no. She had no explanation, just a lot of sleepless nights trying to figure out how this was happening on her shift.

She'd since triple-covered all of her security measures, and prayed to the gods of roulette that she had a handle on things. That's when the unthinkable happened. Last night, twelve of the thirteen gaming tables under her direct supervision had been flooded with counterfeit twenty-dollar bills. Whoever distributed them had taken the casino for close to two hundred K.

Now here she was, standing in her boss's office, listening to him tell her that someone had made an unauthorized entry into the vault using her access card.

For the first time since he'd called her in here, Crystal breathed a sigh of relief. Cameras monitored the vault twenty-four-seven, three-sixty-five. If someone had used her card, it would be clear that it wasn't her. "Check the videos."

"We did." Mark Gilbert, director of casino security, looked grim. "The video surveillance developed a little glitch during the time in question. The tape is blank. Convenient, wouldn't you say?"

Her heart dropped to her knees. "You don't seriously believe I'm stealing from you?"

Gilbert sat behind his massive mahogany desk and stared through her more than at her. "I don't want to, no. But given the circumstances, Miss Debrowski, we have no choice but to place you on leave without pay."

She swallowed back anger and frustration and tears. "I understand." Actually, she didn't, but given the fact that the only case she had to plead was ignorance, what else could she say? As gaming manager, Crystal was the last line of resistance. The security breakdowns had occurred on her watch. That not only made her negligent, it made her suspect.

Gilbert pressed the intercom button on his phone. "Send them in."

The door opened. Crystal looked over her shoulder to see two uniformed LVPD officers walk in.

The blood drained from her head, swamping her with dizziness. *Oh, God.*

She turned back to Gilbert, her heart pounding. "You're having me arrested?"

Her boss had the decency to look remorseful. "I'm sorry."

He was sorry and Crystal was scared to death as the officers Mirandized her and charged her with suspicion of grand larceny and embezzlement before they handcuffed her and led her out the door.

"And here I thought I was the only one who got to use handcuffs on you."

Crystal looked up from the corner of the jail cell to see Johnny Duane Reed grinning at her from the other side of the bars.

Perfect.

Grinning and gorgeous, Reed was exactly the last person she wanted to see, specifically because until today he *had* been the only one who had ever gotten to use handcuffs on her.

A vivid memory of her naked and cuffed to her own bed while Reed had hovered over her was not the diversion she needed at this point in time.

She'd ask him what he was doing here but figured she already knew. "Abbie called you."

"I was visiting the ranch," Reed said. "I was there when you called her."

It figured that Reed would be back in Vegas and not bother to come and see her. Not that she wanted him to. Not that she cared.

"I need a lawyer not a . . ." She paused, groping for the word that best described him.

"Lover?" he suggested with that cocky grin.

"Not the word I was searching for," she grumbled, but let it go at that.

"If you don't want him, sugar, I'll be happy to take him."

Her cellmate shot Reed her best come-hither hooker smile. Reed of course couldn't help himself. He winked at her.

Jesus, would you look at him. Hair too long and too blond. Eyes too sexy and too blue. Body too buff, ego too healthy. Standing there in his tight, faded jeans, painted-on T-shirt, and snakeskin boots, he looked like God's guilty gift—and he knew it.

So did Crystal. What she didn't know was why she was so glad to see a man who played at life, at love, and at caring about her. That was the sum total of Reed's commitment quotient. He played at everything.

"How you holding up, Tinkerbell?" he asked gently.

Oh, God. He actually sounded like he cared.

"Careful, Reed. You might get me thinking you give a rip."

He had the gall to look wounded. "Now you've gone and hurt my feelings."

"Just get me out of here," she said, rising and meeting him at the heavy, barred door.

"Working on it," he said. "Abbie and Sam are right behind me. They'll arrange bail."

"Bail's already made."

Reed looked over his shoulder at the jailer, who sauntered slowly toward them with a set of keys.

Crystal backed away from the bars when the barrel-chested and balding deputy slipped the lock and slid open the door with a hollow, heavy clink. "Someone made my bail? Who?"

He shrugged. "You'll have to ask at processing. I just do what I'm told."

"I've always had this prison-chick fantasy," Reed said confidentially as Crystal squeezed out of the cell. "You know—sex-starved, man-hungry."

"Stow it." Crystal marched past him, ignoring his warped sense of humor. She was tired and terrified and doing her damnedest not to let either show.

"Hey, hey," Reed said gently and caught her by the arm. "Looks like someone could use a hug."

Yeah. She could use a hug. She could use a hundred hugs but now was not the time, this was not the place, and Reed was not the man she wanted to show the slightest bit of weakness to. "What I need is fresh air."

"Sure. But first, do a guy a favor. Make my fantasy complete. Tell me that you and the sister there had a hair-pulling, nail-scratching catfight and I'll die a happy man."

"Screw you, Reed."

He dropped a hand on her shoulder. Squeezed. "Now you're talkin'."

"I want to come with him."

"You're more than welcome to attend," the agent had said. He gave her his card with the address and told her she could follow them in her own vehicle.

She'd glanced at the card.

"Agent Larson, does my brother need a lawyer?"

"I already told you," Cory had said, ducking into the backseat of the car. "I don't want a lawyer."

Because he couldn't afford one. Abbie knew that was his reason. And because he didn't want her paying for one out of her own limited reserves.

Other than her divorce lawyer, who wasn't even with the firm anymore according to the names on the letter accompanying her settlement payment, Abbie didn't know who to call anyway. But she would find one if necessary. She glanced around the room at the hard faces, waiting in stoic silence. If this interview started smacking of inquest and even a hint of the word *criminal* came up, she was getting Cory representation whether he wanted it or not.

She nodded at Crystal, bless her, who had insisted on coming along for moral support. Then she glanced around the table again. Ordinary-looking men with extraordinary responsibilities and enough government muscle to send Cory to prison for a very long time.

It was scary as hell to be a civilian in the midst of all this federal bureaucracy. So scary that Abbie had already forgotten their names, just as in the blur of nerves and concern for Cory, she'd forget their faces when this was over. They'd all introduced themselves, along with the names

25

It was a typical government office, Abbie thought as she sat beside Cory at a long table in the front of a large, windowless room.

Industrial gray paint on the walls. Office furniture circa "several years ago," before budget crunches bit into the workings of the great bureaucracy. The suits lined up around the table were black.

Only Crystal, sitting alone at the back of the room, her wild red hair spiked and shining, her beaded earrings dangling, provided a splash of color in the otherwise black and gray environment.

Abbie wanted this over with, was impatient for it to start. While escorting Cory to a government car earlier this morning, the DEA agent had told Abbie they were waiting for someone else to arrive for "an informal interview."

"He's not being arrested?"

"No, ma'am. Not at this time."

Which implied that he would be at some point.